FIC ORO
O'Rourke, Betty.
The eagle and the rose

DATE DUE

THE EAGLE AND THE ROSE

Couples who fall in love during wartime face particular difficulties, but never more so than when one of them, Ruth Lawson, is an English girl trapped in France during the German Occupation, and the other is Captain Paul Reinhardt of the German Army. Add to this the fact that Ruth is actively involved in working with the local French Resistance, and, inevitably, there must be divided loyalties. A way must be found so that the German Eagle and the English Rose may one day find happiness together.

Books by Betty O'Rourke
Published by The House of Ulverscroft:

NIGHTINGALE SUMMER
PENHALIGON'S ROCK
COPPER ROSE

BETTY O'ROURKE

THE EAGLE AND THE ROSE

Complete and Unabridged

ULVERSCROFT
Leicester

First published in Great Britain

First Large Print Edition
published 2002

Copyright © 2001 by Betty O'Rourke

British Library CIP Data

O'Rourke, Betty
    The eagle and the rose.—Large print ed.—
Ulverscroft large print series: romance
1. Romantic suspense novels
2. Large type books
I. Title
823.9′14 [F]

ISBN 0–7089–4643–7

Published by
F. A. Thorpe (Publishing) Ltd.
Anstey, Leicestershire

Set by Words & Graphics Ltd.
Anstey, Leicestershire
Printed and bound in Great Britain by
T. J. International Ltd., Padstow, Cornwall

This book is printed on acid-free paper

1

The early autumn evening was drawing in, but the two girls, sitting in the tiny back room of the cottage, seemed loath to turn on the lights. Ruth, sitting by the window to catch the last of the light, was writing. Her companion, Annette, sat in her wheelchair with a book on her lap. She had not been reading it for several minutes.

'Ruth, it's nearly time. Draw the curtains so we can put on the light,' she said, glancing at her watch.

Ruth looked up. 'I'll draw the curtains but we'll have to wait for the news. The battery's low; I daren't use it more than we need.'

'Fetch it out, at least.' Annette swivelled her wheelchair backwards, off the rug that covered the centre of the floor. Ruth stood up and twitched the thick curtains across the window, which looked out on to the small garden. 'Why are you so impatient tonight?' she asked, bending down to turn back the rug.

'There might be a message from Simon. Who knows? I worry about him a lot.'

Ruth raised a loose floorboard under the

rug and brought out a wireless set, complete with cumbersome accumulator battery. She rested it on the floor, glanced at her watch, then turned on the set and began to tune it. Moments later, the signature tune of the BBC World Service came softly over the air waves.

'Turn the volume up,' Annette asked, leaning forward.

'Better not. If anyone is in the kitchen they might hear.'

'It doesn't matter. It'll only be Françoise, no one else, and you know we can trust her. She and Michel have been working for my family all their adult lives — they wouldn't say anything.'

'I know we can trust them. But Françoise may have friends dropping in. And she could easily let slip something heard on the wireless without realising it. We simply daren't risk having it confiscated.' Ruth knelt down on the floor beside the set, but turned the sound up a fraction. The announcer's voice came to them, reporting the week's news.

'The Germans have occupied Rome,' Annette whispered in awe. 'What will that mean for us, do you think? The Allies will have a long battle up the length of Italy. They will not have the resources to open a second front across the Channel and rescue France for years yet.'

'They'll come; soon as they can,' Ruth said comfortingly. 'And the Russians are doing well. They must keep the Germans occupied. Meanwhile, until the Allies come, we must do all we can to make life as comfortable as we can for ourselves and as uncomfortable as we can for the Germans. Hush, he's getting to the coded messages now. There might be something for us.'

The news broadcast over, the announcer said blandly 'I have some personal messages now. Henri's aunt thanks him for the apples which she says were delicious, and Marie Artaud wishes her family to know that the baby arrived safely on Tuesday.'

'That's Alain's message!' Ruth said eagerly. 'Marie's baby was a message he sent to England. I don't know what it was about but he asked me particularly to listen out for a birth announcement.'

'What about the apples?'

'I don't know anything about that. It must be meant for another group.' Ruth reached to switch off the set but as she did so, the girls heard a loud knocking on the front door.

'Whoever can that be? Nobody would ever come calling so near to curfew,' Annette exclaimed. 'Quickly, put the wireless back before anyone sees it!'

Ruth whisked the set and its battery back

beneath the floorboards and replaced the loose one over them with a speed borne of much practice, then twitched the rug back in place over it. Annette moved her wheelchair forward over the spot as there came a timid knock on the sitting room door.

'Oui, Françoise,' Annette called, and the door was opened by an elderly woman in a shabby, black dress, covered by a grubby apron. She wore a scarf over her grey hair and looked frightened. She addressed them in a sudden, nervous rush of French.

'Mam'selles, there's a German officer at the door! He's asking for Mam'selle Ruth!'

Annette's hand flew to her mouth, her eyes round with fear. 'Oh, Ruth! What could he want? They've never bothered us before.'

'Don't worry, dear. I'm sure it can't be anything much. I'll explain to him that I'm needed here to look after you and if necessary you can convince him you couldn't possibly manage without me, even though we both know you could, perfectly well, if need be.'

'I *couldn't* manage without you! You keep my spirits up. I'd be lost without you,' Annette insisted.

'That goes for both of us! I'd better see what the man wants. It's sure to be nothing to worry about; nothing important. You know how the Germans make such a fuss about

4

everything.' Ruth scrambled to her feet, giving Annette a reassuring pat on her shoulder before straightening her shoulders, lifting her chin defiantly, and striding out of the room.

The German officer was standing in the small, square hallway. He was tall, almost filling the space and Ruth saw from his shoulder insignia that he was a Captain. She was relieved to note that he was wearing the field grey uniform of the regular army, not the sinister black of the dreaded Gestapo, the German Secret Police who terrorised the civilians and made life difficult for everyone; even, it was rumoured, for their own troops. She also noticed with some surprise that the man looked ill at ease, rather unsure of himself, unusual in one of the occupying force.

'You are Mademoiselle Lawson?' He spoke in English.

Ruth nodded.

'I am Captain Paul Reinhardt.' He clicked his heels and Ruth resisted the urge to giggle. Germans being formally correct always reminded her of musical comedy. It would be dangerous to offend this man, though it didn't seem as if there was likely to be anything seriously important about his visit.

'You are, I believe, an Englishwoman, living

here in France since before the beginning of hostilities?'

'That is so.' He must know all about her, anyway, because the records about her nationality and background were in the Town Hall, which the Germans had taken over as their headquarters.

'Why are you still in France, Mademoiselle? Why did you not leave before France was occupied? You must have had sufficient time and opportunity to return home, after Britain declared war on Germany?'

'I stayed on because my friend was ill and needed me. We were on holiday here, Mademoiselle Annette Brissaud, my brother and I, the summer before war was declared. Mademoiselle Brissaud was involved in a car accident which left her very badly injured. She had no parents or family whom she could call on for help, so I stayed here to look after her. She has now recovered as much as she is ever likely to do, but she is, as you must already know, confined to a wheelchair and needs constant help. At the time when I might have left, she was too ill to risk bringing to England and I was not prepared to leave without her.'

'Your devotion does you credit, Mademoiselle.'

Was there a cynical note in the man's

6

remark, Ruth wondered. Probably it was her imagination; all these questions were making her nervous. He must already know all about herself and Annette, so where was all this leading?

'Your brother, however, did not stay in France too?'

Irritation flared in her at the pointless interrogation. 'No,' she said defiantly. 'He went back to England to join the British Army and help rid Europe of the Nazi scourge.'

A muscle tightened in the corner of the officer's mouth, but he made no comment. 'Your loyalty to your friend is to be commended,' he said smoothly, 'but also somewhat surprising. What about your loyalty to your country? Did you not wish to return to England and, like your brother, serve your own country?'

This was dangerous ground. Was this man trying to trick her into saying that she could help her country equally well in France, virtually admitting that she was doing just that? She looked at him directly, and realised that he was both good looking and young, hardly more than a year or so older than herself. To be a Captain already he must be both bright and competent. She would have to be particularly wary.

'Annette is more than just a friend,' she said. 'She is engaged to be married to my brother. Had the war not intervened they would have married long since. I think of her as a sister.'

'I fear Mademoiselle Brissaud has had a long and rather lonely betrothal,' Paul said. 'Four years apart from her future husband must be hard to bear.' There did not seem anything other than normal sympathy in his words, but then he added. 'Perhaps she will not have much longer to wait.'

Now, what on earth was he implying by that remark, Ruth wondered. Was he trying to draw some response from her? Did he suspect that she wasn't only here to look after Annette and hoped that he might provoke some retort that would tell him that she knew more about the present situation than the German propaganda bulletins released? Ruth decided she had had enough of this dangerous conversation. Her hands felt cold and clammy so she clasped them behind her back. She tossed her head, letting her long, blonde hair fall loosely round her shoulders, and faced him squarely.

'What is the purpose of your visit, Captain Reinhardt?' she asked frostily. 'You must already know the answers to all the questions you have asked me, so how do you imagine I can help you?' She had the satisfaction of seeing him look disconcerted. He dropped his eyes momentarily.

'It is a personal matter, Mademoiselle,' he said, after a moment. 'I do not come in my official capacity as a German officer. I saw your name and nationality in the records at the Town Hall. There are no other native English speakers in the town, and so I thought — I came to ask you if you would consider giving me English lessons?'

'What!'

Ruth was so astonished she could only stare, open-mouthed, at the man. This was the very last thing she had expected.

'It is a straightforward request. There is nothing behind it except a wish to improve my language skills.' He sounded hurt.

'But you already speak English! We're conversing in it now!' For so long, Ruth had spoken only French, apart from occasional brief exchanges in English with Annette when they wanted to say something very private, that she had hardly been aware of responding in her own language when Paul had addressed her in English.

'Regrettably, I am by no means fluent, and I would like very much to be able to improve my accent, which is something that may only be done by conversation with a native

English speaker,' he said.

'You sound as if you speak it well enough already,' Ruth said coldly. 'And I'd say the chances of your needing to speak it in England are really very remote.'

She held her breath. Insulting a German officer was a very dangerous thing to do, but, as the majority of the citizens of Ste Marie de la Croix were agreed, they had not been put on this earth to be polite to Germans.

Again the muscle twitched in his jaw. 'So, you are unwilling to give me English lessons, Miss Lawson? Very well. That is your choice. It was merely a hope on my part that you would agree. I am prepared to pay whatever fee you ask, either in French francs or German deutschmarks, as you prefer. I am sorry if I have offended you by my request, but it seemed harmless enough to me. I bid you good day.' He turned towards the door, having clicked his heels again and saluted her. His hand was on the latch when an idea came to Ruth.

'No, wait!' she said. 'Tell me exactly what it is you want. How can I teach you English?'

He turned back from the door and there was a smile on his face; not, it seemed, of triumph but merely relief.

'As you have pointed out, I speak some English already. It would not be formal lessons that I require, though I would wish you to correct any grammatical errors I make. Rather, it is English conversation I am seeking, to improve both my vocabulary and pronunciation.'

There was no denying it would be pleasant to have the opportunity to speak English again, especially with this pleasant looking young man. He wasn't the distinctively blond, blue-eyed Aryan that she thought of as typically German; he had light brown hair and hazel eyes. But for the uniform, he might have been of almost any European nationality.

Ruth brought her thoughts back to reality. He *was* a German, one of the enemy, and if she were to hold conversations with him she would always have to be careful, very, very careful, about everything she said. But perhaps she could also be very clever, and maybe, if he believed her story that she was trapped here in France solely because she chose to look after her invalid friend, he might not be as careful as she. There could be possibilities . . .

'How often would you require these English conversation lessons?' she asked abruptly.

'Preferably, twice a week. For two hours, shall we say?'

'When?'

'Whenever it is convenient to you. For myself, the afternoons of Tuesday and Thursday would suit very well. Shall we say half past two until half past four? Would that be suitable for you?'

This was all very un-German. Usually, they announced what they wanted and the civilians, the occupied people, were given no choice but to agree. She should have accepted his politeness gratefully, but some demon inside her made Ruth retort, 'It would seem the German army is here only on a part-time basis, since its troops appear to work only in the mornings.'

This time the muscle did not twitch. Paul said coldly, 'I can understand your unwillingness to do any member of the occupying forces a service, Fräulein Lawson. Let me point out that this is not an official request. I asked, as a personal favour, but, understandably, we are, none of us, your taste of the month. I will take up no more of your time.' He turned towards the door again and, automatically, Ruth muttered 'flavour.'

'What did you say?' He spun round to face her.

'It's flavour of the month, not taste.'

For the first time during their conversation,

Paul smiled, a broad, generous grin of pure delight.

'That is exactly the reason I wish to take conversation lessons with a native English speaker,' he said. 'These phrases — these idioms — are not easily found in textbooks.'

Ruth made up her mind. 'Tuesday and Thursday afternoons would be quite convenient,' she said, 'but perhaps two until four would suit better?'

'Whichever you prefer. And if I pay you per lesson, would you prefer francs or deutschmarks?' Paul's eyes twinkled suddenly. 'It might even be possible to offer British pounds, but I doubt they would be of much use to you at present.'

'Neither would deutschmarks,' Ruth retorted. 'And there's precious little to buy in the shops these days, so francs seem pointless. Will you pay me in coffee? I should think a quarter kilo a week would be a fair price. All the francs you could pay me wouldn't buy any in our shops, but I'm sure the German army must have some.'

Paul raised his eyebrows slightly but barely paused before replying, 'Yes, I think that might be arranged. Shall we begin this Tuesday? I shall be here promptly at two o'clock and I will bring you your coffee.'

'Thank you.' Ruth was feeling rather dazed

by the turn of events.

Paul was out of the door and on the path outside when he looked back, to remark: 'Miss Lawson, perhaps you should know that the German army is on duty twenty four hours a day here, therefore, some of us take our off-duty hours while others are working. My off-duty hours are on Tuesday and Thursday afternoons but I assure you I work full time during the rest of the week.'

Ruth flushed. 'I'm sorry I was rude,' she said.

'No matter. It is already forgotten. Until Tuesday, then!' He saluted and strode down the short path to the road.

Françoise came warily from the kitchen and looked anxiously at Ruth. 'What did he want? No trouble, I hope?'

'No, no trouble.' Ruth shook her head, still not quite believing the conversation which had just taken place. She went back to Annette in the sitting room and Françoise followed her, eager to hear everything.

'Well, what was that all about? You were talking to him for ages, and in English, too, though I couldn't hear what was said. Is there some trouble because of your nationality?' Annette demanded at once.

'No, nothing like that. It was nothing to worry about.' Ruth sat down in one of the

14

armchairs, feeling as if her legs would no longer support her. 'He came to ask if I would give him some English conversation lessons. Can you imagine?' She began to laugh.

'I hope you said no. He's probably planning to parachute into England as a spy,' Françoise said sourly.

'English lessons?' Annette said in surprise. 'And you agreed? Ruth — have you thought about this? It could be terribly risky, talking on a non-official level to a German.'

'I know. And I'll be on my guard all the time, you may be sure of that. I suppose we can talk about English literature. Jane Austen ought to be a safe enough topic.' Ruth was beginning to recover, to think about what she had agreed.

'You know, it might not be a bad idea to have a tame German you could cultivate,' Annette said thoughtfully. 'It could prove quite useful. If he's careless, who knows what you might learn from him?'

'Bah!' Françoise exclaimed contemptuously. 'Have nothing to do with any of them, Mam'selle Ruth. It will bring nothing but trouble, you'll see.'

'They're not too bad, I suppose, some of them,' Annette conceded. 'It's the Nazi element that cause the real trouble. At least

15

he wasn't Gestapo.'

'You haven't heard the whole of it yet!' Ruth began to laugh. 'He was prepared to pay for lessons, but money isn't much use these days so I asked him to pay in coffee.'

'Coffee!' Annette exclaimed. 'Do you mean real coffee? Not that terrible stuff we've been forced to drink for years? I can hardly remember what real coffee tastes like.'

'It'll be as real as the German army can offer its troops,' Ruth promised. 'A quarter kilo every week. I don't suppose German coffee is all that wonderful these days either, but I'm sure it will be a great deal better than anything we can buy in the shops.'

'I don't like it,' Françoise grumbled. 'A German, coming here? What if he catches you with that — that — ' She gestured towards the rug. Françoise knew about the hidden wireless, but she rarely listened to the BBC broadcasts herself.

'It'll be safe enough.' Ruth assured her. 'He's coming twice a week, Tuesdays and Thursdays, beginning tomorrow, from two until four. Germans are very precise; I'm sure he'll come at exactly those times and no other. If he does turn up unexpectedly, I shall tell him I can't give him a lesson, I'm too busy. Well, it's true, isn't it?' She turned to Annette for confirmation. 'We both have

16

other, perfectly legitimate activities which take up plenty of our time, teaching at the school and preparing lessons. And even when I don't have a class myself, you need me to take you to the school and bring you back.'

Annette nodded. 'I'm sure it will be all right, Françoise,' she assured the older woman. 'Ruth will be careful what she says and it may prove a useful contact for us.'

'And just think! On Tuesday evening you can be drinking coffee after your evening meal!' Ruth exulted.

Françoise sniffed. 'No German is to be trusted,' she muttered. 'But you must do as you wish, Mam'selles. It's not my business if you wish to encourage the enemy. Just don't ask me to be friendly with any of them.' She stumped out of the room, muttering to herself.

'I won't even ask you to open the door to him,' Ruth called after her. She and Annette exchanged understanding smiles. Françoise had bad memories of Germans in the first world war and hated the whole nation indiscriminately.

'What's he like? Really?' Annette asked, curiously, as they heard the kitchen door slam shut behind Françoise.

Ruth hesitated, considering. 'Young, for a Captain. And quite good looking. Very formal, of course. I was rude to him twice but he took it rather well. He could have had me arrested for insulting him, but he didn't say anything. He's nice, I think. Not all blond and blue-eyed like so many of them. In fact, apart from his uniform he could have been anyone. He speaks very good English already.'

'Then why does he need lessons? Is there something behind this?' Annette asked sharply.

'I honestly don't think so. He's quite fluent, but his word order is more like a German's, and his pronunciation is not all that good. He certainly could do with some practice at speaking, and it would be nice to be using English again occasionally. However, we'll have to see what happens — if it doesn't work out I can always find some excuse to stop the lessons. I'm sure he wouldn't be difficult about that, and in the meantime, we have coffee to look forward to!'

'Will you tell Alain about him?' Annette asked.

'I suppose I must. He will need to be warned never to come here when Captain Reinhardt is visiting.'

'Be careful, Ruth,' Annette said. 'You face more dangers here than any of us, and if anything were to happen to you — how

18

would I ever face Simon if I let harm come to you?'

'No harm will come to me,' Ruth said stoutly. 'But you know I couldn't just live here and do nothing, when I know I can be of some use.' She looked affectionately towards Annette. It was true, what she had said to Captain Reinhardt, she did look on Annette more as a sister than a friend. Had it not been for that accident, and war declared while Annette was still gravely ill and unable to be moved, she would have been married to Simon by now and living relatively safely in England.

Annette's head, with her dark hair, neat as usual, in a smooth chignon, was bent over something in her lap, her delicate, flower face hidden. Ruth saw she held a photo album, filled with snapshots of that last holiday they had taken together. The poignancy of those last pictures of Annette standing by the top of the cliffs in Brittany was hard to bear.

Annette turned the page quickly and stared down at the picture of a young, fair-haired man in swimming trunks.

'It's so long since we had any news of Simon,' she whispered. 'So often I wonder where he is. Is he still in England, do you think, or perhaps somewhere far away? He could be fighting in North Africa or even the

Far East. I wish I knew.'

'It wouldn't be any help to know. You'd only worry about him all the more if you knew he was fighting somewhere,' Ruth said. She looked thoughtful, then added, very quietly, 'Simon has some useful skills; he speaks French and German fluently, as well as knowing France very well. I think it's possible the British Army might make special use of those qualities. They must be planning to invade Europe and rescue the occupied countries soon. They *must* be; they couldn't leave us at the mercy of the Germans forever.'

'You mean, he could be involved in the plans for the Second Front?' Annette whispered, her dark eyes round in wonder. 'Ruth — please tell me! Do you know anything? Have you heard any rumours, any names mentioned?'

Ruth shook her head. 'No, I've heard nothing. No one of our group would know anything like that. I certainly don't know where Simon is or what he could be doing, but it seems to me the powers-that-be in Britain would find his specialist knowledge very useful and would put them to the best possible use. It was merely a thought.'

'You speak German too, don't you?' Annette asked.

'A little. I picked up some when Simon and

I were on holiday in the Black Forest, years before the war,' Ruth replied. 'I'm not anything like as fluent as Simon but I can understand what's being said, most of the time.'

'Will you let your German know that you can speak his language?'

'I don't think that will arise. He's coming to practise speaking English; he's not going to learn it by speaking German. It's quite useful, being able to listen in to the soldiers' comments sometimes. They'd be much more suspicious of me if they thought I knew what they were saying to each other.' Ruth paused, then added, 'Of course, Alain knows. I've translated a few documents for him that have been stolen from the Germans, but I don't let too many people know. The locals might be mistrustful. They're a bit wary of me as it is.'

Annette nodded. 'I know, and it angers me. They ought to realise — you do so much for us all. And you take so many risks — even by staying on here, you were taking a risk. They might easily have interned you, or deported you to Germany.'

'Then they would have had the problem of what to do with you,' Ruth pointed out. 'Fortunately, the majority of Germans seem to have a low opinion of women so they haven't bothered too much about me. That's

21

why they let me stay with you.'

'And gave you the opportunity to show how wrong they were,' Annette said, very quietly. She closed the photo album. 'Such a happy time we all had, that last holiday! I like to remember it; it doesn't make me sad but I do wonder — what will Simon be like when I see him again?'

On Tuesday morning Ruth walked into the small town of Ste Marie de la Croix to buy whatever groceries she could find, for the household. Many of the shops were closed now, unable to find enough goods to sell to justify keeping open, but there were a few market stalls in the middle of the town square doing good trade with second-hand goods. There was an increasing amount of barter these days, money being worth less than goods in most people's minds. One shop which was still open, though only for a few hours each day, was the bakery, situated on one corner of the square, facing the Town Hall. Ruth disliked crossing the main square, having to pass the rows of German staff cars drawn up in front of the Town Hall, and seeing the men in their field grey uniforms, or, occasionally, Gestapo black, going up the steps into the building. She hurried past and arrived outside Claude Rousseau's little shop. It was early and Claude was still fastening the shutter back from his windows, but already there were a group of women gathered outside with their shopping baskets, gossiping while they waited for the bakery to open. Ruth called a general greeting as she joined them; almost all of them were known to her by sight and several by name. They nodded in return but the conversation faded and an uneasy silence followed.

Claude went back inside his shop, leaving the door open and the women crowded in after him. If this had been England, Ruth thought ruefully, they would have formed an orderly queue with very little jostling, but here, all friendships were abandoned as neighbours elbowed each other aside in their struggles to be first to reach the counter.

Claude rationed his sales to two long loaves for each customer, but, even so, his stock, piled on the counter and on shelves behind him, began dwindling at an alarming rate. At last, Ruth reached the counter, more by being pushed there by customers leaving than by her own efforts, but Claude ignored her, serving women on either side of her, even behind her, while acting as if she were invisible. She called to him in a bid to attract his attention, waving a five-franc note in his face, but he seemed determined to avoid serving her.

Ruth became annoyed. She accepted that the local people might be wary of any foreigner in their midst, and the British were not exactly popular ever since Dunkirk, but to refuse to serve her at all was ridiculous.

'Claude! I want two loaves for Annette and Françoise!' she shouted, her British restraint gone now. 'It's my turn to be served! Please give me some bread!'

Claude, however, continued to deal with all the other customers, ignoring her entirely. Finally, there were only two other customers left in the shop and both of them had come in long after herself. There were only four loaves left on the counter.

'Yes, Madame? Two for you?' Claude handed over two loaves to the woman beside Ruth, taking the money from her outstretched hand.

One each for us, then, Ruth thought resignedly, glancing at the one other woman left. She was Madame Duvalle, a rather unfriendly woman who wore a perpetually sour expression and always looked as if she disapproved of Ruth's presence in the town.

'Two for you, Madame?' To her horror, Ruth watched Claude pick up the last two remaining loaves and thrust them into Madame Duvalle's basket. He almost snatched the note she held out to him and pushed her change towards her. Madame Duvalle glanced at Ruth as she turned to leave, a triumphant smirk on her face.

Ruth's temper boiled over. 'I was one of the first customers to come into your shop this morning,' she stormed at Claude. 'Why wouldn't you serve me? If you are going to begin a vendetta against me because I'm British, well, that's your decision, but Annette Brissaud needs bread too, and so does Françoise Leclerc. What have you got against them?'

Claude did not reply. Instead, he came round the side of the counter and opened the shop door, peering out into the street. Then he closed and locked it, hanging a worn 'sold out' notice against the glass. Only then did he smile at her.

'For you, Mam'selle, and for poor Mam'selle Annette, I always have bread.' He took Ruth's basket and rested it on the counter. From underneath the counter he took two loaves, slightly shorter and plumper than the ones he had been selling earlier and which Ruth recognised as being the special ones he made with a small ration of superior flour. No one knew where he acquired it, and no one had ever been rash enough to ask.

Claude covered the loaves carefully with the cloth Ruth kept in the basket for the purpose. When she held out the money he waved it away with a gesture.

'For you, there is today no charge, Mam'selle. I am sorry you had to wait but it could not be helped. I hope you understand. Perhaps you would be so kind as to spare a little more of your time and step upstairs to bid good-day to my wife and family, before you depart?'

Ruth started at him blankly. It was common knowledge that Claude Rousseau was a childless widower who lived alone above his shop. He smiled at her puzzled expression and gestured towards a door at the back of the shop. He opened it slightly, showing a steep flight of stairs immediately inside. 'This way, Mam'selle,' he said. 'Just a few words, for friendship's sake. I beg you.'

Ruth could see she wasn't going to be allowed out of the shop without first going upstairs to see these strange new relations Claude was so anxious for her to meet. Fleetingly, she wondered if the old man had indeed married again recently, but if so, surely the town would have been rife with gossip and Françoise would certainly have told them all about it. Perhaps Claude was becoming a little strange, feeling the strain of years of wartime occupation. Whatever it was, she thought it best to humour him. It would hardly take more than a few minutes and in truth she was beginning to wonder who or what she would find upstairs.

The stairs were steep, wooden and uncarpeted. At the top was another door. Ruth knocked on it and a man's voice answered 'Entrée!'

Seated in a small, rather bare room were two men. As Ruth entered, one of the men gestured to the only other empty chair. 'Sit down, Mam'selle Ruth,' he said, 'we have been wanting to talk to you.'

Ruth knew the man who had spoken. He was Alain, who owned the local hardware shop. The other man was a stranger to her.

'This is Jacques. He is one of us but he does not live in the town,' Alain said, gesturing to the stranger. Ruth looked at him. Bearded, thin faced almost to gauntness and with a sharp, watchful look in his eyes, he looked the part of a guerrilla fighter from the hills. No wonder he was not from the town; his appearance would have drawn attention at once from the Germans.

Jacques addressed her abruptly. 'We understand you had a visit from a German officer recently.'

'Yes, that's true.' Ruth looked surprised. 'I wasn't aware that anyone except Annette and Françoise knew about him.'

'You may be sure that very little happens in this town which is not very quickly known to us,' Jacques said smoothly. 'What did he want?'

'If you already know of his visit — ' Ruth began.

'We know that he asked you to give him English conversation lessons. That is correct, is it not?' Alain asked.

'You are very well informed.' Ruth frowned. It was not particularly pleasant to discover that her activities were under such close surveillance by the local people. The Germans were one thing, but to be spied on by those she thought of as friends —

'What did you tell him?' Jacques asked sharply.

'I agreed. There seemed no harm in it. It sounded like a genuine request to — '

'Good. This is exactly the kind of contact we can use to our advantage. How often will he come for these lessons?'

'Twice a week, Tuesdays and Thursdays. But look, it's very unlikely that I'll be able to get any information from him that would be of use to our group. He's an officer, a Captain, and he'd certainly be on his guard — '

'As you must be, too,' Alain interrupted. 'Be very careful what you discuss with this

28

German, Mam'selle Ruth.'

'I intend to be. I plan to keep the conversation to subjects like literature, classical English novelists perhaps, or the weather.'

'Even discussing the weather has its dangers,' Jacques growled.

'I do know the risks. I'm sure he has no deliberate intention of trying to trick information out of me. If he had, I'm hardly the best person he could have chosen. I know very little about anything that happens in the town.'

'Just as well. It is better you keep it that way,' Jacques said. He gave her a searching look and Ruth had the uneasy feeling he was giving her a warning. Perhaps he did not entirely trust her, because she was not French? She ought not to be too offended by that because these days it was hard to know just who to trust, and probably safer to trust no one.

'You may not be the best person to approach for information, Mam'selle Ruth, but for English lessons you are the only one,' Alain pointed out. 'And, undoubtedly, you will know things about England and the customs of the English that none of us would know. Why do you think this man wishes to come to you to learn English?'

'He said he wanted to improve his accent. He does speak quite good English already but his pronunciation and grammar need polishing. He could well do with some lessons from a native English speaker.'

'So! He speaks English already! Why do you imagine he would wish to improve his accent unless he had plans to slip into England as a spy and pass himself off as an Englishman?'

'I'd hardly think so. I imagine he discovered from the local register of citizens that I was English and thought it was a good opportunity to improve his language skills in his free time,' Ruth said. 'I doubt, even with my tuition, that he'd ever completely lose his accent, and, anyway, his mannerisms would give him away if he tried to pose as an Englishman.' She remembered the clicking heels and the formal manner. Paul Reinhardt might not look typically German but his mannerisms would ensure he wouldn't pass for anyone British, either.

'Mam'selle Ruth, we think this contact with a German might prove useful to us,' Alain said, 'but we must warn you again to be very careful what you say to this man.'

'I've told you. I'll watch what I say. I don't intend to discuss anything that might be controversial, certainly I won't discuss the war at all-' Ruth began indignantly.

'We shall require a report on what has been discussed between you both,' Jacques said. 'The morning after each meeting, when you come here to buy bread.'

'No,' Ruth said. 'If, and it's a very unlikely if, he does let slip anything which I think could be of use to the group, I will, of course, pass it on to Alain. But I'm sure he won't, and you can be assured I won't say anything that I shouldn't, either. If I keep coming here after every lesson it will be noticed and should Captain Reinhardt ever suspect that I have any connection with — with your people, I would at best be deported to Germany. More likely, I'd be shot. I'm here to look after Annette Brissaud; I don't want to endanger that. Annette will always be my first consideration. And if I was suspected of anything, then naturally, I would be of no further use to you, either.'

'She has a point,' Alain conceded.

'How often does she buy bread?' Jacques spoke as if Ruth were not there. 'She will come here more than twice a week anyway. Why should that arouse suspicion with anyone?'

'If Claude makes me wait until everyone else is served and has left the shop, like he did this morning, then someone is bound to notice soon enough, that there is something odd going on,' Ruth snapped impatiently.

Jacques looked annoyed. Clearly, he wasn't used to his orders being questioned, particularly by a woman. 'Well, you are the local man,' he said, turning to Alain. 'You arrange matters as you think fit.' He stood up, indicating that the interview was at an end. 'Au revoir, Mam'selle. Remember what has been said here — but forget who it was who said it. That's safest, is it not?'

Alain stood up as well. 'Report here if there is need,' he said. 'You can tell Claude you wish to see me. Ask how his wife is. That is the code.'

'It's ridiculous!' Ruth exclaimed. 'Everyone in the town knows Claude is a widower!'

'I assume you will not ask him in front of a shop full of his customers,' Jacques said. 'If so, they may possibly misinterpret the remark and imagine you have a personal interest in our baker.'

Ruth did not know whether to laugh or be indignantly angry. Claude must be at least sixty, bald and paunchy. Who in their right minds would imagine that she was having a romantic liaison with him? The thought reminded her. For anyone in the square who might have been watching, she had spent a long time in a locked and empty shop with the baker. An affaire might not be the first thought that entered anyone's head, but certainly it would look strange, and such behaviour might throw suspicion on both herself and Claude, for reasons more serious and nearer the truth.

'I must go,' she said quickly. 'Goodbye, Jacques. Alain, I will see you again before long, I expect.'

Alain nodded, his hands in his pockets, but Jacques held out his to her, and she shook it hesitantly. She decided she didn't like Jacques very much, but it was tough, hard men like him who were needed in the Resistance. Rightly, she guessed that he was in a senior position to Alain, and wondered if they attached some particular importance to Paul Reinhardt's request, since Jacques had come himself to see her. The thought made her even more nervous about the coming English conversation lessons.

She closed the door behind her and went down the steep, bare boards of the staircase, back into the shop. Claude was waiting for her with her shopping basket.

'All well, Mam'selle?' he asked. 'Here, slip out through the back door of the bakery. It leads into a side road, away from the square. Maybe there are some of the old crows still hanging round outside. Best if they don't see how long you have been in my shop.'

As she went through the back of the shop, past ovens and worktables, stacked flour bags and baking trays, Ruth realised she was grateful to the elderly baker. She also realised that she was undoubtedly not the first visitor to be ushered out this way, away from prying eyes in the square. Claude was another, unsuspected member of the group dedicated to making life hard for the German occupying forces.

2

Later that morning Ruth collected together the small batch of English classical novels she had acquired during her years in France. A couple of them she had brought with her on that last, fateful holiday she had spent with Annette and Simon. She smiled ruefully, remembering that she had planned to read some of the collected works of Jane Austen during those weeks. The weather had been glorious, they'd gone exploring and swimming from the Brittany beaches and there had never been time or inclination for reading. When Annette had been knocked down by a speeding car and rushed to hospital, then might there have been time during the long wait to find out the extent of her injuries, but certainly no inclination to try to distract herself with a book. That thick tome, and a couple of paperbacks, had remained unread, and although she had bought half a dozen others from second-hand shops or stalls since, they seemed a poor collection to provide the basis for two hours' discussion with someone who might never even have heard of the authors.

She was nervous, now. Part of her wanted to see the good looking young captain again, and in a social, non-threatening situation, but part of her wondered — was there, after all, as Alain and Jacques evidently suspected, something more behind this request? Did Paul know she had links with the Resistance group in the town, and was this some way of making her give away their secrets? On the face of it, it didn't seem likely. The Germans weren't known for being devious or subtle when it came to seeking out their enemies; far more likely that if Captain Reinhardt had any suspicions he would have had her arrested and questioned at the Town Hall, not used this unorthodox approach.

There was something about him, too, which made her feel instinctively that his request had been genuine. Even so, she must guard her tongue and not unwittingly give him any potentially useful information. She began making a list of subjects they might discuss with safety: certain films, the late summer flowers still blooming in Annette's garden, sports that might interest him. Did he play, or watch, tennis, she wondered? She baulked at the thought of trying to explain the complexities of English cricket.

He came, prompt to the minute, at two

o'clock. She opened the door to him herself, Françoise having grumpily refused to have anything to do with the enterprise. Annette had wheeled herself into the kitchen, to leave the sitting room free for the lesson.

Ruth showed him into the room and he took off his greatcoat and peaked cap, laying them carefully over one of the chairs.

'Please sit down, Captain. I've looked out a few English novels which I thought you might have heard of. I thought perhaps we could discuss them.'

Paul handed her a small packet. 'I thought you might like payment in advance,' he said formally.

The brand was unknown to her, but as she instinctively sniffed at it, the delicious, almost forgotten aroma wafted up her nostrils. 'Thank you,' she said.

'I am afraid it is not very good quality. It is impossible to obtain real coffee anywhere in Europe these days,' he said.

'It certainly smells like real coffee. I haven't smelt anything as good as that in years. The only coffee substitute that we can buy here has no smell at all. I don't even want to think what it might be made from.'

Ruth put the coffee down and turned to the table. 'Do you know any of these books, Captain Reinhardt? Perhaps you have read some of them in translation. Shall we begin with them?'

Paul picked up the books, one by one, glancing at the titles on their spines. 'This I know,' he said, indicating Oliver Twist. 'One of your great Victorian novelists, I believe? And there are others whose authors' names are familiar to me, but I have not read any of them. I am sorry. Perhaps we may discuss books in general? Have you read any German authors? Goethe, or Schiller, perhaps?'

Conversation became an effort, her words becoming formal as Ruth struggled to keep up a conversation about books, but finding that there were few they had both heard of, and none that they had both read.

'Perhaps we should discuss something else,' she said desperately. 'Are you interested in sport, Captain Reinhardt? Or gardening? Or — or-?'

Paul gave a gesture of exasperation. 'This is no good at all!' he exclaimed. 'This is not at all what I had in mind. We shall not achieve anything while it is clear to me that you are frightened of being in the presence of a German officer.'

'I am not!' Ruth said indignantly. 'It's just that — that I don't know what to talk to you about. I don't know what your interests are, or what you are expecting of me.'

'It would be better, perhaps, to be less formal,' Paul said. 'My name is Paul, and yours, I believe, is Ruth. Much simpler to use first names, I think, if you do not object.'

Ruth shook her head. 'No, it's a good idea.' Already the thought of calling him Paul made her less shy of him.

'And please, try to ignore this uniform I have to wear, and let us talk as if we were two people who had recently met and wished to get to know each other.'

That sounded reasonable, though it might lead to embarking on some risky subjects. 'Tell me about yourself,' Ruth said. 'Your family; what you did before the war.'

'Ah, yes! We must not mention the war!' Paul grinned at her, almost teasingly. 'This is a time when we have the opportunity to forget the war for a little while. I shall tell you about myself and my family and my home in Germany, and then you will tell me as much as you wish about yourself.'

This was certainly better. Paul talked to her without reticence about his home in Mannheim, where he had lived with his parents and younger brother. His father had been managing director of an engineering company and his brother a pilot in the Luftwaffe until he had been shot down in the English

Channel. He seemed to have lived a comfortable life before the war, with tennis parties, boating trips on the lake and excursions into the countryside.

'And now you?' Paul said. They had been chatting normally for the past twenty minutes, Ruth asking a question here and there, Paul describing the city and the countryside around his home. 'Is there only yourself and your brother in your family, or do you have other siblings?' he asked.

For a moment Ruth froze. Was this, then, how it was done, lull her into a feeling of relaxed friendship, telling her all about himself, and then letting her tell him too much in return — about Simon, and about England?

'There's just my brother and myself,' she replied. 'My father died a few years ago. My mother lives in a country town. There's really nothing much to tell.'

'Nothing much you wish to tell, perhaps?' Paul said. 'No matter. Tell me what you liked to do when you were a child; what games you played, what plans you made, before the war changed everything for us all.'

This was easier. It was undeniably pleasant to be speaking English again, remembering her childhood on a farm in Hertfordshire. Ruth talked eagerly of things she had done in those days but she did not tell him of her ambitions to travel, and her time studying French and German with this in mind.

It was after three when she next glanced at the clock. 'I think it might be a good time for us to have a break now,' she said. 'I'll ask Françoise to make us some of your coffee, shall I?'

'That would be pleasant, though I doubt your maid would be pleased to offer me hospitality,' Paul said ruefully.

'Françoise will make us coffee if I ask her.' Ruth picked up the packet and went into the kitchen. Annette was sitting in her chair by the table, scraping carrots.

'How is it going?' she asked, looking up.

'He's surprisingly normal, and nice. And easy to talk to, once we stopped trying to force the conversation.'

'Phut!' snorted Françoise, making pastry at the other end of the table.

'Will you make us some coffee, please?' Ruth asked, handing her the packet. 'And have a cup yourselves, of course.' To Annette, she added, in English, 'see she doesn't spoil his on purpose, won't you? He doesn't deserve discourtesy, he can't help being a German.'

When she returned to the sitting room, Paul said, 'Our conversation has been most pleasant, Ruth, but it was not what I had been hoping for.'

'No?'

Had he, after all, been hoping they would discuss subjects where she was likely to give away information useful to the Germans? Ruth felt keen disappointment. She had not thought Paul had been out to trap her.

'No. You let me speak for nearly an hour, yet never do you say 'it is not said like this' or 'it is not pronounced like that'. I know that I make many mistakes, yet you say nothing. Be frank with me, please, Ruth. Is it that you hesitate to correct me because I am a German soldier?'

Ruth could not resist a sigh of relief. 'No, not because of that,' she said. 'I was enjoying the conversation too much. I didn't want to interrupt you. I'm sorry, I'm not earning my coffee, am I? Your English is very good but you have been pronouncing some words strangely. And the order in which you put some words isn't — well, it isn't how we would say it and although I can understand you perfectly well, it isn't grammatical English.'

'I think you would need to correct me every time I speak,' Paul said gravely.

'Perhaps. But then we would never have a proper conversation,' Ruth replied. 'I think we should concentrate for now on improving your pronunciation. Your W's sound like Vees, and your Vees sound like F's. I'm sure with practice you would overcome that. Let me think of some words you could say that might help. I know!' There was an old children's nursery rhyme book in the cottage which had once belonged to Simon. How it came to be there in Annette's home, Ruth had no idea, but she saw at once it would serve her purpose admirably. She took it down from the shelf and flipped over the pages. 'Here, read this!' she held out the book, open at an illustration of a small, pyjama'd boy holding a candlestick. Paul looked surprised, then began to read.

' 'Wee Willie Winkie runs through the town.' No, that is not how you would say it. Those words are difficult for me.'

Ruth took the book back and read the rhyme slowly.

'What does it mean?' Paul asked.

'It doesn't matter what it means. It's a way of making you say lots of words beginning with W,' Ruth explained. 'Try some more. Here's one about three little foxes. See if you can pronounce all the words correctly.'

'If my fellow officers could hear me now!' Paul laughed, after he had recited several rhymes, carefully sounding the words as Ruth directed. 'I should never hear the end of it!'

'They would be expecting you to be discussing serious issues, like the progress of the war?'

Ruth had meant the remark casually, but Paul looked at her sharply. 'Is that what you thought I would want to discuss with you? That is far from my wish. I value the opportunity to forget the war for a brief time, when I can relax and hold a normal conversation for once. And my fellow officers would have no opinions, because none of them knows of these lessons. It would not be approved. Of that I am certain.' He put the book down, then said, as if the idea had just occurred to him, 'You did not think, I hope, that I came here with the intention of discussing the war with you? Of perhaps obtaining information from you?'

Ruth felt a hot rush of colour burning her cheeks. 'Why should I think that?' she asked. 'I know very little about what is happening with the war. I know nothing that could possibly be of interest to you. For me, too, it is pleasant to be able to forget such things for a few hours, and speaking English again reminds me of my home. It reminds me of the life I had before all this began.'

Paul nodded sympathetically. 'I understand, Ruth. It is like that for me, too. But we must also make sure that we keep to the lessons. So, now, you will read one of these strange poems which seem to have meaning understood only by an English child, and then I will try to read it as you do, and my F's and W's and Vees must sound as yours do.'

They ended the two hours laughing together over Paul's efforts, and Ruth's attempts to explain some of the rhymes.

'I am sure we must have similar nonsense poems in German,' Paul said. 'It is so long since I heard any. There are no young children in our family.' He reached for his greatcoat and cap. 'You are agreeable that I come again on Thursday?'

'Yes. I shall look forward to it. And I'll plan the time better. I'll think of lots of things we can talk about, now that I know you better.'

'And you will no longer be shy of saying my words are all in the wrong order?' Paul smiled at her and held out his hand. 'Goodbye, Ruth. I have enjoyed today.'

He's not at all formal, really, she thought, as she saw him to the door. She couldn't think of him as the enemy now that she felt she was beginning to know him. She was looking forward to his next visit; already planning what they might talk about.

The following day, Annette said, 'Ruth, take me out as far as the crossroads, please. It's a nice day and I'm tired of staying indoors.'

Ruth fetched Annette's coat and her own, and a rug to go over her friend's knees and pushed the wheelchair along the country lane, away from the town.

'Tell me, what is your German really like?' Annette asked curiously. 'We heard you laughing together. Françoise could not believe her ears. She hates all Germans, as does Michel, because of what happened in the first war.'

'Paul's easy to talk to,' Ruth said. 'It doesn't seem to matter that he's German, he's just a person.'

'Françoise and Michel won't be the only ones to disapprove of his coming to the house, when word gets around,' Annette warned. 'And people are sure to notice; they always do.'

'I know,' Ruth sighed. If it wasn't German soldiers staring at them, it was the local women, and everyone seemed to be watching everything she did.

Annette said no more, but noticed that 'Captain Reinhardt' was now 'Paul.' And there was no denying, from the brief glimpse of him she'd had through the crack in the kitchen door, that he was a pleasant looking, open-faced man. Annette sighed. When she and Ruth's brother had decided to marry, she

46

had thought how nice it would be if Ruth could have found herself someone too, and at the time the chances had seemed to be that it would be someone French, since Ruth was spending much of her time in France. But the idea of Ruth falling for a German, someone from the enemy's occupying forces, was distasteful and disturbing. Annette put the thought resolutely out of her mind. Captain Reinhardt might be transferred away from here, or become too busy on more important matters and lose interest in improving his English. She hoped one or the other might happen before the locals came to hear about the English lessons and voiced their disapproval. In general, the citizens of Ste Marie de la Croix were not fond of foreigners, though they had become used to seeing Ruth around, over the years, and accepted her, mainly because she spoke French almost as well as themselves.

'Let's go as far as the War Memorial,' Annette said suddenly. 'That's if you don't mind pushing me so far.'

'Course not! It's not all that far and the road is level. I feel like some exercise myself,' Ruth answered.

The War Memorial was an elaborate, stone-carved monument erected to commemorate those men from the town who had been killed during the 1914–18 war. Two of Annette's uncles were recorded among the list of names on the plinth. The monument itself portrayed a group of weary soldiers and sailors, with, behind them, an angel stretching wings protectively over them.

'Oh, look!' Annette exclaimed in dismay. 'The figures have been damaged! The Germans must have been using it for target practice!'

Ruth shook her head. 'No, don't you remember? It was a few months ago. Some German soldiers were chasing a group of local boys they suspected of sabotaging one of their staff cars. They caught up with them here and they were all shot, blasted with automatic rifles. Some of the bullets must have hit the memorial.'

Annette shuddered. 'And that dark stain on the side of the memorial — '

'It's all over now,' Ruth said gently. 'I heard that it was something even some of the Germans regretted afterwards. The boys wanted to do something to annoy the soldiers, but they didn't think of the possible consequences.'

'They have destroyed part of the angel's face,' Annette said, looking up at the memorial. 'It always looked such a beautiful, peaceful face. Now it's ugly, with part of it blown away. The angel has a sinister look, but it's still a face. It reminds me of someone.'

'Madame Duvalle,' Ruth said, studying the angel. 'I think it looks just like her now. How odd! And she does look rather ugly and sinister.'

'Yes, you're exactly right! It is like her,' Annette agreed. 'I don't think I'll want to come up here now I know what happened on this spot, but every time I see Madame Duvalle in the town I shall be reminded of a sinister looking angel.'

'Let's call it the Duvalle statue,' Ruth said, turning the wheelchair back towards home. 'No one else will know what we mean. That woman gives me the creeps, she's always staring at me with suspicious looking eyes. I wouldn't be surprised if she was an informer, spying on everyone and passing on information to the Germans.'

When Paul came again on the following Thursday, Ruth felt less nervous about the coming two hours. She had planned this lesson, written some notes about subjects she thought she could safely mention, and there was coffee set out ready on the table.

Françoise opened the door to him, scowling, though he seemed not to notice. He greeted Ruth warmly, tossed his greatcoat on to a chair and settled himself in another with every sign of being at ease.

'What are we to talk about today?' he asked, smiling.

'Coffee first, I thought. If this were England, I would probably be offering you tea, but France has never been good at that, and now it's impossible to obtain. Anyway, I'm sure you prefer coffee.'

'Yes, I do. Though we drink tea at home, and with milk and sugar as you do in England.' Paul accepted his cup and sipped it. 'I don't suppose it's readily obtainable at home now, any more than here.'

They could drift into a discussion on German rationing quite easily, Ruth thought, and perhaps that might be useful information to pass on to Alain, but she didn't want to compromise Paul.

'I looked out some more books,' she said. 'French ones this time, which I think are more likely to have been translated into German, so you might have read them. Or do you read French anyway?'

Paul smiled. 'I know enough French to converse with the local people here, but it's not enough to read French novels in their original. Let me see what you have, and I'll tell you if I know them.' He crossed to the table and picked up one or two, reading their titles and glancing inside. Then he noticed

Ruth's notes on possible subjects, and picked it up.

' 'Playing tennis; American films; classical music,' ' he read aloud. ' 'Avoid Mendelsohn.' What is this? Are we to avoid Mendelsohn because he was Jewish? Is that what you think?'

Ruth flushed. 'Those are my notes for today's lesson. They weren't meant for you to read.'

'Do you really think I would not wish to hear music merely because it was written by a Jewish composer?' Paul asked. 'That is a Nazi attitude. I am not a Nazi. I thought you would have realised that.' He sounded hurt.

'I'm sorry. I — I was being careful,' Ruth blurted out.

Paul sighed. 'You still do not trust me, do you? You have the attitude that all Germans are monsters, with unhuman feelings.'

'Inhuman,' Ruth said automatically.

'Quite so. You cannot see me as a person, an ordinary man who happens to have been born in a country whose government is at war with your government. That need not concern you — '

'How can you say that!' Ruth burst out. 'It's all very well for you! You are in authority here — for the present time, at least — and your word is law. If I offend the German

51

military, I shall be in grave trouble. I *have* to be careful what I say and do, every moment of the day. I have to be even more careful than anyone else, because I'm not French and I could be deported to Germany on the slightest pretext. And if I offend the local people, I shall be in almost as much trouble. They don't like foreigners of any kind, and if they knew I was friendly with a German soldier they could make life impossible for me. I dare not forget that we are at war and you are one of the enemy.'

Paul looked taken aback by her outburst. Then he said, 'I'm sorry. I should have realised the problems you were likely to face. I did not think of the effect it might have on your relationship with the local people. Perhaps I should not have asked you to give me English lessons.'

'It doesn't matter. I have little to do with most of them, anyway,' Ruth shrugged. Already, she was regretting her outburst and embarrassed by it.

'Would you prefer me to go? Shall we forget about the lessons for the future?'

She shook her head. 'No. Why should I care what the local people think? I enjoy speaking English again for a little while and it has nothing to do with anyone else, whom I invite to this house. Except Annette, of course. It's her home, but she has already said she has no objections to your coming here.'

The lesson proceeded. Paul insisted on listing all the musicians, composers and writers of the past who were Jewish, but whose works he admired. 'There! I hope that convinces you that I do not hate Jews!' he said finally.

'What a long list! How do you know that all of them were Jewish?' Ruth asked, intrigued.

'The Gestapo keeps a list. We are not supposed to read or listen to their works, but of course, many of us do. It is quite ridiculous to try to ban them. All the same, we have to be careful. They would report us for misconduct just as readily as they report the local citizens for a crime. I can tell you, the Gestapo are not at all liked by the Wehrmacht, the regular army.'

To change the subject, Ruth suggested they opened the french windows and sat outside in the tiny garden. The day was mild for once, and the garden still full of late flowers.

'This is a beautiful, peaceful place,' Paul said. 'Someone has cared for this garden.'

'Annette used to be a very keen gardener, before her accident,' Ruth explained. 'We used to bring her English plants and bulbs every time we came over, so you may see flowers that are not common in France. Now, of course, she can't do anything, but Michel, Françoise's husband, keeps it tidy for her. He works at the farm nearby; he's too old to do much but they are so short of labourers he is still needed.'

They sat on a wooden bench seat under an arbour of climbing plants that Michel had built so that Annette could sit out in her chair in the shade. Conversation turned to the holidays they had both enjoyed as children.

'It seems we both liked similar things,' Paul said. 'What a pity we never met, making sandcastles on a beach somewhere! I am sure we would have been friends then.'

How would I have felt, had I met and made friends with you before the war? Ruth thought. Life would be even more complicated, worrying about you fighting as well as Simon. And you and he might have met in a battle! I suppose you both still might, before this war is over.

'I must go,' Paul said, standing up. 'The time for my lesson is over.'

'You could stay longer if you like. It doesn't matter.' Ruth was reluctant to break the peaceful spell of the garden.

'Unfortunately, I cannot. I have shortly to be on duty at the Town Hall.' He walked back down the path to the sitting room, then said shyly, 'You cannot imagine how even these two sessions have helped me.'

'Yes, I've noticed that your English has improved since I first spoke to you,' Ruth replied innocently.

'I did not mean that. I was — war weary, I think you could say. Tired and depressed and undoubtedly homesick. To come here and talk for a few hours with someone who is both friendly and beautiful and treats me like a normal person, not an enemy, that means more to me than I can ever express — in any language.'

Ruth was not sure how to reply, but he seemed not to expect her to say anything. His coat and cap on, he took her hand and raised it to his lips. 'Auf wiedersehen, Ruth,' he said, then straightened up and was about to give his formal salute when he stopped himself.

'No! I must remember! The clicking of the heels is not done in the presence of English young ladies. It makes them laugh too much and then they are embarrassed at their lack of manners.'

'I've never laughed at you!' Ruth exclaimed indignantly.

'No? You laughed with your eyes, that first time when I came to ask for lessons. You could not hide what you thought of me, and I thought — ' Paul hesitated.

'Yes?'

'I thought they were the most beautiful, expressive eyes I had ever seen and I wanted to do anything that would give me the chance to see them again and get to know their owner.' He put a finger under her chin, raising it slightly. For a moment, Ruth thought he might be going to kiss her, but then he seemed to recollect himself, and turned away abruptly.

'Until next week, then!' His smile made her feel unaccountably weak in her legs. At the door, he said, 'Now, do I click my heels to make you laugh again, when there is so little to laugh about, these days, or do I preserve the dignity of the great German army? I could have had you arrested for mocking a German officer, you know.'

'I know. I was very rude to you, that day you first came here. I was surprised you didn't arrest me.'

'I surprised myself, too, that day,' Paul said enigmatically. He saluted her, but not formally and strode down the path.

'Your German is becoming less formal, less *German*,' Annette remarked, after Paul had gone. She had been sitting in the kitchen doorway, watching them. 'He seems quite relaxed now. This may be the time when he begins to say things which may be of interest to Alain and the group.'

Ruth shook her head. 'No, he won't. We don't ever discuss things that would be of the slightest interest to Alain.'

Annette gave her a long stare, and Ruth snapped irritably, 'And before you say it, yes, I am careful what I say to him. But I'm quite sure he doesn't come here with the intention of pumping me for information. He genuinely wants some English conversation. And also a chance to forget about the war for a little while. We are just two people talking together. It's unimportant which country we were born in.'

'Huh!' Annette said scornfully, wheeling herself back into the sitting room. 'They are never off-duty, these enemies of France.'

3

It was the day when Ruth wheeled Annette along to the local school, where, in the absence of most of the regular teachers, they both helped out. Annette taught reading and writing to the youngest pupils while Ruth attempted to teach English to a group of unwilling and rather slow-witted older girls. The head teacher had been deported to Germany the previous year, and most of the other teachers had left, either escaping to join the Free French forces under de Gaulle in Britain, or disappearing into the mountains with the freedom fighters. The school was now struggling to keep going with the help of a few local volunteers, overseen by Père Joseph, the elderly parish priest.

This morning, Ruth found her pupils particularly difficult to handle. 'Come along, Lisette,' she coaxed. 'Surely you can tell me the past tense of 'I go'?'

'I don't want to learn English,' Lisette sulked. 'What's the point?'

'The point is that one day the war will be over and you will be able to visit England. It's hardly any distance away, across the Channel. It's a beautiful country and you will enjoy being there so much more if you can speak the language a little.'

'I shall never want to visit England!' Lisette burst out. 'I hate the English! My papa said that the English betrayed us. He said that at Dunkirk — '

Ruth looked at her severely. 'That is enough, Lisette. Perhaps you should learn some historical facts before you say things like that. However, we're supposed to be having an English lesson, not a history one, so you will please pay attention and try to learn some irregular verbs.'

It was a difficult lesson, with the other girls taking their cue from Lisette and either pretending not to know the answers to the simplest questions, or giving wrong answers when Ruth was quite sure they would have known the correct ones weeks ago.

When the class was over, she felt relief, but also anger. Did these girls think they could behave as badly as they chose, just because there was no one in real authority here to stop them? She would speak to Père Joseph about their rudeness and inattention, though she doubted that the gentle, inoffensive old man would be able to make much impression on them.

Ruth found him in the classroom where Annette had been teaching. He looked sad and rather embarrassed, putting his hand affectionately on her shoulder as she prepared to wheel Annette home.

'My dear, I wanted to have a few words with you about your English pupils,' he began.

'Yes, I'd like a few words with you about them, too,' Ruth replied crossly. 'What is the matter with them lately? They used to be quite well-behaved and keen to learn, but today they have been really difficult. This morning it was certainly no pleasure to teach them.'

'Then perhaps you won't mind very much giving up your English classes here?' Père Joseph said gently.

'What?' Ruth stared at him in astonishment. Teachers were hard to come by, with so few younger people left in the town. Père Joseph had been delighted when Annette, who had taught infants before the war, suggested that as well as bringing her, Ruth should stay and help with the older girls. Someone able to teach them English had seemed an unexpectedly fortunate bonus.

'I am so sorry, Ruth, but some of the parents have been objecting to you teaching their children. It's ridiculous, I know, but there is a good deal of anti-British feeling in the town.'

'Lisette's parents, I suppose. She as good as said she hated everything English.'

'Grandparents, as a matter of fact. Her father was killed shortly after the Dunkirk withdrawal, and her mother was deported to Germany for offending the occupying forces here. I'd prefer to call it for services to the French Resistance.' Père Joseph smiled ruefully. 'You can understand their feelings, perhaps, though it is unfair to condemn you personally.'

'It is completely ridiculous!' Annette said angrily. 'If they did but realise — surely they know the British are on their side! And can they not see, from a purely practical point of view, what a splendid opportunity the children here have to learn English from a native speaker? Ours must be the only school left in France that can claim such an advantage.'

'Unfortunately, the situation is a little more complicated than a matter of mere prejudice.' Père Joseph fidgeted with the end of the cord round his cassock; clearly he found it difficult to explain further. 'It is not only Lisette's grandparents who have spoken to me. It seems — it seems there are others in the town who think you are becoming too friendly with the Germans here. They suspect you may be an informer.'

'That's the last thing Ruth is!' Annette burst out angrily, before her friend could reply. 'If they only knew! Ruth gives English conversation lessons to a German officer, that's all. He sought her out and asked her, and you know perfectly well she couldn't have refused! The Germans can demand anything they want; everyone is aware of that. He comes to the house for lessons, nothing more. I can vouch for that myself.'

It wasn't quite as she would have explained it herself, but Ruth was grateful that Annette had spoken up so forcibly in her defence.

Père Joseph nodded sadly. 'Yes, I am quite sure myself that Ruth could never do or say anything that would help the Germans. In fact,' he hesitated for long enough to make Ruth wonder just how much he knew about her contacts with Alain and Claude the baker. 'I *know* Ruth is a loyal friend to France. But these people . . . ' He sighed and shrugged. 'They say they have seen a German officer coming to your house and they have put the worst possible interpretation on it. They have told me they will withdraw their children from the school if Ruth remains as teacher.'

'Pshaw! This German officer could equally well be coming to see me!' Annette exploded indignantly. 'Why don't they condemn me as well?'

Père Joseph's cassock cord was becoming frayed between his nervous fingers. 'It is because you are French, Annette, and Ruth is a foreigner,' he blurted out. 'It is unfair, I know. But what can I do? If I insist that you stay, you will have no pupils to teach.'

'It's all right. I understand,' Ruth said quickly. 'It's natural for them to condemn anyone who is different, whom they don't entirely trust. I'll give up teaching willingly, if it's going to cause trouble for you. But will they still object if I continue to bring Annette here? She can hardly manage to wheel herself all the way very easily.'

'They needn't think *I* shall come any more if *you* aren't wanted!' Annette said fiercely. 'I'm sorry, Père Joseph, but you'll have to find another teacher for the little ones. If Ruth isn't allowed to work here, then I won't, either.'

'But Annette — ' Ruth began, then stopped when she saw the stubborn expression on her friend's face.

Père Joseph rested his hand on Annette's shoulder. 'I can understand your feelings, Annette, and I applaud your loyalty. But there are families with little children who have not spoken against Ruth. It is sad they will not have the opportunity to learn anything. I don't know where I shall find another teacher for them, and this war may go on for a long time yet. Would you, perhaps, consider visiting them in their homes, to make sure they don't forget how to read and write?'

'I'll consider it,' Annette conceded. 'But only if they have no objection to Ruth coming with me. I don't want to have anyone else pushing my wheelchair if I go to visit them. Is that understood? Perhaps you will speak to some of the parents, Père Joseph, and tell them the situation. And if you let me know who would like me to visit them, I will try to arrange it.'

On the way home Annette said to Ruth, 'You know, visiting some of the children in their homes is not such a bad idea. It gives me an excuse to get out of the house and when you have messages to deliver for Alain, who is to say whether we are visiting one of my little ones or you are going to one of your secret message drops? It could be perfect cover for you.'

Ruth agreed. Now she had time to think about it, no longer teaching at the school felt more of a relief than a disappointment. It also meant that Alain might find more work for her to do. So far, she had carried messages, passed on information heard on the BBC

World Service, and translated a few German documents, but little that could be considered important, dangerous work. She shamelessly eavesdropped on conversations that the German soldiers had together, in the hope of picking up some useful information, but so far she had heard nothing more than a few grumbles, comments about girls and some chit-chat about their families back home; typical soldiers' talk containing nothing of interest to Alain and his group.

'Don't let's go straight home,' Annette said suddenly. 'Wheel me to the end of the main square, where the market is. We might be lucky and be able to buy some fish. At least, we can look at what everyone is selling. There might be some bargains.'

Ruth turned the chair down a narrow street that led into the square. Most of the shops were closed, shuttered and empty, but there was a small crowd round some rows of trestle tables, displaying everything from vegetables to second-hand household goods and clothing. There was precious little of use or value for sale. Privately, Ruth thought it reminded her of the leftovers from a rather down-market jumble sale in England. She supposed that someone might have a use for some of the objects offered for sale, but if not, it provided an excuse for the stall holders to come into the town and gossip with their friends.

At a small table on the end of one row, they were lucky enough to be able to buy three eggs and some rather limp carrots. 'Françoise will be able to make something with this,' Annette said confidently. 'There'll be some herbs in the garden she can use, too.'

As they moved slowly down each row of trestles, Ruth became aware that they were receiving hostile stares and that people were nudging each other and muttering amongst themselves.

'Let's go home now, Annette,' she urged, feeling uneasy.

Annette didn't seem to be aware of the attention they were provoking. 'We haven't been round everything,' she protested. 'There may be something interesting among the books at the far end. You're not in a particular hurry, are you?'

Ruth pushed Annette's chair between the rows, conscious of both a silence as they passed and a muttering behind them. As they neared the end of a row, there was a hissing sound from someone at one of the stalls. Even Annette heard, and tried to turn in her chair to see what the matter was. It was followed by a shout:

'Collaborateur! Traiteur! Keep away from

our town, English!'

'Oh, that's horrible! Who said that? Turn me round!' Annette exclaimed. The next moment Ruth felt something strike her between her shoulder blades, and a rotting turnip fell beside her.

'We're going home, Annette. Don't try to turn round; they're throwing things at us.' With as much dignity as she could muster, Ruth pushed the chair towards the edge of the square. Something soft and decaying flew past her shoulder and landed with a splat on the road in front of them.

'What's happening?' Annette gasped. 'Why are they doing this? Stop the chair, I want to demand an explanation from them!'

'No, not now.' Ruth kept on walking, resisting the urge to run, and sheltering Annette as much as she could from the rotting fruit and vegetables that were being hurled after them. They were out of the area of the stalls now, and out of range of the missiles, though they heard the sound of two or three falling on the stones behind them. Ruth turned into a lane leading off the square and kept on for some fifty yards before risking a glance back. The lane curved; they were out of sight of the stalls and those throwing the vegetables had lost interest.

'Who were they? Did you see?' Annette asked.

'I didn't see who threw the rotten fruit and veg,' Ruth replied, 'but the people just behind us looked like the same people who were outside Claude's bakery the morning I met Alain there. They didn't seem unfriendly then, though I noticed they stopped talking when I joined them.'

'They didn't know about your German captain then,' Annette said. 'Word must have got round about him coming to the house. They are all jumping to the wrong conclusion.'

'I don't see what I could do differently,' Ruth said indignantly. 'If they know that Paul comes to the house regularly they must have been watching for him. It's horrible to think I'm being spied on, and by people who are supposed to be friendly. No one was ever like this when we stayed here before the war.'

'The Occupation has changed people,' Annette replied. 'Now no one trusts anyone any more. No one can be sure who is in the pay of the Germans or who would betray a neighbour for a few groceries. Ruth, do you think it will ever return to the pleasant, friendly little town it used to be, before all this happened?'

Though she tried to brush off the incident

as the act of a few troublemaking locals, Ruth was shaken more than she wanted to admit. She wondered if it would be possible to continue to collect their bread from Claude's shop in future, and if not, how she was going to contact Alain if need be.

When they arrived back at the cottage, Françoise opened the door to them, her face blotchy and red from crying, her hands continuously twisting nervously in her apron.

'Oh, Mam'selle Annette! Mam'selle Ruth! I am so relieved you are back at last! Something terrible has happened! Michel has been arrested!'

'Arrested? Whatever for?' Annette demanded.

The Germans kept a check on all the men still in the town, but Ruth had always imagined that someone as elderly as Michel would be largely ignored by them. He was long past the age when he should have retired from work, but with the acute labour shortage, he was still in demand to work on the farm.

'Tell us what happened.' She manoeuvred Annette's chair into the kitchen and made Françoise sit down at the table. Then she began to prepare a strong cup of Paul's precious coffee and put it in front of the elderly woman. Through sobs and sniffles

Françoise gradually told them as much as she knew.

'He was up at the farm, working as usual, when two soldiers came in an army truck and took him away. They never said why. Phillipe, who was working with him, said they told him he was to be taken to the German Headquarters. You know what that means. He'll be deported to Germany and I'll never see him again.' She began to sob noisily into her apron.

'Don't cry, Françoise. Here, drink your coffee. It's good and strong, almost as good as we used to have it. It will make you feel better,' Annette urged.

'They wouldn't deport him,' Ruth tried to reassure her. 'The Germans know we need people like him to bring in the harvest. And why on earth would they arrest him, anyway? There's no reason for it. They must have mistaken him for someone else. He'll be released as soon as they realise their mistake, you'll see.'

'But suppose he has been betrayed?' Françoise wailed.

'Betrayed? But how could anyone betray — ?' Ruth stopped, realisation slowly dawning.

'Why would you think anyone would wish him harm? He's an old man; no threat to anyone,' Annette asked innocently.

'We thought no one knew. But someone always knows what goes on in a small place like this,' Françoise said.

'You thought no one knew what? Oh — I see!' Annette exchanged glances with Ruth. It was clear neither of them had had any idea that Michel had been involved with the Resistance. The knowledge came as a shock; if the Germans knew about this, then anything might happen to him.

'We must ask around among his friends, among the people he worked with,' Annette said briskly. 'Discreetly, but we must find out if they've arrested anyone else. But please don't worry, Françoise. You know the Germans are always arresting people for no reason. They do it to frighten them. They hold them for a few hours, then release them. It's always happening in the town. They *can't* know anything about what Michel has been doing; even we didn't.'

Eventually, they persuaded Françoise to stop crying, but she was in no state to prepare their evening meal. Ruth made an attempt to produce something, using the eggs from the market, but none of them felt much like eating.

'I'll walk up to the farm and ask around,' Ruth suggested. 'I can be there and back before curfew. And someone may have had more news by now.'

'I'll come with you. They may be less willing to talk to you, but everyone at the farm knows me. I've lived nearby ever since I was a child,' Annette said.

'No! Please, Mam'selles — don't leave me!' Françoise began to cry again. 'What if they come here and ask me questions? What if they want to arrest me, too? I've never done anything — I've never been involved, but Michel has told me things sometimes, when he has had to go out after curfew and I've been worried, and now, if they were to ask me anything, I could let something slip and betray him myself.'

'You know nothing,' Annette said sharply. 'No one will come and question you, I'm sure. But if anyone does, then your husband is an elderly farm worker, nothing more. He is clearly too old to take any active part in the war. Why, he is barely able to pick potatoes or milk a cow.'

'My Michel is not as useless as that!' Françoise said grumpily.

'You know that; we know that, but there is no reason for the Germans to know it,' Ruth explained patiently. 'We'll stay with you for now. I don't suppose anyone is likely to come, but if anyone does want to ask any questions, you must weep and wail so much that they'll give up. I'm sure the Germans can't know anything. It must all be part of their policy of trying to intimidate the local people. They can't keep him for long; the farm needs his labour and the Germans must know that.'

In spite of her reassurances, Ruth began to be worried about Michel. She couldn't imagine he was seriously involved with the Resistance; at his age he would surely not be able to do more than take messages, but even that, if discovered, could lead to dire consequences. There had been plenty of stories she had heard, of people in the town, who had been arrested, for apparently trivial reasons, or even no reason at all, and several had been deported to Germany and not heard of again.

They were almost too dispirited to listen in to the BBC on their secret wireless, but Ruth hoped there might be some good news to cheer them a little. There was a report that the Allies had entered Naples and there was news of the unconditional surrender of Italy, which was very cheering, considering that the German reports had spoken of 'stiff resistance' from the German army and the news released to the French had been of Germans fighting back the British invaders throughout the whole of Italy.

Françoise never listened to the BBC broadcasts, but was eager to hear any news the others passed on. Tonight, however, she seemed uninterested in any of it, sitting in her rocking chair in the kitchen, her apron thrown over her face, sniffing dolefully.

After the broadcast, Ruth and Annette sat with her in the kitchen to give her some company, but she seemed locked away in her own world, oblivious to anyone or anything. She didn't seem to want to go to bed, and both Ruth and Annette were loath to leave her, so they sat in the darkening room, not talking now, each wrapped in her own thoughts.

It was after midnight when they heard the sound of footsteps scraping on the cobbles of the yard outside the back door. Françoise sat up with a jerk. 'It's them!' she cried, with a little scream. 'They've come for me! Mam'selles, please don't let them take me away!'

'Germans don't creep round the back of the house, they'd hammer on the front door,' Annette said. 'Go and see who it is, Ruth. Just open the door a crack, first.'

'Who can it be if it's not the Germans? It's long past curfew,' Françoise muttered uneasily.

Ruth went to the back door and, shielding

the light from inside, opened it a few inches. She heard the sound of scuffling footsteps and a shadow, darker than the surrounding darkness, moved along by the side fence.

'Who's there?' she called.

There was a flicker of movement and a man came out of the shadows, towards her.

'Mam'selle Ruth?' he whispered.

By the light spilling out from the kitchen she saw that it was Marc, one of the men at the farm who worked with Michel. He was one of the few young men left in the town but had been rejected for military service because he was epileptic.

'Have you any news of Michel?' she asked. 'Come inside. We're all still up. None of us wanted to go to bed until we knew what had happened.'

Marc sidled in through the gap in the door, shutting it quickly behind him. He took in the faces of the two women sitting at the table, looking anxiously towards him.

'Have you brought news?' Annette asked.

Marc nodded. 'Some news, but not good, I'm afraid.'

Ruth drew out a chair for him and he sat down with them at the table.

'Well?' Annette asked. Françoise seemed too frightened to say anything.

'Michel was arrested with two other men.

We were told he'd been taken in for questioning but no one would say what about. The good thing is that we don't know the other men and they don't know Michel, so there's nothing they could say to incriminate him.' Marc paused, fidgeted on the chair, then continued, 'The worrying thing is that the other men were both released just before curfew, but they are still holding Michel. I've spoken to them, but they could tell me nothing. They weren't even questioned about Michel, so we've no idea what's going on.'

Françoise gave a sob. Her eyes had never left Marc's face.

'These other men,' Annette said thoughtfully. 'Were they involved with any group, do you know?'

Marc shook his head. 'I don't know. If they were, they were not with us, and one never knows who is or who is not, involved elsewhere. I could not ask them; it would not be right. All I know is, I had never met them before and never heard their names mentioned by anyone.'

'Where is Michel now?' Ruth asked.

'As far as we know, he is still being held at the German Headquarters. There are cellars underneath the Town Hall that they use for prisoners — and interrogations.'

'Is there nothing we can do?' Françoise moaned.

Marc looked at Ruth. 'I've been talking with — some of the others. Some of our friends,' he said hesitantly. 'Alain says you know one of the German officers rather well. He thinks it might be possible for you to find out exactly why Michel has been arrested, and what is likely to happen to him.'

'But I couldn't ask!' Ruth gasped. 'Paul — Captain Reinhardt — comes here for English lessons. We don't, ever, discuss the war or anything to do with the Occupation. I don't even know what kind of work he does at headquarters. He may have nothing to do with anyone who they arrest.'

'But you're friendly with him? You could ask, as a favour to a friend? Even if it isn't his province, he would be able to find out some information for you, more than we could discover ourselves.'

Ruth was aware of Françoise staring at her, the expression in her eyes suddenly full of hope. She dropped her own, embarrassed. 'He wouldn't tell me anything, even if he knew,' she muttered. 'He's an officer — he's schooled to be discreet. And, as I said, we never discuss — '

'He would tell you,' Annette broke in. 'Of course, he wouldn't tell you confidential information, but he'd reassure you if — if it wasn't anything too serious they were holding Michel for. And he'd warn you if Michel was really in trouble. That's what friends are for, surely?'

'It's not like that,' Ruth said desperately. 'Paul wouldn't — couldn't — do anything. And I couldn't ask him.'

Françoise's eyes were brimming with tears again. 'Please, Mam'selle Ruth,' she begged. 'You are our only hope. Please speak to your German. Make him believe my Michel is nothing more than a harmless old man. If he is sent to Germany, I shall die.'

'Ruth, you could at least try to ask him what the situation with Michel is,' Annette urged. 'If he can't, or won't, tell you, we shall understand, but at least speak to him. It's the only chance we have.'

Ruth felt trapped. 'Very well,' she said reluctantly. 'I'll tell him about Michel and how worried we all are. But he may refuse to discuss him at all and I couldn't make him.'

'We understand that. But he may want to reassure you,' Annette said.

'He'll be coming next Tuesday. I'll speak to him about it then.'

'Tuesday! That's far too long ahead!' Marc said anxiously. 'Anything could have happened by then. No, you must go and see him at the Town Hall, early tomorrow.'

'But I couldn't go and see him there — ' Ruth began.

'Please, Mam'selle Ruth. We are all depending on you.' Françoise stretched out her hand, her work-roughened fingers gripping Ruth's arm. 'Please do this for me,' she begged.

Ruth took a deep breath. 'All right,' she said. 'I'll see what I can do. I can't promise anything will come of it but I'll go to the German headquarters at the Town Hall tomorrow and try to talk to Paul.'

4

It was some time since Ruth had been inside the Town Hall. She had gone there to register as a foreign national when the Germans had first occupied Ste Marie de la Croix, but that had been more than three years ago now. At that time, the building had looked little different from the Town Hall as she had known it in peacetime, but now the Germans had expanded their operations and the place fairly hummed with the comings and goings of German soldiers.

Ruth's knees began to tremble as she mounted the short flight of stone steps leading up to the main doors. She had no idea what she would say; no idea even if she would be allowed to get as far as seeing Paul.

There was an armed soldier standing guard at the entrance. She noticed two Germans ahead of her, flash passes and walk inside unchallenged. Then she was in front of the guard, who barred her way.

'Your business here, Mademoiselle?' he asked, in heavily accented French.

'I — I wish to see Captain Reinhardt.'

'For what reason?'

'I — it's a confidential matter.'

The guard gave her a searching look. 'It is most unlikely the Captain will see you. He does not deal with civilians.' He gestured to her to leave, but Ruth stood her ground.

'I think he will see me when he knows I am here,' she said, with a confidence she did not feel.

The guard shrugged. 'You can try asking at the desk inside.' He stepped aside and motioned her to enter, but his tone and attitude suggested that she was unlikely to fare any better there.

Ruth stepped into the large vestibule, shabbier than she remembered and very bare. Against the far wall was a semi-circular counter on which were two telephones, a contraption that looked like an ancient internal switchboard and, at the back, filing cabinets topped with an untidy pile of ledgers. Manning the counter was a bored looking corporal. He glanced across at her as she came towards him and a flicker of interest passed briefly over his face. He didn't have occasion to deal with many young women, certainly none as pretty as this one.

'What is your business, Mam'selle?

'I wish to see Captain Reinhardt, please.' Ruth spoke in slow French for his benefit.

'What is the nature of your business with

Captain Reinhardt?'

'It's private.'

The corporal regarded her contemptuously. 'Captain Reinhardt is a busy man and he does not deal with civilians.' It sounded as if both he and the guard outside had learnt the same standard phrases in French, but then he added, 'If you state your business it might be possible to see someone else.'

'No. It has to be Captain Reinhardt. Please ring through to his office and tell him that Mademoiselle Ruth Lawson wishes to see him.' Ruth tried to sound as haughty and arrogant as she could, knowing that the German soldiers were used to being given orders in that manner.

'I cannot telephone him. He will not wish to be disturbed.' The corporal turned away and began fiddling with some filing cards, expecting her to give up and leave. Ruth moved nearer.

'He will want to see me when he hears my name. This is not disturbing him. He will be annoyed if you do not tell him I am here.'

The corporal stared at her insolently. 'I cannot contact him. He is at a meeting.'

'At what time will the meeting be finished?'

'I have no idea. Mam'selle, there is an officer who deals with all matters relating to the civilian population, Lieutenant Kaufmann. It is he you should see. Shall I ask him if he will see you?'

'No, it has to be Captain Reinhardt and the matter is private and confidential,' Ruth replied icily. She noticed a long bench against the wall over to the left, and indicated it. 'I shall wait there until Captain Reinhardt has left his meeting and is available to see me. When he is free, you will please inform him that I am here.'

The corporal shrugged dismissively and continued with his filing. He muttered something in German that sounded like 'you'll have a long wait' and turned his back on her.

Ruth sat down on the bench. Away to her right was the main staircase to the upper floors and in both directions long corridors led away from the main hall. Surely, Paul would come past here eventually? At the very worst, he must come this way at lunch time and she'd be able to stop him before he went out of the main door.

There was a clock on the wall above the counter and she watched the minute hand move slowly round the face. A few civilians came up to the counter and were either dealt with by the corporal or diverted to wait on the bench nearby. They all ignored her and each other and were eventually called back to the counter, to be given documents, rail travel permits or vouchers for special medical needs, it seemed, or escorted by another soldier to some office down one of the passages. Disconcertingly, none of these people reappeared.

After nearly an hour, Ruth was becoming desperate. She could wait here all day and still, perhaps, miss Paul. It was clear the corporal had no intention of informing him that she was here.

At eleven o'clock, when she had been sitting on the bench for over an hour and her bottom was aching with its hardness, the corporal was relieved at his post by another soldier. For the last fifteen minutes an idea had been forming in her mind, and now, with someone new at the counter, it seemed a good time to put it into operation. It was risky; if it didn't work she would have to give up any further attempt to see Paul or try to help Michel, for she was likely to draw suspicion of the worst kind on herself. She waited until there was no one else in the vestibule, then approached the new soldier on duty.

'Young man!' she said sharply, speaking in German. 'This is quite ridiculous! I have to see Captain Reinhardt on urgent, confidential business and he will be most annoyed when he learns that I have been kept waiting. Please show more efficiency than your colleague and inform him at once that he has a visitor.'

The soldier gave her his full attention. It was unusual for any of the local civilians to know any German. If they did, they did not choose to speak it. Nor did they address members of the occupying force in such an authoritative manner. This young woman facing him, glaring at him furiously, didn't look like one of the usual Frenchwomen; in fact, with her blonde hair she could easily be taken for one of his own nationality. Her German was well-spoken, too, without a trace of French accent. He decided to play safe and treat her with more respect than he usually gave the locals. However, he dared not disturb the Captain against orders.

'What is the nature of your business with Captain Reinhardt, Fräulein?'

Ruth noted with satisfaction that he sounded almost deferential when he replied to her, in German.

'I have some information for him,' she said haughtily.

He raised an eyebrow slightly. This could be interesting, but still he had strict orders about not letting civilians further than the entrance hall, without precise instructions.

'Captain Reinhardt does not interview informers. If you have information concerning anything or anyone, that is the province of the Gestapo, who have offices in this building. You should ask to speak to Lieutenant Kruger.'

The Gestapo were the last people Ruth wanted to become involved with. She watched in horror as the man lifted a telephone receiver. If he summoned someone from the Gestapo she would be in serious trouble and she would be likely to make Michel's situation far worse, too.

'No!' she said sharply. 'My information is not for the Gestapo. It is for Captain Reinhardt's ears only. Please call him and tell him — ' she had a sudden inspiration — 'tell him Wee Willie Winkie wishes to speak with him.' Germans, she knew, liked code names and this soldier might think it was a password used by Captain Reinhardt's personal informant.

The soldier put down the receiver. He looked at her thoughtfully for a moment. This girl was certainly no local Frenchwoman and her ready use of German made him think she might indeed be an undercover agent for the Reich. If she was one of Reinhardt's own informants, the Captain would be furious if the Gestapo learnt her information first.

There was certainly no love lost between the Wehrmacht, the regular army, and the secret police.

He lifted the other telephone, pushed a switch on the switchboard and cranked a handle on its side, which emitted a faint, whirring sound. Moments later, he spoke into the telephone mouthpiece, turning away so that Ruth could not hear what he was saying. There was a pause, then, 'The Captain says he will see you. I will send for someone to escort you to his office,' he said.

'Danke.' Ruth was so relieved she almost forgot to inject a note of arrogance into her thanks. The soldier pressed a buzzer and another soldier appeared from a door behind the counter. They exchanged a few muttered words, then the second soldier came over to her and indicated she should follow him up the stairs.

'This way, please, Fräulein,' he said politely.

He led the way along a long, uncarpeted corridor. These had once been the comfortable offices of the Town Hall staff but now the place looked bare, uncleaned and uncared for. Ste Marie de la Croix still had a mayor, but these days his office was in name only and his staff virtually non-existent.

At a door towards the end of the corridor,

the soldier stopped and knocked. Clearly, Ruth heard Paul's voice answering within, and a great surge of relief swept over her. It had been so difficult to get this far, surely now Fate was on her side and she would be able to help Michel.

The soldier pushed open the door and stood back, gesturing her to enter. She saw Paul sitting behind a large desk, spread with maps and files. He looked up, registering astonishment when he saw her.

He said nothing until the soldier had closed the door behind her, then exclaimed, 'Ruth — what on earth are you doing, coming here? When the clerk rang through, I wondered — but I thought it couldn't possibly be you. Why are you here? Is something wrong?'

'Paul, please — can you help us? I'm sorry to have tried to see you in this way, but I didn't know what else to do. We're all so terribly worried and you were the only person we could think of who would help us.'

'What is it, Ruth?' Paul came round the side of the desk and pulled forward a chair for her. Thankfully, she sank down on it, her knees shaking so much she doubted they would have supported her much longer.

'It's Michel, Françoise's husband,' she said. 'He's been arrested. We have no idea why. He's an old man, quite harmless, but

Françoise is terrified that he will be deported to Germany. That would kill both of them. Please, *please*, can you find out what is happening and help us?'

Paul looked at her sympathetically. 'I can see that this must be a worry for all of you,' he said 'but truly, there's not much that I can do. It's not my department, and if he's been arrested by the Gestapo then there certainly is nothing I can do. They run their own department, quite separate from the army and they would not welcome any interference. Any inquiry might end up making things worse for him, in fact.'

'But couldn't you find out *why* he's been arrested? We can't imagine that there could be any real charge brought against him,' Ruth said desperately.

'Tell me what you know. When was he arrested; where and by whom?'

Ruth told Paul the little she knew. 'He was working at the farm when two soldiers came in a truck and took him away. The men who were working with him, said the soldiers didn't say why he was being taken. No one else was arrested; only Michel.'

'Hmm! Two soldiers in a truck doesn't sound like the way the Gestapo operate. They tend to make a more impressive arrival.' Paul made a rueful face. 'If the Gestapo aren't involved, then maybe I can make a few discreet enquiries and find out what it's all about.' At Ruth's eager expression, he continued, 'But further than that I could not go. I have no influence in matters concerning the civilian population, and, even if I had, I could do nothing for him. You do understand that, don't you? Though I would, very much, like to help you, I cannot.'

Ruth nodded. 'Even finding out why he was arrested, would help. We'd know then how serious things were and perhaps what was likely to happen to him.'

'I will do whatever I can, but I'm afraid it can be very little,' Paul said. 'You know, you should not be here at all. Civilians are not allowed in these offices, certainly not without special permits. You risk being arrested yourself.'

'I know. And I'm sorry I had to trick the young soldier downstairs into letting me see you. It wasn't his fault, but I was desperate. Françoise is beside herself with worry and I didn't know what else to do.'

Paul smiled at her. 'It was brave of you, and a very resourceful trick. It intrigued me enough to order him to send you up, whereas had you merely given your name, I could not have seen you. Now, I will speak to the officer who is in charge of these matters and see what I can find out. One moment, please.' He picked up the telephone on his desk and asked for an extension number. Ruth gazed round the room and tried not to look as if she was listening, or give any indication that she understood what was being said. In fact, she could glean little from the conversation, for, having asked for information about those currently held in the cells, Paul said little more and she could hear nothing of the other speaker.

'Michel Leclerc, is he not?' he asked finally, putting the receiver down. Ruth nodded.

'He was arrested with some others yesterday on suspicion, the charge says. Of what, I do not know. He is being questioned but I know no more than that, and that is hardly more than you know yourself.'

'But what can they possibly suspect him of?' Ruth asked. 'An old man like him? There were others at the farm, younger men, but the soldiers left them alone. Why should they bother with Michel?'

'I do not know. Lieutenant Kaufmann, who deals with these matters, is not a particular friend of mine. Since I have no reason for asking details about civilians who have been arrested, he has no reason to give me any. I am sorry, Ruth, but I cannot do more. If I were to persist in enquiries, it could well lead to awkward questions being asked in return and perhaps make the situation more serious for Françoise's husband.'

'I understand.' Ruth accepted his words, but she was deeply disappointed. She had hoped, all along, that Paul would be able to do something to help them. He had seen Françoise; he must know her husband would not stand up to the rigours of being kept for long in a cell, and questioning could only confuse him.

'Now, you must go at once. I will show you out the back way; it might be awkward if you were seen up here by the wrong people,' Paul was saying. At the door he paused, hand on the doorhandle. 'I am so very sorry I could not help, Ruth,' he said. 'I hope this will not mean — are you still happy that I come for the conversation lessons, as before?'

'Of course!' Ruth replied at once. 'It's not your fault that Michel was arrested. I shouldn't have come here, I've put you in an embarrassing situation. But I didn't dare risk waiting to speak to you until you came for your lesson.'

'No matter. No one will know why you came.' He smiled at her and just before opening the door, added, 'Your visit has enlivened a particularly tedious morning. You have made the sun shine for me.'

He led her on, further down the passage, away from the main staircase to a narrow, spiral staircase at the end. 'There is a one-way door at the bottom. It will bring you out into a quiet side street where no one is likely to see you,' he said.

'Goodbye, Paul. And — thank you for trying to help. I know you have done as much as you could,' she whispered.

'I will see you next week. That is, if Françoise will forgive me enough to let me into the house. Tell her I am truly sorry about her husband.'

Ruth walked as quietly as she could down the staircase, trying not to let her feet clatter on the iron treads. At the bottom was a blank wall with a small door in it. The door had a bar across the centre, like a fire door, and when she pushed it it opened stiffly, just enough to allow her to slip through. It swung back with a click and she saw on the outside that there was nothing to indicate this was an exit of any kind.

Ruth found herself in a narrow, cobbled street with the blank walls of the backs of buildings rising up on either side. One way looked like a dead end, so she turned in the opposite direction, assuming she would come out into one of the side streets that led off the main square.

Half way towards the end of the street she had the distinct impression that someone was watching her. Uneasily, Ruth glanced over her shoulder. She'd been sure the street had been empty when she had come into it, but now standing across the cobbles was a woman in old, rusty black clothes with a shawl over her head, watching her.

As she looked, the woman turned her head and Ruth saw it was Madame Duvalle. A cold shiver ran down her spine. The woman did not speak or make any gesture, just stared after her, her expression hostile.

That woman really is sinister. She's like a witch, Ruth thought. She resisted the urge to run, and continued along the cobbles until she came to the junction with a second, slightly wider street, where there were houses, shops and the comforting sound of people passing by.

She must have seen me come out of that door, Ruth thought. It wouldn't take much to work out that it's a discreet exit from the German Headquarters. Now word will get round to all the old women of the town that I must really be an informer in the pay of the enemy.

She was still shaken by the time she arrived back at the cottage. Françoise opened the door to her, desperate for news, and it was hard to have to disappoint her. Annette took a more phlegmatic attitude. 'Well, I suppose we were hoping for too much, thinking Paul could help us. He has his job to do; he's a German soldier, after all. Though I believe he would have helped us if he could; he seems a good man.'

Françoise, once she realised that Paul could not help, seemed to accept that nothing else could be done, and accepted the situation with a deep, silent gloom which was almost as hard to bear as her earlier hysterics. Annette stayed with her in the kitchen, giving silent comfort by her presence, but Ruth, feeling illogically that she was to blame for failing, stayed in her room or out in the garden, reading.

They ate early in the evening, mainly because Françoise was persuaded that preparing the meal would take her mind off her worries. Afterwards, they sat over the last of Paul's coffee, talking little, each engrossed in her own thoughts.

It was dusk, about half an hour before curfew, when they heard the sound of footsteps in the yard outside.

'What now?' Françoise muttered. 'Have they come for us, now? If they try to take me away I shall defend myself.' She picked up a rolling pin and turned to face the back door, brandishing it menacingly. It opened and Michel stood there, his arms flung wide and a huge grin spread all over his face.

'They released me,' he said. 'Just like that. No word, no explanation. They just told me to go.'

Françoise flung herself at him, sobbing again with relief. He let her embrace him for a moment, then pushed her aside. 'I'm back safe, woman, and they didn't harm me. No need for any waterworks. Essentials first. They have even worse food in the cells than we have, so how about some of your cooking? I haven't had a decent meal for twenty four hours.'

Françoise ran to warm up the remains of their own meal, adding whatever delicacies she could find, to implement it. 'Perhaps Captain Reinhardt used his influence after all,' she whispered to Ruth.

Ruth thought it unlikely, in view of what Paul had said. This must be no more than a coincidence. Perhaps they had been intending to release Michel anyway, had arrested him only to discourage and frighten his friends and those who worked with him, from involving themselves in any anti-German activities.

Later, some time after curfew, when it was completely dark, there were more sounds of footsteps in the yard, and Marc and Alain sidled in through the back door. They nodded to Michel, who was enjoying his pipe, filled these days with a mixture of poor quality tobacco, dried weeds and shreds of rope, and drew up chairs to sit at the table with him. Françoise left the room but Ruth stayed, hovering by the door. She had been about to wheel Annette into her ground floor bedroom on the other side of the hall, but waited to hear what the men had to say.

'What questions did they ask you?' Alain asked. 'Do you think they knew anything?'

'Hard to say,' Michel shrugged. 'They established that the other two they picked up at the same time, were not known to me, or I to them. I suppose they must have suspected something, but could not prove it.'

'Since when has lack of proof ever bothered them?' Marc said scornfully. 'Did they put you in the cells for a few hours to frighten you, perhaps?'

'It certainly did that, I can tell you! But I gave them no cause to think they were on to anything. They got nothing out of me,' Michel declared stoutly. The food had revived him; he was back to himself again.

'They must have thought there was

97

something, or why you? There are others, more likely targets, whom they left alone,' Marc said.

'It's because he looks too old to be a danger to them that they think he is,' said Alain, with complicated logic. 'They'll be watching you closely now to see who you contact, who you run to. You'll have to lie low for a while, act like the useless old man you want them to believe you are.'

'But he can't do that!' Marc exclaimed. 'There is the pickup in four nights' time! It has been arranged for him to do it.' He suddenly became aware that they were not the only ones in the kitchen, and turned anxious eyes on Ruth and Annette.

'It's all right, Marc. We are all friends here.' Annette smiled at him. 'You and Alain should know that.'

Alain nodded, but he glowered at Marc. 'Someone else will have to do it,' he said. 'It would be asking for trouble for Michel to attempt anything so soon. We need someone who is not suspected at all.'

'But there is only Michel,' Marc argued. 'The others — ' he hesitated, shrugging his shoulders. 'The others cannot go. You know that.'

'He'll be watched from now on. Sure to be, which means he'd be bound to be caught.

And most likely with the goods on him,' Alain persisted.

Marc glanced at the two girls. 'What about Mam'selle Ruth?' he asked. 'She could do it.'

'A woman?' Alain looked doubtful. 'She has never done this before. I don't know.'

'Someone has to go,' Marc said. 'And you know that it cannot be either you or me. Who else do we have?'

'What is it that needs to be done?' Ruth asked. She was beginning to be nettled by the way they were discussing her without including her.

'It is a pickup,' Alain said unwillingly. 'There is something which needs to be collected, at night, after curfew.'

'It sounds simple enough,' Ruth said impatiently. 'Why do you doubt I can do it?'

'Is it dangerous?' Annette asked. She put a hand protectively on Ruth's arm.

'Only dangerous if you're caught,' Marc growled. 'She'll have to go. There's no one else and it's straightforward enough.'

'You'd better tell me what it's all about,' Ruth said. 'I'm prepared to go if you want me to. It's not all that risky, being out after curfew. I've done it before. It's easy enough to hide from patrols.'

'It's a rendezvous,' Alain said. 'With someone from a boat. Meet on the beach.

They're bringing a package — supplies for us which have to be collected.'

'But no civilians are allowed anywhere near the beach,' Annette protested. 'There is barbed wire everywhere. And surely, there would be guards, too.'

'Not at night,' Marc told her. 'You can get very near to the beach by going through the woods. That's safe; they only patrol the roads. We'll need someone who knows the way, it's very dark. There will be no moon and it would be too risky to use any lights.'

'I know my way through the woods quite well. We used to go to the beach that way most times when I was on holiday here before the war,' Ruth said. 'I haven't been that way recently, though. You can't easily push a wheelchair along those paths.'

'Ruth, are you sure about this?' Annette said fearfully. 'If you are caught, you could be shot.'

'It's safe enough, if you're careful,' Michel reassured her. 'I've done it before, several times. What you need to know is how the patrols work. Being Germans, they keep to a regular routine. If you see one lot going past, you know you'll be safe enough until they come back, and they never vary their timing.'

'Tell me what I have to do,' Ruth said. 'I'll do it. Who do I meet and where? And how will we know each other?'

'You'll be told the details on Tuesday afternoon. Best you know as little as possible until the last moment.' Alain stood up. 'Thank you, Mam'selle Ruth. We appreciate what you are doing for us.'

'Just a moment!' Annette exclaimed. 'Tuesday is the day when Captain Reinhardt comes. Don't come near the house until well after four o'clock.'

'Reinhardt? That's the man who comes for English lessons?' Marc asked.

'Yes. Ruth went to ask him for help when Michel was arrested,' Annette said. Alain, on the point of leaving, swivelled back sharply. 'You went to see him, Mam'selle? At the German headquarters? You actually managed to see him and ask for his help? When was this?'

'This morning,' Ruth said unwillingly. 'He said it wasn't his department, dealing with civilians, and that he couldn't interfere — '

'Yet Michel was released only a few hours later,' Alain said musingly. 'That could hardly be a coincidence, I am sure. Keep this German sweet, Mam'selle Ruth, it looks as if he could be very useful to us in future.'

'But I don't — '

Annette silenced her with pressure on Ruth's arm. 'Say nothing,' she muttered in

English. 'Let them think as they please. This way they will not think ill of your friendship with Paul.'

Tuesday afternoon Ruth felt very uneasy as she waited for Paul's arrival. She wondered if he would say anything about Michel's release, but more seriously, she felt concerned about the activities of the coming night. Even though Paul was one of the enemy and she was committed to doing all she could to help the local members of the Resistance, she hated the thought that she was deceiving him. If he ever suspected that she was involved with them, their friendship would count for nothing and he would have her arrested, she was sure. By now, Paul's friendship had come to mean a great deal to her and she hated having to jeopardise it.

He came, prompt to the minute as usual. He did not mention Michel or her visit to his office and Ruth, sensing that he wanted to forget anything to do with his work for these two hours, said nothing either. It was only when a beaming Françoise brought in coffee and some home made cake, half way through the lesson, that the subject was, of necessity, brought up.

'Monsieur, you are most welcome today!' Françoise put down the tray with two steaming cups of coffee on the table. She had made a big effort to produce a cake with some hoarded ingredients and presented it to him proudly.

Paul looked startled. 'This is a bit different from her usual reception of me,' he remarked to Ruth in English, knowing Françoise would not understand. 'I thought she hated all Germans without exception. Is the cake poisoned, perhaps?'

Ruth laughed. 'I doubt it! Annette has already tried some and to prove it's safe I'll eat a piece myself. Françoise wishes to show her appreciation to you because Michel has been released and she is sure it was all due to your intervention.'

'But I did nothing! I am pleased for her that her husband has been restored to her, but it was not due to anything I did. I told you, did I not, that the arresting of civilians is not my department and there was nothing I could do to help him. His release is a coincidence; nothing to do with me.'

'I'll tell her but I doubt if she will believe it,' Ruth said. 'Bask in her gratitude. It's better than having her glower at you whenever you come here.'

'It is indeed! Now I shall not, perhaps, feel that I risk a carving knife in my back while I am here.' Paul was laughing with her, but then he took her hand and added, 'I always thought, though, that the carving knife would be used to protect your honour, rather than because Françoise and Michel suffered at the hands of my fellow-countrymen during the last war. After all, I was barely born then. It would be illogical to hold me responsible for my country's excesses at that time.'

'I don't think logic plays much part in Françoise's thinking,' Ruth replied. Was their maid really concerned for her honour, as Paul had rather quaintly put it, she wondered? If she were to become too fond of him . . . She thrust the thought from her. They were friends, but as to anything else — . That way, problems abounded. She must not think of Paul in that way, and yet he'd taken her hand and the unexpected contact had sent a pleasant sensation through her fingers.

They sat in the garden, discussing Annette's flowers, comparing the common names of some of them, deciding which grew naturally in France and which were rare, brought from England on one of Ruth's visits before the war. Paul seemed to want to stay longer and at any other time, Ruth would have encouraged him, but today she was on tenterhooks in case Alain appeared. He worked so actively for the Resistance that she felt sure he must be one of the Germans' suspects and it would not do for Paul to see him at the house. As it was, Alain normally came only after dark when he wanted to see Michel, or there was a small job for her to do, like a message to deliver or some German papers they wanted translating.

It was nearly half past four before Paul rose reluctantly from the garden seat. 'I must go now, Ruth,' he said. 'I have stayed far longer than my lesson time permits.'

'It doesn't matter,' Ruth said quickly. 'I don't think of it as a lesson now, just a conversation between friends.'

'I am glad you think of it like that. I, too, feel that I am conversing with a friend. Although you must admit that my English has improved a great deal. So much so, that you rarely correct it now. It is no longer a lesson, is it?'

'I'm sorry I forget to tell you. I don't like to interrupt you to point out mistakes.'

He turned hazel eyes on her and she saw they twinkled with humour. 'Sometimes I make a mistake on purpose, to see if you notice. Mostly, you do not.'

Ruth blushed. 'I'm sorry. I forget, because I don't want to stop you.'

'And all I want to do is sit here with you and talk about flowers, or books, or pre-war films and forget the rest of the world for a little while.' He gazed down at her. 'Forget the lessons. They are not important. What is important is that we can have these few hours out of time, out of this tormented world. It means a great deal to me, more than you can imagine.'

Ruth nodded. She was not sure how to reply but no answer seemed necessary, for he leaned towards her and kissed her gently on her lips. 'In appreciation,' he murmured. Then, before she could speak, he rose to his feet, made her a formal salute and walked quickly back through the french windows. When she followed him inside he had already let himself out of the front door, calling a farewell and thanks to Annette and Françoise.

Ruth avoided joining them in the kitchen straight away. She needed time to herself, to think about things. Paul was a serious young man; flirting would not be in his nature, she was sure, which meant that he, too, was beginning to view these conversation lessons as developing into something more than friendship.

She pulled herself up with a jerk. She had been thinking 'he, too'. It was clear now that Paul had become very important to her, and that could lead to a difficult situation. Alain, Marc, Claude and the others would strongly disapprove; they would be justified in feeling they could not count on her complete loyalty to France and the aims of the Resistance. She must always remember, as they had warned her at the beginning, that Paul was an enemy soldier. She must not let her feelings and emotions overcome her duty and patriotism. But already, she feared that it was too late for that.

5

Alain arrived in the early evening, coming through the fields from the farm and in at the back door, to avoid being seen on the road. He began briskly, without preamble. 'You have some dark clothes? Trousers? Sweater? A flashlight?'

'I have black slacks and a black pullover. I can borrow a knitted cap from Annette. Should I blacken my face?'

'Don't overdo it. That would be hard to explain if you were caught. If you are careful and sensible, there is no reason for anyone to see you, but if you are unlucky, spin them a tale of needing urgent medicine for Annette. Doubtless she suffers sometimes from stiffness of the joints, sitting all the time in that chair. There is no better treatment for that than to wrap the limbs in damp seaweed, but it has to be freshly gathered.'

Ruth laughed. 'I must remember to tell her that!'

'It is true. An old remedy used by my grandmother, and she was agile up to a great age. But warn Annette that she must be prepared to back your story if necessary.

Now, I will tell you exactly how you are to reach the rendezvous and how you are to pass the barbed wire and get on to the beach.' Briefly he gave her instructions. Ruth knew the area well, she was sure she would have no difficulty finding the exact place on the shore, even though she had not been there for some time.

'When you come out of the woods you will be beside the coast road. Opposite you is a narrow lane which leads directly to the beach. At the end of the lane, on the left hand side, is a large post. There is wire on your right, so keep well clear. Go forward fifteen paces to your left, past the post, and you will find a gap in the wire. This will enable you to walk down the shore to the water's edge.' He grinned. 'Even the Germans have to make it possible for their troops to reach the sea. When you are at the water's edge there is no more wire and you will be able to walk along the edge of the shore. At precisely a quarter past twelve, give three quick flashes out to sea. Watch for one answering flash. Do not use your light for any other purpose. A rowing boat will beach as near to you as it can manage. Someone will hand over a package in a holdall, or a rucksack. Bring it back with you and leave it under the hay in the barn at the farm. It will be collected later.'

'What will be in it?' Ruth asked curiously.

'Better if you do not know. It will not be too heavy for you, I am sure. If all goes according to plan, you will be safely home and in bed by one o'clock. These people you are to meet are very reliable. They will be there, without doubt. If you are not, they cannot risk waiting. And we cannot afford to wait for these — supplies. Do not fail us, Ruth.'

'If they're expecting Michel, how will they know that I'm the right person to hand over these supplies to?' Ruth asked.

'Well, they will not be expecting a woman, that's for sure,' Alain said. 'But the boat will be launched from a small fishing boat in the Channel. The crew are likely to be British so once they hear your voice they will doubtless be reassured. The codename of your contact is 'George from Dover' and the person he will be expecting to meet will be codenamed Jean. Is that clear? Do you have any further questions?'

Ruth shook her head. 'No, it seems quite straightforward. I know my way through the wood and Michel has explained how the patrols work. The road and the beach look like the only dangerous places, and I'll be particularly careful then.'

'Don't stay around talking to your

compatriots when you meet,' Alain warned. 'Every unnecessary minute you and they are on the beach, puts everyone's lives in danger. Go quick; come back quick. Bon chance, Ruth.'

When Ruth went to help Annette to bed as usual, her friend was unwilling to go. 'I want to stay up until I know you are safely back,' she protested.

'Stay awake by all means, but go to bed. If anyone should come, they'd think it odd if you were still fully dressed. If you are in bed it will be easier to pretend you know nothing about where I am.'

'I wish you were not doing this!' Annette muttered. 'What you have done in the past was risky, but this is downright dangerous!'

'No it isn't; not if I'm careful. And think: Michel has been doing this kind of thing on several occasions and we never suspected at all!'

At half past eleven Ruth let herself out of the back door and walked through the fields at the back of the cottage, towards the woods which stretched along one side of the coastal road. The road itself was out of bounds to all civilians, being too near the beach, and technically, the woods were too, but the Germans rarely entered them. Ruth felt quite confident that she was safe as she walked

111

silently along the mossy paths, finding her way by the darkened outlines of the trees on either side. She wondered if the RAF would be flying over tonight; they came mainly on moonless nights. It might cause a diversion if they did, but she wasn't sure if that would help her or not.

She reached the part of the wood running parallel to the coastal road. There was a grassy slope leading down from the trees and a few yards along the road was the lane which led directly to the beach. An empty house stood at the top of the lane; the occupants had been moved out some time before and the building, a small holiday cottage, was now becoming derelict. Ruth could see the outline of its roof, a darker black against the dark sky, and this showed her exactly where the lane was. Before she left the shelter of the wood, she turned her flashlight on the face of her watch, shielding the light. It was five minutes past midnight.

The road was the tricky part. At the edge of the trees she stopped to listen. The night was silent, not even broken by the sounds of small animals rustling in the undergrowth. She slithered down the grass slope and followed the road, walking along the grass verge to deaden the sound of her footsteps.

Fifty yards along, she came level with the

house and the entrance to the lane. Still no sound of any patrols, or vehicles, broke the silence.

Ruth turned into the lane and was startled by the hooting of an owl, and something large flew low past her. If that's all that's out at night round here, I won't have much to worry about, she thought, laughing at her fears.

The lane was no more than a couple of hundred yards long, but it was surfaced with loose stones and Ruth had to walk slowly and carefully to avoid making a noise. Alain and Michel had warned her that it was possible there could be soldiers on the beach, either a patrol or a lone man there for purposes of his own. If there was anyone, she must wait in hiding, and hope they would leave. The boat she was meeting would not come inshore unless they saw her signal. If she had to wait more than half an hour, the boat would turn back and another rendezvous would have to be arranged. Alain had impressed on her that, if at all possible, she must collect this mysterious package tonight, because the contents were urgently required by the group.

Ruth found the post without difficulty and stood close to it for a few moments, listening for the sound of anyone on the beach. She could hear nothing except the regular hiss and rattle of the waves pouring over the shingle and sweeping back again.

Out at sea the sky was fractionally lighter, though she could see nothing except the occasional flicker of white spray on the waves. Nearer at hand was a dark shadow, like an unkempt hedge, but which she knew was the line of spiralling barbed wire.

Fifteen paces to the left of the post, Alain had said. She counted them carefully, then tentatively put out a hand. She touched wire in front of her. Had Alain been wrong? Perhaps there was, after all, no gap here? There were other places, over the dunes all along this stretch of shoreline, where there could be ways on to the beach, but she'd never find them in the dark.

She listened again and heard nothing but the swish of the tide, nearer now. It must be nearly at its height at this hour and would come only a few feet short of the wire. Shielding her torch again, she took a second glance at her watch. The minute hand was well past the twelve; they would be looking for her signal in less than three minutes. Where *was* this gap?

Ruth inched forward cautiously. It occurred to her that Alain or Michel's paces could well be longer than hers. She took two more paces and felt ahead. Nothing. She had reached the gap. She moved forward and had the sensation of walking down a tunnel, wide enough for a rowing boat or three men to march abreast, no more. Then the tunnel melted away and she was beyond the wire, the water lapping at her feet.

She looked out to sea. The whole expanse seemed completely empty. She listened; there was no sound from the land but out at sea she thought she caught the sound — once — of an oar creaking in its rowlock.

Ruth pointed the flashlight out to sea and gave the signal, three quick flashes. Half a minute later there seemed to be an answering flash, so brief in the darkness ahead of her that she wasn't certain whether she had really seen it. And then she heard, clearly this time, the creak of oars again.

The little boat must have been quite close in to shore, though she had been completely unaware of it. Within a couple of minutes there was the grating sound of a keel on the stones, a soft splash and a dark shape came wading through the water towards her, a rucksack slung over one shoulder.

'Hallo!' she whispered into the darkness. 'I'm here. In front of you.'

The man had almost reached her. He began to speak in stumbling French but she stopped him.

'It's okay. I'm English. My name's Ruth.

Are you George from Dover?'

'Good God, a woman! And English, too!' Came an unmistakable British voice out of the darkness. 'I was expecting a chap, a Frenchman called Jean.' He stopped, suddenly wary, and she saw his hand go to his belt.

'It's all right. Jean couldn't come. We suspect the Germans are watching him so we couldn't risk sending him.'

The man visibly relaxed and stepped out of the water beside her. 'Yes, I'm George from Dover,' he said, 'but what's an English girl doing here in France?'

'It's a long story,' Ruth said, laughing. 'I live in France for the moment. And I can't tell you how good it is to hear an English voice again. Is this what I'm to collect?' She gestured to the rucksack.

George handed it to her. 'It's not heavy, but be careful how you handle it. How are things here?'

'Not too bad, compared with some places. The town is swarming with Germans but we're learning to live with it. How are things in England?'

'Bearing up. Morale is good. Seems as if we might have the Jerries on the run in Italy, and the Russkies are defeating them on the eastern front. Do you get much news?'

'Officially, only German propaganda. We hear the BBC World Service but it's illegal to listen so it's always a bit risky. There aren't many wireless sets in the town and it's dangerous to know too much about what's really going on.'

'I want to tell you — we're all very grateful for what you chaps — and women, too — are doing to make life difficult for Jerry. Look, good as it is to talk to you, mustn't hang about here. Chaps in the boat want to be away sharpish. Good luck, Ruth. Just hold on in there; we'll be coming to rescue France and kick Jerry out, soon as we can. That's a promise.' He saluted her, then began wading back through the water. She stood listening until she heard the grating of the boat against the pebbles and a soft thud as George from Dover climbed aboard.

Ruth turned away. The conversation, brief though it had been, had lifted her spirits. She hadn't spoken to another fellow countryman for nearly four years and it was good to know they were still there, not all that many miles away, across the channel and still free. She almost laughed aloud as she hefted the rucksack on to her shoulder and began the trek back up the shingle, between the barbed wire hedges. She had done it! She had collected Alain's precious package and had

had a conversation with someone from Britain, a ridiculous conversation, just as if they'd met on a street corner in England and then he'd had to hurry off to catch a bus.

Ruth reached the lane and strode up it, still feeling elated. Twenty minutes more and she'd be safely back in the cottage, perhaps half an hour to include leaving the rucksack safely hidden in the barn.

She reached the end of the lane and stepped on to the road without pausing. She had hardly gone half a dozen paces when, round the corner beyond the lane, came one of the German patrol cars, driven fast.

Ruth dived back against the hedge at the side of the road, praying she had not been seen. The patrol car, a small military truck with a canvas top, had masked headlights shaded so that they could not be seen from the air. They were little use for seeing very far ahead either, their main use being to alert other vehicles coming in the opposite direction.

Perhaps they hadn't seen her. Ruth pressed herself into the hedge. At her feet was a ditch, overgrown with brambles. She slid the rucksack off her shoulder and dropped it, nudging it with her foot so that it slipped to the bottom of the ditch, out of sight. Unless they'd already seen her carrying it, Alain's supplies would be safe and if she were challenged she had a chance of bluffing her way out of trouble if she could spin them a convincing enough tale.

Until the very last moment, Ruth thought she hadn't been seen, then the truck slowed to a stop just beyond her, reversed back and three soldiers leapt down from inside and with rifles unslung, ran towards her.

A bright flashlight shone in her eyes, dazzling her. A man's voice shouted in bad French: 'Don't move! You are under arrest! Raise your hands!'

Obediently, Ruth raised them, forcing herself not to glance down into the ditch. Two men stood in front of her, their rifles pointing at her. A third searched her briefly, discovered her torch and kept it. He jerked his head to indicate that she should get into the back of the truck, and to make sure she understood, one of the soldiers prodded her towards it with his rifle. Once inside, her arms were pulled roughly behind her and a pair of handcuffs snapped on them. The soldiers scrambled back inside the truck and the driver shot off again at speed.

Ruth decided that her best response was to remain silent. These were ordinary soldiers, with a corporal in charge. They probably wouldn't understand French and wouldn't need to; their job was to deliver her to an officer at the German headquarters. Meanwhile, she had time to think up a convincing explanation for her presence on a banned road, long after curfew.

They hadn't noticed the rucksack; that was one enormous relief and if they had been intending to drive down the lane to check the beach, she had distracted them from that. Now, their only concern seemed to be to return to the town and hand her over to the authorities. She prayed it wouldn't be the Gestapo.

Ruth dismissed Alain's suggestion that she should claim to be gathering seaweed. Even to her mind, it sounded far-fetched, especially as she had no seaweed with her, or a bag in which to stow it. Better, too, that they didn't think she'd been intending to go on to the beach itself. She could pretend she was a bit simple, hadn't realised the road was out of bounds. It was a feeble excuse; it would hardly stand up when she was probably a familiar enough figure in the town, pushing Annette's wheelchair. They'd soon know all about her.

A lover. Yes, that was it. She'd say she had a lover, someone the rest of her household disapproved of, so she had to meet him at night, secretly. It wasn't a very good story and wouldn't stand up to much investigation, but if she could convince them that she was a simple, love-struck girl, the Germans, with their low opinion of women, just might let her go with a stern lecture and a warning. There were girls like that in the town, she knew. She'd even taught some of them. They were harmless, foolish and naïve, and surely the Germans wouldn't want to waste time arresting them and keeping them under guard when there were far more serious trouble-makers to be caught.

The truck pulled into a parking bay beside the Town Hall and she was hustled in through a side door and down a flight of stone steps to the cellars. Her handcuffs were removed and she was pushed into a small, windowless room barely bigger than a cupboard. It was pitch dark inside and she had no time to get her bearings before the door was slammed shut and she heard the key turn in the lock.

The room was completely bare, with brick walls and a concrete floor. Ruth sat down with her back to the wall and found, with her arms outstretched, she could touch the other walls either side of her and in front. High up on one wall was a tiny grille which let in air but was far too high to reach, let alone try to see out.

She couldn't judge how long she was kept

in the cell. Without her torch she couldn't see her watch. It felt like hours, and she was cold and uncomfortable. She spent the time perfecting her story. The lover, someone who didn't live in the town — she'd met him casually and only knew his first name, Didier. She chose the name because she didn't know anyone of that name, so there was less chance of involving anyone else. She didn't know this man very well, but she was absolutely smitten by him. His description — he was handsome, so handsome! She pretended a vague, girlish answer — she couldn't describe him in detail, he was someone who made her pulses race and she would do anything to see him again. He'd arranged to meet her, in the dunes by the sea, but he hadn't turned up — yes, that was it! And so she'd been on her way home. How was she to know that road was out of bounds to civilians? Didier had said to meet her there, where it was quiet and dark and they would not be disturbed . . .

She was well into embroidering her story, almost with a picture of the non-existent Didier in her mind, when she heard the key turn in the lock and a bright shaft of light from outside, dazzled her momentarily.

'Komm! You are to appear before the Duty Officer!' A soldier, his rifle slung across his back, pulled her to her feet and marched her upstairs. Stumbling and dazed, Ruth was taken along a passage with several doors on either side, interrogation rooms, she guessed. Although these were on a higher level than the cells, they still felt as if they were underground.

The soldier halted outside one of the doors, knocked, then opened it and pushed Ruth inside. 'The prisoner, Herr Kapitän,' he announced.

Ruth found herself in a small room, bare except for a desk, telephone and one chair behind the desk. When she looked at the man behind the desk, she didn't know whether to be relieved or horrified. All her carefully thought-out cover story was useless now. Tonight's Duty Officer was Captain Paul Reinhardt.

For a moment, his eyes widened in shock as the soldier pushed her forward. Then, he took control of himself, making his expression blank and his voice bored and impersonal as he asked the guard: 'What is the charge, Corporal?'

'The woman was found at 24.30 hours on the coast road near the beach lane. She gave no explanation when arrested.'

Paul nodded. 'Thank you, Corporal. You may leave us. I shall interrogate this woman myself.'

The corporal saluted, the leer on his face showing clearly how he imagined the interrogation would be conducted. Officers often preferred to be alone with prisoners if they were young and pretty, and this one certainly was.

Paul waited until the door had closed behind the soldier, then leapt up from his chair and came round the side of the desk towards her.

'Ruth! What in Heaven's name did you think you were doing, out after curfew and in a restricted area?'

'Oh, Paul, I'm sorry!' She meant that she was sorry to have embarrassed him in this way, but he misunderstood.

'But why were you there?'

'I can't tell you.' There was no explanation she could possibly give him without implicating the others and jeopardising the pick-up. And Paul was the one person on whom she could not use her cover story of the fictitious lover.

'Can't, or won't?' His voice sounded harsh, unlike his usual tones.

'Can't and won't.' She knew there were methods the Germans used to make prisoners give information, but surely Paul wouldn't? But he was a German officer, after all, and that and the safety of his troops must come first with him. If he suspected the real reason why she was near the beach, and it wouldn't take much thought to work it out, then he'd have no option but to hand her over to the Gestapo, or the SS, to be dealt with. At best, that could only mean deportation to Germany but the more likely outcome would be that she would be shot.

'You realise that your refusal to answer leads me to only one conclusion — that you were there for some purpose connected with actions against the Occupying Forces here?'

Still she kept silent. She *couldn't* lie to Paul, she realised, but then neither could she betray Alain and the others.

'Ruth, do you not see how foolish you are being, to associate with these — these amateur troublemakers? They and their actions can cause you nothing but harm. And harm for you means harm to your friend Annette, who depends on you so much. You may think it is a form of patriotism; you may be misguided enough to believe that what they do will shorten the war, but I assure you that it will not. In fact, their actions will almost certainly have the opposite effect. They think they can stab the German Army of Occupation in the back, but all they can achieve is no more than the sting of an insect, briefly annoying but doing little harm. And what do we do with an insect when it stings us? We kill it, destroy it completely. That is what we shall do to these foolish people who try to resist us. Be assured, they will never succeed in any of their impractical schemes.'

Ruth nodded but still kept silent. In truth, she had no idea what to say. There wasn't anything she *could* say.

'You realise,' Paul continued, 'that if you have anything more to do with these people, then our friendship must end. That would be most sad for me, and for you too, I think?'

It suddenly dawned on Ruth that Paul thought this was her first encounter with the Resistance; that he had no idea that she was already involved with them, had been almost since the Germans had occupied the town.

'I'm sorry, Paul. I didn't intend to embarrass you,' she whispered. 'I realise how bad this must look, but I meant no harm — '

'What were you doing there? You know that area is completely out of bounds!' he burst out angrily. 'And in the middle of the night! Were you being totally stupid? I can't believe that of you and I don't want to believe anything worse!'

He'd force an explanation out of her; she wouldn't be able to avoid answering him eventually, Ruth knew. She thought quickly. She couldn't lie to him but she could

126

encourage him to believe that she had very little to do with any members of the Resistance.

'I've never done anything like that before, never gone out after curfew to a restricted area,' she said. 'It was a — a sort of test. To see if it was really as difficult as everyone says. I know I was being very stupid, Paul.' Yes, stupid to walk straight out on to the road without first checking that there was no one around.

'I'm relieved to hear you say you have not done this before,' Paul said, calming down a little. 'I must beg you not to have anything to do with these people. They will involve you in grave danger. They are fanatics, obsessed with destruction. In peacetime, they'd be thugs, criminals and murderers. You wouldn't think of associating with people like that, would you?'

Ruth thought of Alain, Michel and Marc, even Claude the baker, all solid citizens who would have been shocked at the idea of breaking the laws of France in peacetime. 'No, I wouldn't,' she whispered meekly.

Paul stood in thought for a moment, then, lifting his head as though coming to a decision, said, 'It seems to me these people were trying you out. Had you succeeded in avoiding our patrols, it would inevitably have led to your becoming more and more embroiled in their schemes. Think yourself lucky that the patrol picked you up. You have failed their test. They will be less inclined to use your services now and that is your opportunity to free yourself from them. You already have enough to do, looking after Mademoiselle Annette and teaching English to — to anyone who wishes to learn.' He smiled, for the first time that evening. 'Promise me that you will have nothing further to do with these people, Ruth. You are too important to me to take such risks.'

With overwhelming relief, it dawned on Ruth that no one had realised she was on her way back from the beach. No one had seen the rucksack. With luck it would stay safe in the ditch until someone could collect it. The patrol had reported finding her walking on the road and it hadn't occurred to them or to Paul that she was on her way home, with mission already accomplished.

'What will you do with me?' she asked him.

'Oh, Ruth, I don't know!' Then she was in his arms, his cheek against hers, stroking her hair. I must look a terrible mess, she thought, hours in that cell.

'Promise me that you will not do anything like that again!' he said, against her hair. 'Promise me you will have nothing more to do with these people.'

She couldn't, dared not, promise that. She was too much involved already. 'Paul, I — ' she began.

'I am so afraid for you,' he whispered.

'I promise that from now on I'll make it my first priority to look after Annette,' she said at last. 'I won't do anything to jeopardise her. After all, she is the only reason I am in France at all.'

He seemed satisfied with that, though Ruth felt she was bending her promise almost to breaking point. Paul kissed her on her lips, a long, slow kiss that was disturbing, yet sweet and wonderful. She hadn't known that a kiss could make her feel as intensely as this before. There had been several of her brother's friends, in those far-off days before the war, who had kissed her, but never had she felt like this. But she was ashamed, too. She was deceiving Paul, and he was the very last person she would have wished to treat in this way.

'I will send you back home and make up some reason on the report,' Paul said, finally releasing her. 'But if ever you are arrested again, I will not be able to help you. I would have to deny our friendship completely.'

'I understand and I'll not embarrass you.' She realised then that Paul did not want to risk having her charged with anything for his own sake, too. If her actions tonight were reported, it would soon become known that he had been a regular visitor to the cottage. He would be in serious trouble himself.

Paul moved to sit behind his desk again and pressed a buzzer on it. The corporal entered, saluted and glanced at Ruth with a smirk. It was clear what he was thinking.

'I have interrogated this woman,' Paul said to him in German, 'and it seems her behaviour was no more than a show of bravado, aimed at testing the efficiency of our patrols. Now she has learnt a hard lesson. You are to be congratulated, Corporal, on seeing her and bringing her in.'

'Danke, Herr Kapitän.' The man's grin widened.

'However, I suspect she may be trying to impress certain of the rougher elements who call themselves resisters. I am letting her go, after cautioning her, of course, and then we shall see if she is approached by any of our known suspects who may plan to recruit her. You can release her for now; it is dawn and the curfew is raised, so she can find her own way home.'

'Jawohl, Herr Kapitän!' The corporal saluted again, then added, 'She is a small fish as bait to catch a big one, Sir?'

'Something like that.' Paul nodded dismissively. To Ruth, he said sternly in French, 'Go home, and do not break curfew again, or it will go very badly for you.'

'Merci, Monsieur,' Ruth replied meekly, letting the guard prod her towards the door. She had not looked at either of them during their conversation, pretending she had not understood any of it. It was a clever explanation but she wondered uneasily if Paul believed any of it himself.

Never had the fresh morning air felt so wonderful as she took great gulps of it from the steps of the Town Hall. The sky was streaked with colours from the coming sunrise and she thought she had never seen a more beautiful dawn.

It occurred to her that she could pick up some bread from Claude's shop on her way home, but she hesitated to do so, in case she was really being watched. He and Alain would need to be told what had happened, and soon, but if she went there now she risked drawing suspicion on him. Now, all she wanted was to be home, with a hot bath and a few hours' sleep. Besides, she remembered as she crossed the square, she had no money on her.

6

'Ruth, what on earth happened? Why have you taken so long? We were expecting you back by half past one. I've been worried sick; we all have been.' Annette, lying on her bed with the door open to the hall, called to her as she came in through the front door.

'It's all right. I'm safe. But I was stupid and was caught by a passing patrol.'

'What! Oh, mon Dieu — what happened?' Françoise, coming from the kitchen, caught the word 'patrol' though Ruth and Annette were speaking in English.

Briefly, she told them both what had happened. 'I don't know whether it was a good thing or not, that Paul happened to be on duty,' she said. 'He let me go, but — '

'Of course it was a good thing!' Françoise exclaimed. 'What could he do but let you go? It would be impossible for him to have you arrested. It would all have come out that he has been visiting here, and that would be the end for him.'

'I had to promise him I wouldn't have anything more to do with the Resistance,' Ruth said. 'Fortunately, he thought this was

132

the first time I had done anything for them.'

'Bah! A promise to a German means nothing!' Françoise snorted. 'Will you have some coffee, Mam'selle Ruth, or do you want to sleep first?'

'I'm exhausted,' Ruth admitted. 'I'll help Annette get up and then I'll sleep for a few hours.'

'No need. Françoise will help me. I can manage most things if she will move my chair to the side of the bed,' Annette said. 'I am so glad you are safe, Ruth.' She giggled mischievously. 'For a moment, I wondered if you had not taken the chance and gone back to England with your contact. I would not have blamed you; it is far safer there.'

'I wouldn't have done that unless I could have taken you with me,' Ruth replied. 'It was good to be exchanging news with an Englishman but I'd sooner be in France. There's more excitement here — more everything.'

'Huh! I doubt there's more food here,' Françoise grumbled. 'There's the last of the German coffee for breakfast. Will your captain come again, do you suppose, or has this episode frightened him off?'

'He didn't say he wasn't coming any more.' Ruth yawned. 'I must get to bed. Will you ask Michel to pass on a message to Alain that I need to see him, please?' She began to climb the stairs, the exhaustion brought on by the stresses of the night having finally caught up with her.

Two hours later, Françoise was shaking her awake. 'Mam'selle Ruth — Alain is downstairs in the kitchen. He is very worried about you. Will you come and tell him what happened last night?'

Ruth staggered out of bed. She could have used more time, but she had to see Alain as quickly as possible, so that he could arrange to retrieve the rucksack.

He was drinking coffee at the table. 'I heard you were caught by a patrol last night,' he said at once. 'I feared the worst when I did not find the package in the barn. What happened? Didn't you make the rendezvous? If they had found the package you would not be here now. Where is it, back in England with the man from Dover?'

'No. I made the rendezvous. When the patrol caught me I dropped the rucksack into a ditch. They didn't see it. It must be still there, in the ditch beside the entrance to the lane leading down to the beach.'

'Mon Dieu! In a ditch!' Alain threw up his hands in horror. 'No water in this ditch, I hope?'

'What was in this rucksack, that's so

134

precious and secret?' Ruth demanded.

'Detonators. There is a certain job to be done, but we are very low on supplies. Once we have them, we shall really be able to put a spanner in the German war machine.'

'Detonators!' Ruth shivered. If she had been caught with a rucksack full of detonators she would never have been able to explain herself and Paul would not have been able to save her. In fact, she would have put him in the gravest danger, too, had their friendship even been suspected.

'We need bread this morning,' Françoise announced. 'Will you go to Claude's shop today? Don't take Mam'selle Annette with you, you will be quicker by yourself.'

'Yes, and a friendly word with Claude's wife will be appreciated, I'm sure,' Alain added.

'Claude's wife? But you — ' Ruth stared at him.

'There is someone else at the bakery who wishes to speak with you. Go and buy your bread, Ruth. You will understand when you get there.'

Jacques? Ruth wondered, but she knew it was no use asking Alain. She would have to wait until she was in the baker's upstairs room. Well, this would be an opportunity to explain that she couldn't do any more work for the group. She had given Paul her word and besides, it would be far more dangerous, now that she had been caught once.

Claude's shop was sold out of bread and the 'sold out' notice was hanging in the window of the door. Ruth debated whether she should go round to the back and see if she could enter through the bakehouse, but then she saw him inside the shop, sweeping the floor, and tapped on the window.

Claude opened the door a few inches. 'Ah! You come on a social visit to see my wife and children, do you not, Mam'selle?' he asked. 'Come inside quickly. There is no one outside who will see you, is there?'

Ruth was about to tell the baker that she thought his code was ridiculous; that everyone knew he didn't have a wife or children and would be even more curious about him if he kept inviting her to meet these non-existent people, when she paused. Perhaps not many people knew about his personal life after all, and if they did, either they guessed the true situation and kept their mouths shut, or they suspected he had a few lady friends and in true broad-minded French fashion, shrugged their shoulders and made no comment. Rather, she should be prepared to let people think she was one of them, than suspect the true reason for her visits; it was far safer.

Jacques was alone in the little room above the shop. He looked thinner and more gaunt than ever, and was eating some bread and cheese that Claude must have provided. He looked as if he hadn't had a decent meal for some time.

'I heard you were picked up by a patrol last night, and arrested,' he greeted her. 'What happened?'

'A patrol truck came round the corner at speed while I was on the road. They'd seen me before I had time to hide. If I'd run off, they'd have fired at me.'

Jacques nodded. 'So they would have done. You were foolish to let this happen. Were you not told, always to keep in the shadows?'

'Yes, but it was very dark anyway. The truck didn't have proper headlights — '

'If they had, you would have stood no chance. Tell me, where were you? Were you going or returning? Had you been to the rendezvous?'

'I was returning from the beach. But they were not to know that. They wouldn't have been able to tell which direction I was coming from.'

'So you had collected the package from the contact? What happened to it?'

'I dropped it into a ditch. It seems they

didn't see it. They made no move to retrieve it and didn't ask me anything about it.' Ruth was beginning to be irked by the questions. She had already been through much the same interrogation from Alain.

'In a ditch! And did you know what was in the package?'

'I didn't then, but Alain has told me. Detonators.'

'Dangerous things to drop,' Jacques said laconically. 'You may be reassured they will be retrieved when it is safe to do so. You have succeeded in your first mission, Ruth in spite of being caught. Well done. You were very fortunate that the Duty Officer that night was known to you and not disposed to treat you in the regulation manner. You live to fight again! There will be more rendezvous in future and now we know that you will take greater care — '

'No,' Ruth said. 'I can't do any more. I can't be involved in any more missions like that.'

'Not immediately, of course. The Germans will undoubtedly be watching you now. But you have shown resourcefulness, and it is useful to have an Englishwoman meeting our British contacts. It gives them more confidence in us.'

'You misunderstand me,' Ruth said. 'I can't

ever do anything like that again. I gave my word to the German officer, Captain Reinhardt, that I wouldn't.'

'Your word to a German!' Jacques spluttered with laughter, picked up a half full bottle of wine from the table, and took a long drink from it. 'Your word to a German means nothing! They are the enemy. Or did you think, in your English way, that it was 'not sporting' to deceive them?'

'Captain Reinhardt is my friend and I gave him my word. It would lead to an impossible situation for him if I were ever arrested again. He'd be shot as a traitor, almost certainly. I couldn't risk that. I can't do anything at all to help the Resistance any more, Jacques. I'm sorry. Of course, I'd never betray any secrets and anyone I knew who was involved — '

'Just a minute!' Jacques looked at her savagely, and fleetingly Ruth thought how terrifying it would be to come up against him in a fight in the mountains.

'You cannot resign from the Resistance as if it were one of your *so English* sporting clubs. You have said you are with us, and that is a commitment for life, or until we kick every German off French soil and take back our country again. You are under orders, Ruth, make no mistake about that, just as bindingly as if you had sworn allegiance to your British King to fight for your own country. You cannot turn back.'

'But what if I refuse?'

Jacques looked at her contemptuously. 'What do you suppose happens to a soldier who refuses to carry out orders in wartime?'

Ruth gulped. 'I see,' she said.

'You would not last five minutes if you refused to obey your group leader's instructions,' Jacques said blandly. 'There are plenty who would be only too pleased to dispose of anyone they thought might betray them or their loyal French comrades. And what of your friend Annette then? How do you think your brother would feel, if he learnt that his sister had been executed by the Resistance because she was thought to be a traitor?'

'I'm not a traitor!' Ruth cried angrily. 'I'm as loyal to France as I would be to my own country if I were there.'

'Prove it then,' Jacques said. 'Go now, but be warned. We will make allowances for the fact that you had something of a shock, being arrested. We know that it would not be wise to expose you to further risks straight away. But to allow you to withdraw your special skills altogether — never!'

Facing him, Ruth knew she could not argue further. The man meant every word he said. He would not hesitate to order her death if he had any doubts of her total commitment to the group. She was under orders as rigorous as those in any military regime. She had to submit.

When Paul came for his English lesson the following Tuesday he did not mention her arrest, for which she was deeply grateful. When he had taken off his coat he laid two small packets on the table.

'What's this? A double payment of coffee?' Ruth asked.

'I had the opportunity to acquire a little sugar, and I thought Françoise might find it useful.'

'Sugar! We haven't seen proper sugar for ages!' Ruth gasped, her eyes widening. 'Thank you very much indeed.'

'I don't know if you consider this 'proper' sugar,' Paul said, smiling ruefully. 'German rations for the Wehrmacht are not any more of the best quality, but I know we have more than the civilian population here.'

'It's good of you to share with us,' Ruth said.

'It is not sharing, it is payment for English lessons,' Paul replied patiently. 'But the sugar is a present, an extra thank you because I will not be able to come here again for some time.'

'Oh!' Disappointment showed in her face.

'Paul, is it because of what happened the other night? I realise — '

'No, it has nothing to do with that. I hope that we can both forget that that situation ever arose. But I am summoned to Berlin and I leave late tonight. I hope I shall be back here in a few weeks, but in wartime one never knows what will happen, where one will be posted next.'

'I shall miss you,' Ruth said. The words sounded inadequate to express how she felt.

'I, too. I shall miss these conversations but, even more than that, I shall miss seeing you, Ruth. I think we have forged a friendship together. I would say, perhaps, something much more than a friendship.' He took her hand, stroking her fingers gently while he spoke. 'If it had not been for the war, who knows? We could have enjoyed each other's company without fear of consequences. But had it not been for the war, would we even have met? I do not think it likely I would have travelled to France, and you, my English rose, would have no occasion to travel to Germany while your friend is here in France.'

'Fate plays some strange tricks,' Ruth murmured. 'Cruel tricks, sometimes.'

'It was no trick of Fate that brought us together,' Paul said. He hesitated, then added, 'For a long time I have wanted to tell you this. It is true I wanted the chance to improve my English and you were the ideal — well, the only competent teacher in the town, but it wasn't only for that reason that I came to ask for lessons. There was another reason.'

'Another reason?' Ruth felt suddenly cold. Had all this been an excuse to check on her activities? And had the other night's incident provided him with all the proof he needed to arrest her? She looked at him in dismay; her illusions shattered.

'Yes. Back in the summer I saw you pushing your friend in her wheelchair across the Town Square and I thought — I thought I would like to get to know that girl as a friend. I made enquiries. I found out you were not French, but English. That pleased me because my English is a great deal better than my French, so I decided I would ask you for English conversation lessons. Then we could meet and talk, and get to know each other.'

'So you didn't really want English lessons?'

'Assuredly I did. As you noticed then, my English was by no means perfect and it was, as I told you at the time, a genuine request for you to give me instruction to improve my grammar and pronunciation. I think you have done an excellent job with that, and earned every grain of coffee I've brought. You must notice for yourself how I have improved. But it was to give myself the chance to meet you and get to know you, that was my main concern.'

'Oh, Paul! And I did wonder — ' Ruth stopped.

'You thought, perhaps, that I wanted to prise information out of you? That was never in my mind. When I saw you in the Square with Annette, you looked — well, I think I fell in love with you there and then, before I knew who you were, or anything about you. Then, discovering you were English, made things easier. Friendships with the local population are strongly discouraged, as you know, though there are some of our soldiers here who have French girlfriends. When I came to the house to speak to you I was nervous; I did not know how my request would be received.'

'I know. You looked ill at ease. It was that which puzzled me. The Germans are usually arrogant and expect to get what they want.'

'By no means did I expect to succeed automatically,' Paul said. 'I could see you did not like us, any of us, and why should you? But when you asked for payment in coffee, not money, my heart was yours. Such a brave, proud request.'

'Such a practical one!' Ruth laughed. 'Annette and Françoise so longed for a reasonable cup of the stuff and at last it was

144

something I could provide for them. For myself, though I drink coffee here, a cup of tea would be preferable.'

'I will see if I can get you some when I am in Berlin,' Paul said.

'I have a little, hoarded away. I was keeping it, either as a celebration, or, if things became really depressing and I needed the comfort of a memory of home,' Ruth said. 'Would you like a cup now? I think it might be an appropriate time, because I am going to miss you dreadfully.'

She made the tea herself, not trusting Françoise, who would not have known how to do it properly, and they sat drinking it in the garden, in the little arbour seat which had been made for Annette.

'I will come back,' Paul said. 'I promise. Even if I am ordered to another sector after Berlin, I will come back and see you. But there is a meeting I must attend in Berlin. It is not to brief me about another war sphere — '

'Don't tell me what it's about,' Ruth said quickly. 'I don't want to know.'

'In truth, I hardly know any details myself. All I know is that I leave very late tonight and that I will be away for two or three weeks. Perhaps more, perhaps less.'

When it was time for him to go, he took her

in his arms. 'All I have said is true, Ruth,' he said. 'I saw you, was attracted to you, planned how I might get to know you, and, having done so, all my hopes have been confirmed. I was right to fall in love with you on sight; nothing has caused me to change that feeling.'

'Paul, I feel the same way,' Ruth said. 'You've become so important to me.'

'Then for both our sakes, I must say again what I said the other night, which I want to forget ever happened, because it makes me so fearful for you. Have nothing to do with the Resistance here, Ruth. It will lead you into untold danger. I know I thought of my own position, too, if you were involved and caught, but now, for your own safety, I beg you.'

'Paul, I do understand your concern.' She couldn't commit herself either way. If she promised Paul, Jacques would never let her honour that promise. With Paul away, perhaps the situation would be easier. But it was another, added incentive never to be caught.

Françoise, though she had warmed to the German captain ever since she believed he had been instrumental in securing Michel's release, was relieved when she heard that Paul would not be coming to the house again.

'I can hold my head up in the market place

146

now,' she declared. 'Some of those old crows have had the nerve to accuse me of being friendly with the enemy. Most of them would betray their own mothers for a half kilo of butter.'

Michel shrugged. 'There goes the best source we had of acquiring useful information, or using the German to our advantage. But there will be other opportunities, no doubt, and now it will be safer for you, Mam'selle Ruth, to work for us again.'

Only Annette understood Ruth's true feelings. 'I know you two were very close,' she said. 'I saw it in his eyes when he looked at you, and you - well, being in love with Simon I can recognise the signs in others. But Paul was playing with fire, while you are so involved with Alain's people. He is, at least, safer in Berlin.'

That night, Ruth was awakened by a loud explosion that made the windows of the cottage rattle. She slipped on her dressing gown and went to see if it had disturbed Annette.

Annette was wide awake, her eyes two round saucers with fear. 'What was that?' she whispered. 'Have the RAF dropped a bomb on us? It sounded so loud. It must be near, whatever it was.'

'I didn't hear any aeroplanes,' Ruth replied.

'And no gunfire. We shall find out what it was in the morning, no doubt. Can I make you a warm drink, since you're awake?'

'What time is it?' Annette asked.

'Just after midnight. I wonder if . . . ' Ruth paused. A single explosion, without the sound of aircraft or the big anti-aircraft guns, pointed to the most likely cause, some sabotage by the more militant activists in the Resistance; Jacques' men, she supposed. But what was there to blow up in a town like this? There were no factories or aerodromes nearby; no suspicious German bunkers which might house large stockpiles of weapons, as far as she was aware. Then she remembered — there were the gun emplacements all along the coast, not more than a couple of miles from the cottage. It had to be one of them, though the explosion had sounded very loud and she didn't think it had come from the direction of the coast.

While she was in the kitchen, warming some milk for Annette, the back door opened and Michel slipped into the room. He looked startled at first, on seeing her, then grinned and rubbed his hands with pleasure when he realised who it was.

'Hear that explosion? That was us. Our group. A very successful night's work and everyone got away safely.'

148

'What did you do?' Ruth asked.

'Blew up the railway line. We set a charge to go off when a train passed over the bridge near the canal.'

'The railway?' Ruth asked uneasily.

'You may take some credit for that.' Michel opened a cupboard and brought out a half full bottle of wine. He pulled out the cork with his teeth and took a long drink, straight from the bottle.

'You brought in the detonators we needed from the man from Dover. Without them we'd have been unable to mount a decent explosion. It was a good one, was it not? Best show of fireworks since the last pre-war Quatorze-juillet.'

'You blew up a train?' Ruth's heart began beating faster.

'The eleven-thirty, going into Germany. Full of troops going on leave and stolen goods from France which they were shipping back to Berlin. Now we've stopped all that. There are only two trains from here to Germany in a week, but there won't be any to anywhere for a while yet. We messed up their plans good and proper — the line is a shambles, with bits of coach strewn everywhere. Plenty of dead Germans, too. A lovely sight, that. Pity it was too dark for a proper look and we didn't fancy hanging around to watch.' Michel took another drink, then wiped the neck of the bottle with his sleeve and held it out to her. 'Join me in a celebration, Mam'selle Ruth?' he offered. 'Here's to us, the freedom fighters of Ste Marie de la Croix! We've shown 'em!'

Ruth stared at him, frozen with horror. A train, one of only two a week, leaving for Germany, and they'd blown it up. Paul would have been on it, for certain. He might be lying there in the wreckage now, badly injured or even dead, and she could do nothing. She couldn't go and see, she couldn't even risk making enquiries. And what was worse, she had had a hand, albeit unwittingly, in causing the devastation. The rucksack containing the detonators would never have reached Alain and his group if she had not collected it for them from the man from Dover.

The hot milk boiled over in the pan without her noticing. Mechanically, she wiped the stove and poured the milk into a beaker. She couldn't think, her mind was numb with shock.

Annette tasted the milk and wrinkled her nose as the burnt flavour reached her, but she said nothing. 'What's the matter?' she asked Ruth. 'You look as white as a sheet. Who were you talking to, in the kitchen?'

'Michel. They've blown up a train just

outside the station. I think it must be the one Paul was intending to take, travelling to Berlin. He said he was leaving late last night.'

'Oh, my God!' Annette held out her arms and Ruth, unable to control her emotions any more, sobbed on her friend's shoulder.

'It is war. It happens,' Annette soothed, stroking her friend's hair and back. 'He might have been killed any time, any of us might. You knew that.'

'But I was the one — I was responsible!' Ruth sobbed.

'You were not to know, cherie. You did not know what that packet contained when you were asked to collect it. And you could not know how they would be used,' Annette comforted.

Ruth released herself from Annette's arms and sat back on the bed. 'Could he be injured, or killed? How can I find out? I can't bear not to know.'

'You can't find out,' Annette replied. 'Any wounded German soldiers will be taken to the German military hospital, not our local one, that's for sure. You can't go there to ask. For one thing, they wouldn't tell you, and for another, it would be a great embarrassment for Captain Reinhardt if he was known to have a woman friend from the local civil population, asking after him.'

'But what *can* I do?' Ruth moaned.

'If he's all right, surely he will let you know. Even if he's injured, he'd get a message to you somehow. You will have to be patient. Don't fret, Ruth dear. I feel sure he's all right. He'll be round to see you, or send word somehow. He wouldn't let you worry if he could help it. Paul's not that kind of person.'

With that Ruth had to be content. If he was injured, he'd let her know, even if she couldn't see him. But if he was dead, there would be no one to tell her that.

Days passed. There was such tightening of security about the little town that it was barely possible to leave the cottage. The Germans were angry, very angry, and took their anger out on the local population by making life as difficult as possible for everyone.

News came via Michel's friends that the railway line was unlikely to be usable for several weeks. There were carriages and goods wagons strewn everywhere, and many dead. The Germans took two days to clear away all the bodies from the track.

Ruth shuddered when she heard. There was no way she could find out if Paul was amongst them, but the fact that she had not heard anything from him, seemed to indicate that her worst fears were confirmed. As

Annette had said, he would never leave her to worry if he was in a position to reassure her. He must have died in the explosion.

Gradually, the drama died down and things began to return to normal in the town. There had been reprisals; a dozen young men rounded up arbitrarily and publicly shot in the Town Square. All the citizens within the area at the time were arrested and forced to watch. Françoise had been one of them, but both Annette and Ruth stayed indoors for the weeks following the explosion.

It was two weeks later that Alain appeared in the kitchen of the cottage, asking for Ruth.

'I have a job for you,' he said, when she came in.

'No! I can't,' she replied at once. 'It was because of me that all those people were killed and injured on that train, and the subsequent reprisals resulted in the deaths of a dozen more, innocent young men. I can't — '

'Don't become emotional about it,' Alain said harshly. 'If you had not collected the detonators, someone else would have done. Or we'd have found some other way to derail that train. Don't think you were responsible; you did very little.'

'I promised Paul — Captain Reinhardt — ' she began.

'A promise to the enemy means nothing. Besides, from what I hear, he's dead now so any promise you made is cancelled. You can't just leave the group as if we're some kind of social club. I thought Jacques had already made that clear to you.'

'Yes, he did. But Paul's death has changed things.'

'One German's death doesn't change anything, except for the better! I would have thought that now you would feel more free to work with us without any reservation. It is a very simple job I am asking you to do. Nothing dangerous, nothing that will result in death or even damage to property. It is simply the delivery of some messages, something you can do without any risk to yourself or compromising your oh-so-British promises to the enemy.'

As Ruth hesitated, Annette pushed her way into the kitchen. Her chair had been in the doorway and she had heard Alain's words.

'I will take the messages,' she said. 'Ruth needn't be involved. I can do it just as easily.'

'But, Mam'selle Annette!' Alain floundered, astonished. 'How can you possibly do that? You cannot leave your chair, can you?'

'I can wheel myself perfectly well along the road,' Annette said coolly. 'I may be a little

154

slower than if Ruth were pushing me, but I can manage.'

'And if you are seen, by yourself, without Mam'selle Ruth, what are people to make of that? You are a distinctive couple about the town, Mam'selle Annette. Alone, you would draw attention to yourself, invite speculation, the last thing we need.'

'I could let it be known that Ruth is unwell, hurt her leg perhaps,' Annette said wildly. 'I could do it. I know I could.'

'But you won't have to, my dear,' Ruth said gently. 'I couldn't let you go out by yourself for any long distance. Whoever actually delivers these messages is immaterial. I'll push your chair wherever you need to go.'

'That's settled, then,' Alain said with satisfaction. 'Here is the first message, ladies, and here are the details of where you are to deliver it.'

7

Ruth pushed Annette's wheelchair along the rough, dirt track road. The weather was dry, crisp and cold, reminding her of winter days back in England in the countryside she missed so much these days. In less than a month it would be Christmas, the fifth wartime Christmas she had spent in France with Annette. Five and a half years since that terrible accident, and it didn't look now as if Annette would ever be free of her wheelchair. If only I could get her to a good doctor who specialises in such injuries, Ruth thought wistfully, for the hundredth time, but such doctors were all concerned with treating soldiers at the Front; the only doctors left to treat civilians here were the elderly, whose methods and knowledge, though adequate for most things, were somewhat out of date.

'I don't remember ever coming along this road before,' she remarked, pushing Annette up a slight incline.

'No, it's not the best of roads for pushing my chair along,' Annette replied. 'One day, Ruth, when the war is over and we can go to England, do you think we'll find someone who can make me walk again?' It was the first time Annette had spoken of her injuries with the sound of despair in her voice.

'Of course; why do you think I've been keeping your muscles in good order?' Ruth said stoutly, 'massaging your legs every day? After the war anything might be possible. The doctors will have learnt so many new skills and techniques from their experiences of battle injuries. You'll see.'

'There's the chateau!' Annette changed the subject to point ahead. On their left was a high, ancient wall, bounding the grounds of a good sized estate, but the house itself was not yet visible, set back from the road.

'There's a place just along here where the wall has fallen down, so Alain says,' Annette continued. 'There's a loose brick round the back and we have to leave the note under it. You'll have to do it, you'd never get my chair over the rough ground.'

'I can see where he means,' Ruth replied. 'Just a moment, there's someone coming. I can see a bicycle in the distance behind us.' Ruth manoeuvred the chair towards the side of the road. 'Do you have those lesson books well in sight? Remember, we're supposed to be visiting one of your pupils, but I forget which one.'

'Emilie,' Annette said absently. 'Keep

pushing. We may have to go past the chateau and turn back after they've gone, whoever it is.'

'Does anyone live in the chateau now?' Ruth asked curiously. They had reached the lop-sided iron gates leading on to a weed infested, neglected driveway, having passed the broken wall without pausing. They could both now hear the whirr of the bicycle wheels coming up behind them. 'The place looks almost derelict.' She paused to look towards the building, visible at the end of the drive. It had once been an impressive home, but now all the windows were shuttered and the roof was damaged at one end.

'The Comte still lives there, as far as I know,' Annette replied. 'His family have lived in the chateau for generations. They've always been rather reclusive; we never saw much of any of them, even before the war.'

The cyclist caught up with them and, riding slowly, turned the bicycle in between the gates. 'Bon jour, mes demoiselles,' she said, halting and glancing back over her shoulder. She was a tall woman, probably in her early forties, Ruth surmised, and noted that, even on a bicycle in workaday clothes, she had a look of elegant chic about her.

Automatically, Ruth replied to the greeting, but Annette said nothing. To her surprise, the woman said, in excellent English, 'It's a good, crisp morning for a walk or a cycle ride, isn't it? Perhaps we may meet again, and get to know each other.' She mounted the bicycle and pedalled off, down the drive.

'Who was that?' Ruth asked. 'I've never seen her around. And no one in the town has ever spoken to me in English before.' She had the feeling that the words had been addressed solely to her; that Annette had been ignored, even as her friend had ignored the newcomer.

'That's the Comtesse,' Annette said flatly. 'I know her by sight but I've never had much to do with her socially. She's the present Comte's wife, Comtesse Giulia. She's Italian.'

'Italian?' Ruth said, in some surprise.

Annette's face was set. 'Yes. A foreigner. I don't trust her.'

Ruth burst out laughing. 'Annette! How can you say that? I'm a foreigner too, remember?'

'That's different, of course,' Annette shrugged. 'You're British, one of our Allies! But one can never trust the Italians. Look how they have changed their allegiance.'

'How long has she lived in France?' Ruth was still staring down the drive towards the derelict looking chateau, but the Comtesse

159

and her bicycle had already disappeared out of sight.

'Since she married the Comte — must be twenty years ago at least, I should think,' Annette said, considering.

'Heavens! Then she must be as French as he is, by now! What possible reason could you have for not trusting her?' Ruth had noticed that the Comtesse had spoken both French and English without any trace of accent. She might just as easily have been French — or English, except that her smart elegance looked out of place for either nationality these days.

'I don't know why I don't like her. I just don't. You could call it some instinct, or even sheer prejudice if you like. There's just something about her that I don't like,' Annette said impatiently. 'Look, we can't stay here staring at the chateau all day. Let's go back and drop the message in the wall before someone else comes past.'

Ruth turned the chair round. She said nothing further to Annette about the Comtesse, but a rebellious thought rose in her mind. She'd instinctively liked the woman. It had been a pleasant surprise to be addressed in English and she found she wanted to take up the suggestion that they might meet and get to know each other. Now that she would never talk to Paul again, she found she was missing hearing English spoken.

When they reached the part of the wall where the bricks had fallen, leaving a gap that could easily be scrambled through, Ruth looked carefully up and down the empty road before she took the folded piece of paper Annette handed to her, and clambered over the broken rubble.

She found the loose brick easily enough and was about to pull it out when she paused. Something made her open the paper and look at it. She never normally made a habit of reading letters destined for someone else, but this was exceptional..

The sheet consisted of half a dozen rows of letters and numbers, clearly a code which she didn't understand. If anyone other than the intended recipient found it, it would mean nothing. Who the recipient was, Ruth had no idea. Alain had told her nothing more than she needed to know, which was undoubtedly safer for everyone.

Ruth slid the brick back into place, with the note tucked beneath it, paused by the wall to look out and make sure there was no one in sight, then rejoined Annette.

'There! That wasn't too bad, was it? Really, Ruth, I don't know why you made such a fuss about doing something like this for Alain and the group,' Annette said. 'It isn't as if he's likely to ask you to take delivery of any more equipment. That would be far too risky for them as well as you, after the last time.'

'I know,' Ruth said. 'It's just that — I promised Paul I wouldn't do anything, and the fact that I helped to kill him — '

'No, you didn't!' Annette spoke sharply. 'You didn't know what they were going to do with those detonators. You didn't even know what was in that rucksack when you collected it. You were obeying orders, as we all have to do in wartime.'

'But if I *had* known . . . ' Ruth paused. What would she have done, had she known that the men of the Resistance were going to blow up the very train on which Paul would be travelling into Germany? She simply didn't know what she would have done under those circumstances. It was better not to speculate.

'If you were in England now, would you be helping the war effort there?' Annette asked.

'Well, of course.'

'And is this so very different?'

I wouldn't have met Paul if I'd been in England, Ruth thought. Perhaps this was her punishment for having fallen in love with an enemy soldier, that she would forever feel torn by guilt; guilt that she had had a hand in

162

Paul's death; guilt that she was not whole hearted in her efforts to help the local Resistance group. She made up her mind. 'Paul's dead,' she said. 'Nothing I can do will change that. It was for his sake that I promised I wouldn't have any more to do with the Resistance but that doesn't apply any more. The best thing I can do is to do everything I can to help them bring this war to a speedier conclusion. That way, there may be fewer men killed, of any nationality. I'll tell Alain I'll do anything to help, that he wants me to.'

'Good for you!' Annette said approvingly. 'You'd better wheel me along to Emilie's house and I'll hear her reading for an hour. Time's getting on, but if we don't go, someone is sure to notice that we set out and didn't arrive. I don't want to draw any unwelcome attention to us.'

After Annette had helped the child Emilie with her reading, and Ruth had tried to teach a few words of English to the child's mother, who wanted to learn but found it difficult, they walked back towards the cottage. It was long past midday and the day had closed in, cloudy and grey now. Ruth tried to hurry, but she was tired and the chair was heavy to push. Their way led past the crossroads where the damaged war memorial stood.

'Stop a moment, please,' Annette said. 'I want to have another look at that angel, see if it still looks like Madame Duvalle.'

Ruth was glad to stop, flex her aching shoulders and sit down for a moment on the stone plinth. Annette looked up at the group of carved stone figures. 'Yes, it really does look like her,' she said. 'Even more so, I think, now the damage has weathered a bit.'

'It gives me the creeps,' Ruth confessed. 'That woman seems to haunt me. Every time I go to Claude's for bread — even if it *is* only for bread and not to visit his mythical family — she's there, watching me. I'm sure she spies on me.'

'She's nothing more than a foolish, lonely old woman. She can't do you any harm,' Annette reassured her.

'I'm sure she's spying for the Germans,' Ruth persisted.

'Pshaw! The Germans wouldn't take any notice of anything someone like that said. They must realise she's probably a bit touched in her head.' Annette tried to comfort her friend, but in her mind she was only too well aware that it was the thoughtless prattle of old women such as Madame Duvalle that so often led to the arrest and imprisonment of those waging the secret war against the Germans.

'We'd better go,' she said. 'Otherwise we won't be home before curfew. I've no fancy to be arrested. Even though it would be interesting to see a patrol trying to get my wheelchair into one of their trucks.'

A few days later, Ruth was by herself in the Town Square when she heard the tinkle of a bicycle bell behind her. She turned round and saw the Comtesse cycling slowly towards her.

'Hallo,' the Comtesse called. 'I was wondering when I would run into you in the town.' She dismounted and continued, 'It's strange we hadn't met before the other day, in a small place like this. I'd heard of you, of course. You must be the only other non French civilian in the town, apart from the German Secret Service.'

'I suppose so.' Ruth was surprised; she hadn't been aware that there were civilian Germans in Ste Marie de la Croix. The thought made her feel nervous; who knew who might be lurking here, watching everyone? She wondered briefly how the Comtesse knew about them.

'Look, Ruth,' the Comtesse said hesitantly. 'I may call you Ruth, may I not? Tell me, do you ever have time off from your nursing duties? I mean, you always seem to be pushing your friend in her wheelchair, and I was wondering . . . '

'I haven't Annette with me now,' Ruth laughed. 'I'm not her nurse. I'm looking after her until the war is over and she can come to England and marry my brother. They were engaged in June, 1939, but the war intervened before they could arrange the wedding.'

'I hadn't realised you were practically related to her. Now, what I was about to ask may seem terribly rude, but I was wondering if you would care to come to tea, just yourself, one day this week? It would be so nice to speak English for an afternoon. I'd so appreciate it if you'd come.'

'I'd like to, very much,' Ruth said, somewhat taken aback. 'Thank you very much, Comtesse.'

'Giulia, please.' The woman smiled at her. 'I know England fairly well. Where did you live before you came here?'

'Broxbourne,' Ruth replied. 'It's a country — '

'Hertfordshire,' Giulia interrupted promptly. 'I know the area quite well. A pleasant market town, isn't it? Very English. I know St Albans well. I stayed there for three months when I was learning English.'

Ruth felt a warm glow of pleasure. She hadn't had the opportunity to make many friends since she had begun to look after Annette. In truth, the local Frenchwomen had not seemed particularly friendly, but Giulia looked to be just the kind of person she needed to lift her spirits.

'How about the day after tomorrow? Your friend Annette won't mind too much about your leaving her alone for the afternoon, will she?' Giulia asked.

'Annette won't mind at all. She is quite happy to sit and read or paint, and she wouldn't be entirely alone. She has Françoise and Michel Leclerc, two old family servants, living in the house with us. She can push her chair for herself for short distances, too, if she needs, but that is tiring for her.'

'Poor girl! Such a tragedy! A car accident, wasn't it?' Giulia sympathised. 'Well, I must get on. See you the day after tomorrow. About three, shall we say?' She mounted her bicycle and rode off, turning to wave before rounding the corner.

It occurred to Ruth that the Comtesse seemed to know a great deal about her and Annette, without ever having spoken to them, or even seen them. She remembered Annette expressing her dislike of Giulia and wondered if she would be hurt that Ruth had been invited by herself to the chateau.

Annette wouldn't be as small-minded as

that, Ruth told herself, dismissing the thought. Annette has so often said that she worries about me being stuck here in France because of her. She'll be glad I've found some congenial company outside the cottage.

Annette, when told of the invitation, made little comment. 'It'll be nice for you to be able to chatter away in English,' she remarked, 'With someone other than me for a change. But be careful what you say to her, Ruth. She may appear friendly, but we don't really know where her true sympathies lie.'

'I'm hardly likely to tell her what I do for Alain and his group,' Ruth retorted. 'I wouldn't even mention Paul, though I suspect she may know something about him. She seemed to know a great deal about both of us.'

'I don't much like the idea of that,' Annette said. 'But I suppose gossip is rife in a place like this where there's precious little else to entertain folk. I thought she was virtually a recluse in that chateau but she must go out more than I realised, if she has seen us about often.'

At half past two Ruth left the cottage and took the unmade track that led to the chateau. She had dressed carefully, putting on one of her pre-war frocks which had been smart when new, and comparatively expensive. She hadn't had much occasion to wear it since living with Annette in the cottage.

As she walked down the weedy, neglected drive, she studied the rambling bulk of the chateau in front of her. It had been a beautiful place once, and was still impressive. Annette had told her that it had been in the Comte's family for many generations. What would happen in future was doubtful since Giulia had no children and was probably into her forties already.

'I suppose it will go to some distant relative eventually, if the Germans don't wreck it completely before they leave,' Annette had said. 'They damaged it with artillery fire when they first occupied the town, but, surprisingly, they've never commandeered it for accommodating their officers. It's strange, that. It's the only very large house in the area that they haven't taken over, and the Comtesse can hardly need all of it for herself and the Comte. One would think the Germans would have grabbed it with both hands, but they have so far ignored it. I find that surprisingly odd.'

Ruth reached the imposing, iron-studded double front door, which swung open before she even had time to look for a bell or knocker. Giulia stood in the doorway. 'Come in; you are most welcome,' she said. Ruth guessed she must have been watching out for her and thought the Comtesse must be a lonely woman, in need of friends.

Giulia led her through the vast, stone floored entrance hall, down gloomy, damp passages to the back of the chateau. Here she opened a door and Ruth could not help uttering a gasp of surprise and delight. The room into which she was being ushered was lovely, a modern, tastefully furnished sitting room, with chintz covered sofas and arm chairs, matching curtains at the tall windows and a deep piled carpet in a luxurious shade of blue. Bowls of flowers, early spring daffodils and snowdrops, stood on a beautiful, polished bureau and a low table beside the chairs, the perfume of them filling the air.

'What a beautiful room!' Ruth exclaimed.

Giulia smiled, looking pleased at the praise. 'I practically live in it. It's the most comfortable room in the house. Really, the only comfortable room, to tell the truth. I hardly use the rest of the chateau. This was always my favourite place. It had magnificent views over the gardens. It still has, of course, but they're terribly neglected now, hardly worth looking at.'

Ruth wandered across to the central of three long windows, reaching nearly from floor to ceiling. Outside, she could see a weed-covered terrace, with what had been a lawn and flowerbeds once, but were now overgrown and neglected.

'I called this part of the grounds my English garden,' Giulia said, joining her at the window. 'I so liked the little gardens attached to all the houses in St Albans, when I was there. In Italy, gardens are so formal, so unfriendly and aloof. Do you know Italy, Ruth?'

'I've only been there on holiday a couple of times, years before the war,' Ruth replied. 'I thought it a beautiful country.'

'It has a certain appeal, perhaps, but I am not sorry I left and I have no desire to return, especially now, when it has been so cruelly damaged. War is so pointless, isn't it? Games for little boys, who want to destroy everything.'

'That's certainly one way of looking at it,' Ruth said diplomatically. She hoped the Comtesse was not going to talk about the politics of war; it could become awkward when she didn't know the woman's real allegiances.

Giulia gestured to an arm chair beside a low coffee table. 'Come and sit down and I'll bring in some tea. I can't manage cucumber sandwiches or chocolate cake, I'm afraid, but

I do have Lipton's tea and I do know how to make it in the proper, English way. That's one useful thing I learnt as a student in your country.'

'Real English tea! I haven't tasted any since the summer of '39,' Ruth said, astonished. 'Where did you get it? Tea is in short supply even in England these days, I've heard.'

'I have my sources. You see, I too, developed a taste for it, in preference to coffee. And coffee in France is undrinkable these days, don't you think? Unless you have a special source of supply.'

Ruth looked at her warily. Was she hinting that she knew about the arrangement with Paul and the English lessons? No one except Annette, the Leclercs and Alain were supposed to know about that. No one, in fact, apart from the trusted few, was supposed to know anything at all about Paul's visits to the cottage, though, judging by the abuse and rotten vegetable throwing she had been subject to during that time, Ruth suspected that some of the local women knew and disapproved. Madame Duvalle was most likely to have been responsible for spreading that nugget of gossip, she thought ruefully.

Giulia seemed unaware that she might have said something tactless. She was half way out of a door at the side of the room as she spoke, and Ruth, looking towards her, could see a kitchen beyond, modern and well-equipped.

Moments later, the Comtesse returned, bearing a large tea tray laden with beautiful china, a silver teapot and plates of tiny sandwiches. There was cake, too, a beautiful sponge, unlike the cakes Ruth had seen in France.

'So nice to have company and an excuse for real English tea!' Giulia handed her a plate and a lace-edged linen napkin. She poured tea, dark and strong, and handed Ruth a cup. 'Do you know, although I prefer tea, I actually rarely drink it except when I'm alone. My husband, Jacques, never touches it. Like a typical Frenchman, he considers it suitable only for medicinal purposes.' She poured herself a cup, handed the sandwiches and sat down in a chair facing Ruth. 'My husband is away at present, like most of the men in this country. He's not with de Gaulle in Britain, like so many of his compatriots, he's fighting his own private war, up in the mountains. He comes home occasionally, when he wants a bath or a change of clothes.' She laughed. 'He's in his element, out there with his own rabble army. He'd be no good as a conventional soldier, having to obey orders. What he'll do when the war is finally over, I cannot imagine. Find another war, and offer himself as a mercenary, I shouldn't wonder!' She shrugged her shoulders. 'As I said, war is a game for little boys, and Jacques has always enjoyed games.'

Jacques, Ruth thought. The man she'd met in Claude's upstairs room, who was living in the mountains with the freedom fighters. Could it be the same person? It seemed likely; she could imagine the gaunt, bearded man as an aristocrat, someone whose family had dominated affairs in the town for centuries. He had exuded that air of authority when he had spoken to her.

She could hardly say anything. 'I believe I've met your husband' would inevitably lead to explanations that would give away her own connections with the Resistance. Giulia might not sympathise with them, or, worse, have German sympathies. Any mention of the Resistance could be dangerous, both for herself and Jacques. She said nothing, but glanced around the room in the hope of seeing a photograph which would confirm her suspicions.

'You are admiring my flowers?' Giulia asked, misinterpreting her. 'They are sent from the south, especially. Everything is far more advanced there, but you probably know that.'

'I'm amazed that things like flowers can be

sent here in wartime,' Ruth confessed.

'You can get anything you want, even these days, if you know how,' Giulia replied casually. 'But you weren't only looking at my flowers, were you? You were looking for something else, I think?'

She's very perceptive, Ruth thought uneasily. Aloud, she said, 'I wondered if you had any photographs, family groups, that kind of thing. People often do.'

'I have no pictures of any kind,' Giulia said, abruptly. 'Somewhere in the chateau are oil paintings of Jacques' ancestors, but they are stored away for now. I have no photographs, no modern pictures. Not a good idea, I think.'

Of course not, Ruth mentally chided herself. Jacques was undoubtedly a wanted man, a thorn in the flesh of the Occupying Forces, whom they would be glad to capture. A picture of him would be of great help to them. Giulia had probably destroyed them all.

They chatted together like a pair of English ladies at a polite, pre-war tea party. Ruth was wary, but it really didn't seem as if Giulia had wanted to seek out information from her about her activities in France.

'It's so nice, having someone to talk to, really have a girlish chatter with,' Giulia said suddenly. 'I've kept myself shut away here far too long. I was practically talking to the walls with boredom, but it wasn't much better when I went out and tried to make friends with the locals. They're not at all friendly. Have you found that? Even when I can speak their language as well as — and even better, sometimes than they can speak it themselves, they cold-shouldered me, all of them. They talk of the British being unfriendly with strangers, but I can tell you, they've nothing on the people of Ste Marie de la Croix. If you are not French, they simply don't want to know you. I suppose I ought to accept that, since I'm Italian and therefore they look on me as a pro-German alien. But, I ask you! I've lived in their country twenty years and married to a Frenchman, for heaven's sake! I've as much right to be considered one of them as anyone. What about you? At least you can claim to be one of their Allies, but since Dunkirk the French seem to hate and mistrust anyone who isn't French.'

Ruth remembered Annette's words about not liking or trusting Giulia. But Annette was surely not as narrow-minded and prejudiced as some of the local people? She would hardly be planning to marry an Englishman if she felt like that about foreigners.

'I've found some of the locals rather

difficult,' she admitted reluctantly. 'Perhaps they're not used to foreigners. I'm the only non-French civilian in the town, or at least, I thought I was until I met you.' She recounted the incident of the parents at the school, and poor Père Joseph's struggles to find suitable teachers who were acceptable to the parents.

'Ach, they're nothing but peasants!' Giulia said contemptuously. 'If they don't like foreigners in their town, they've certainly acquired plenty now! There must be nearly half as many German soldiers in the garrison as French civilians, these days. See how they like that! It serves them right!'

Ruth was surprised by the vehemence in the Comtesse's voice, but decided that, after having lived in this great mausoleum of a house for so long, entirely by herself, she was entitled to be resentful about the unfriendliness of the local people. Giulia was plainly very lonely; probably had always found it difficult to make friends with 'ordinary' people and missed the fact that there were no other aristocratic households living anywhere nearby. Ruth made up her mind that, whatever Annette's opinions were on the matter, she would visit Giulia again and try to make friends with her.

Abruptly, Giulia said, 'Enough about all this complaining! Look, it's Christmas in less than a month's time. What do you usually do for it?'

'Nothing very much,' Ruth admitted. 'Françoise manages to hoard some special goodies and Michel brings a chicken from the farm. It's always just the four of us and we invariably end up talking about England and France as they were before the war. Rather a nostalgic event, I suppose.'

'I feel like having a party!' Giulia announced. 'A party for Christmas night! What do you think about that? Would you and Mademoiselle Annette come?'

'Of course we would! We'd be delighted to!' Ruth said at once. She had been wondering about inviting Giulia to join them for Christmas lunch, but, knowing how Annette felt, and the fact that Giulia seemed rather too aristocratic to contemplate sitting down at the kitchen table with Françoise and Michel, she had said nothing.

'Six o'clock on Christmas evening,' Giulia announced. 'Perhaps the Commandant can be persuaded to waive the curfew for the night. He might as well; there'll be plenty of people breaking it and his troops won't want to be out patrolling the streets on that night.'

'We'll look forward to it,' Ruth said sincerely. 'But, since he hasn't altered curfew regulations for tonight, I'd better be off.' As she rose to leave, Giulia added, 'I'll invite just a few people, perhaps a dozen. Some interesting ones, I think you'll find.'

As she left the chateau, Ruth wondered who would be the 'interesting' guests Giulia had in mind. Unlikely to be many of the townspeople, she thought, given the Comtesse's scathing opinion of them, but who else did Giulia know to invite? It promised to be an intriguing evening.

Annette was not as enthusiastic about the party as Ruth had hoped. 'The Comtesse? Having a party at the chateau on Christmas night? Who on earth will she find to come? And how are we going to manage to get either there or home afterwards, when curfew begins as soon as it's dark?'

'She suggested the Commandant might lift it for Christmas night. Give us an amnesty and his patrol troops a night off,' Ruth replied.

'And is she going to ask the Commandant herself?' Annette sneered. 'I wouldn't be surprised if he turned out to be one of her guests. That woman is not to be trusted.'

'So you won't go to her party?' Ruth asked. 'Judging by the splendid tea she gave me, I would think it would be worth going for the food alone. And I've heard you say you'd like to see inside the chateau.'

'I said I would have liked to,' Annette said crossly, 'in the days when it was a real family home. Now it's nothing but an empty shell, half of it a ruin and the rest derelict. You said yourself she appears to live in only one room of it.'

Ruth sighed. If Annette refused to go to the party, she could hardly leave her on Christmas night to go by herself, and she found that she did, very much, want to meet the Comtesse's interesting guests.

'We haven't been to a party for years,' she said regretfully. 'I think it might do you good to go. You hardly see anyone except me and Françoise. There must be other local people, whom you knew before the war and perhaps you'd be able to renew acquaintance. Living here all your life, you must have known plenty of people when you were a child.'

Annette, however, proved remarkably stubborn about refusing to attend the Comtesse's party. 'If you really want a party, we can invite people ourselves for Christmas night,' she said. 'I'm sure Françoise could make some canapés if we give her plenty of notice, and Michel always seems to be able to find bottles of wine. Who shall we invite? Anyone except Madame Duvalle. Or perhaps we ought to invite her especially, since it's Christmas and we should be friendly to everyone.'

Ruth forbore from pointing out that if Christmas was a time for friendliness with those one felt less than friendly towards, it was a good time to start with the Comtesse, by accepting her invitation. She didn't want to quarrel with Annette, so she said no more, and shelved the idea that had been in her mind, of visiting Giulia regularly. Was Annette jealous, she wondered? It seemed too petty a notion to attribute to her friend, but the fact was that Annette saw hardly anyone other than the four of them, these days, and there were times when Ruth felt herself almost suffocated by the restrictive life she was forced to lead. She would never leave Annette until she could come to England and marry Simon, but, at the same time, Ruth wanted — needed — some life of her own, apart from Annette. Paul had been her lifeline, more than she had realised at the time, but Paul was dead, and she would never risk becoming friendly with one of the enemy soldiers again.

About a week before Christmas, Ruth realised that she would have to call on Giulia for politeness' sake and explain that they couldn't come to her party. She had hoped that she might see the Comtesse on her bicycle around the town, but she had seen nothing of her since her visit. Accordingly, while Annette was busy sketching and didn't appear to need company, she slipped out of the house and took the track away from the town, towards the chateau.

It was very cold, with a bitter wind blowing across the open fields. Ruth was glad when she reached the place where the boundary wall of the chateau grounds gave some slight shelter. Passing the place where the wall had crumbled, she remembered the message she had left there, weeks ago. Who had it been for? Could it have been Jacques, on one of his visits home, she wondered. Since then, there had been other messages to be delivered to secret locations, but not another at this place. She was almost tempted to look and see if it was still there, in case the intended recipient had not been able to collect it. It was dangerous to leave messages too long in their secret 'post boxes.' The German patrols were learning the whereabouts of some of them and could easily intercept them.

There was nothing under the brick. Ruth straightened up, looking over her shoulder towards the chateau, half hidden by trees. It might be pleasanter to walk to it this way, through a small copse, rather than continue along the road and up the drive. She set off, noticing that there was a faint track leading through the trees towards the house. Other people must come along this way regularly, though she doubted it would be an easy route for Giulia on her bicycle.

Ruth had reached the edge of the trees and was about to step out on to the drive, when she stopped in surprise. There was a car drawn up outside the main doors, and one glance told her it was a German staff car.

Was Giulia in trouble? A visit from the German authorities was rarely good news. She drew back into the shelter of the trees but kept watch on the car. Someone was getting out of the back seat and she saw the distinctive black uniform and highly polished boots of a Gestapo officer, one of the Secret Police.

A cold shudder of fear ran through her. It looked as if Giulia was about to be arrested, and there was nothing she could do to help her.

The German was middle-aged, beginning to go to fat in the way that Army officers seemed to avoid, but then Gestapo officers had largely desk-bound jobs; at least the higher ranking officers. It must be serious if someone as senior as this man had come to interrogate her, though if she were to be arrested it was surprising there was only this one man, with, presumably, his driver.

Before he had walked round the car and reached the front door, it opened and Giulia stood on the threshold. The German reached her, stopped, clicked his heels and bowed formally, taking her hand. Ruth's eyebrows raised in surprise. The Gestapo certainly did not have a reputation for politeness, especially when it came to dealings with the civilian population, but perhaps this man might make an exception for a Comtesse.

Ruth could hardly believe her eyes at what happened next. The German moved closer, enfolded her in his arms and gave her a long, lingering kiss!

Finally, they broke free, and Giulia made a few little dancing steps towards the door. The German followed her and before they disappeared inside, patted her bottom seductively.

After the front door closed, the driver of the staff car began to reverse the vehicle and return along the drive towards the gate. Ruth dropped to her knees and crouched behind a tree, concerned that he might see her watching, but he drove past at speed and, beyond the gate, turned right, towards the town.

There was no question of staying longer. Ruth scrambled to her feet and ran through the trees to the broken wall. She looked carefully out to see that the road was empty before she stepped on to it. The staff car was already long gone out of sight.

It looked, now, very much as if Annette's instincts had been right, and Giulia's loyalties lay with the Germans. Desperately, Ruth tried to think back to what she had said during their tea party, for it looked now as if the woman had been befriending her with a view to prising information from her.

Ruth's footsteps dragged as she made her way home. She had been so delighted to have found a new, English speaking friend who knew her part of England and seemed the ideal companion. Now, she knew Annette's gloomy words were true; you couldn't be sure who you could safely trust these days.

As she reached the outskirts of the town, no more than a couple of hundred yards from the cottage, another thought struck her like a sledgehammer blow. She was virtually certain that Jacques, the Resistance leader, was the Comte, Giulia's husband, but if Giulia herself was on close friendship terms with the Gestapo, where did that leave Jacques?

8

Christmas Eve, and they were all in the kitchen, making preparations for the following day. Michel had been persuaded to cut some holly branches and Annette was busy fashioning them into wreaths and garlands. Françoise was at the other end of the table plucking a chicken from the farm, a rare treat. Ruth was working on some plans of her own, to give the festivities a special, British touch.

'Was that someone at the back door?' Annette's sharp ears had caught a sound and she paused, looking up from her work.

'It's the wind,' Françoise muttered. 'No one would come visiting at this hour. It's past curfew.'

'There are some who would,' Michel said. He put down the branch of holly he had been trimming for Annette and went out to the tiny passageway off the kitchen, where the back door was located. Moments later, he came back, followed by Alain.

'Come to help us with the festivities?' Françoise asked. 'A glass of wine, perhaps? I still have some of the pre-war vintage I made.'

'Thank you, but I didn't come on a social

visit.' Alain sat down on one of the chairs, accepted a glass of wine from Françoise, and addressed Ruth.

'I'm sorry to come when you are busy with your preparations for the festival,' he said, 'but I have a particular job to be done, and I need your help.'

Ruth regarded him doubtfully. 'Not more supplies to be collected?' she asked. 'Surely not at Christmas! I'm willing to do what I can, but — '

'No, I am not asking you to collect any more packets containing detonators.' A ghost of a smile passed over Alain's usually dour features. 'But it is a collection, in a sense. This time, you will not be alone.'

'What is it? What do you want me to do?' The others paused in their work, all eyes turned towards Alain.

'I have not asked for your help for anything more than delivering messages for some time now,' Alain said. 'I — we — felt that perhaps your loyalties might be divided. Since the railway incident — '

'Ruth is one of your most loyal members!' Annette broke in angrily. 'You have no reason to doubt her in any way! You know she had no option but to agree when the German Captain came here and asked for English lessons, and, in fact, his friendship with her proved most useful to you. Naturally, Ruth was upset when she realised he must have been on that train that you derailed. Anyone would be. There was a good Frenchman who was the driver who died as well. It was a shock for her to realise that the goods she had collected in good faith were to be used for that purpose. Anyone would be upset by that.'

Alain looked abashed at Annette's outburst, but Ruth said quickly, 'No, it's all right. I made a promise to Paul that I wouldn't work actively for the Resistance but now that he's no longer alive, that promise doesn't hold any more. I'll do whatever you want of me. In fact, I'll be glad to do anything I can if it helps shorten the war.'

'We are expecting a delivery, in the evening of the day after Christmas Day,' Alain said. 'But it is the delivery of a person, not a package. London is sending us one of their agents to help co-ordinate all the groups in the area in preparation for the invasion of the Allies, which we know must happen before long. A plane is coming from London and it will be necessary for several of us to be ready with lights to guide it to the right landing place. I also think it would be helpful to have someone who speaks English, present. I would not wish to interrupt your festivities tomorrow, so I have come tonight. I will give you further details on the evening of the twenty sixth.'

'Someone from England?' Ruth's heart gave a leap. 'It will be nice to have another English person here, but how will you explain his presence in the town? He will be impersonating a Frenchman, I assume.'

'He will not be staying in Ste Marie de la Croix. He will be taken to the mountains as soon as possible after his arrival. They need him there, but here is the only place where he may be landed safely.' Alain stood up. 'I must go. I have other visits to make and, though it is the Eve of the Nativity the Germans have made no concessions for those who would wish to visit their friends and family this night.' With a polite 'bonne nuit' to Annette he slipped out of the back door as silently as he had come.

'I suppose we must be grateful this person is not arriving on Christmas Day,' Françoise grumbled, turning back to her chicken.

Annette looked thoughtfully at Ruth. 'You haven't done much more than deliver messages for weeks now,' she said. 'Alain knew you wanted to stay in the background ever since Paul was killed. He understood how you felt about that.'

'He didn't trust me,' Ruth said bluntly. 'He thought if I'd known what they were going to do, I'd have warned Paul. And I believe I would have tried to, if I had known he was going to be on that train. But he has no reason not to trust me now. There'll never be anyone like Paul, ever again. All my energies are going to be channelled into helping our group fight against the Germans.'

'Good for you, Mam'selle Ruth!' Michel applauded. 'I'm glad to see you are whole-heartedly back with us again. I did not like it that you began to like that German officer so much. He might have been better than many of them, but he was still a German. You want to find yourself a good, solid Frenchman and there'll be plenty of them home soon, once we've kicked the Boche out of France.'

Ruth smiled, but the thought of Paul was still painful. Her heart ached for him. The thought that he was dead and she had been in some measure responsible, weighed heavily with her. She promised herself that she would never again allow herself to become close to anyone, while the threat of losing them was so real.

They planned their Christmas lunch for mid afternoon the following day, the four of them gathered round the kitchen table. It would probably be the only meal they had that day, so leaving it late meant they had less chance of going to bed hungry. Ruth told Annette about seeing the Comtesse with a German officer at the chateau and Annette had nodded, unsurprised.

'I always thought there was something odd about that woman,' she said, 'though I admit, I never saw much of her, before the war. She never seemed friendly and I thought then it was shyness but now I'm convinced it was simply because she disliked the French.'

'Perhaps we should have gone to her party after all,' Ruth suggested, half joking. 'At least, if there were German officers there the food and wine would have been good and who knows, once they'd drunk enough we might have learnt things that Alain would have been pleased to know.'

Annette looked at her in horror. 'No! That would have been terribly dangerous! If you think it's the Comte her husband who is the leader of the guerrilla fighters in the mountains she might well be a double agent. She probably knows of your links with the group here and she could have planned to set you up at the party to betray you to the Germans.'

'It's a disappointment, though,' Ruth said, speaking in English so that Françoise and Michel would not hear her 'I was looking forward to seeing her again, and having some fun. The chateau is a fascinating place, even though it's been damaged and a ruin in places. Lord, I'm so sick of this war! When is it going to end? This is the fifth wartime Christmas we've had. Surely it must be the last?'

'There's something you could do to make things better,' Annette said thoughtfully. 'This plane that's coming tomorrow - why don't you ask them to take you back to England with them? I can manage here with Françoise's help, and conditions in England are much better than here. You'd be free, you wouldn't have to see German uniforms everywhere — '

'No!' Ruth exclaimed. 'Don't even think it! I'm not leaving France. I'm not leaving you.'

'But I can cope quite well by myself now. There's no need — '

'It's not only you. I think that at last Alain is beginning to trust me again and I've said I will do whatever he asks of me. I want to do more than delivering messages and there may be exciting things happening next year. They can't delay invading Europe much longer, and then the Allies will need all the help on the ground that they can get. I want to be part of that.'

'I wish I could do things for the group like you,' Annette said sadly. Then she brightened.

'Perhaps I could! You could take me with you tomorrow; I could hold a torch in a corner of the field, same as anyone else and if anyone saw us you could pretend I was sick and you had to take me to a doctor or the hospital. No one would imagine that someone like me would be anything but genuinely ill, so I'd be the perfect cover for you.'

'Annette, you're incorrigible! Can you see us trying to convince a German patrol in the middle of the night, in the middle of a field, that we were on the way to a doctor?'

They both began to giggle, then Ruth glanced at Françoise, who was looking at them with a puzzled expression, wondering what the conversation was about.

'I have a secret surprise for us all,' she told the older woman. 'I've decided that this year we'll have a real English Christmas, with crackers and paper hats.'

'Crackers and paper hats? Where on earth will you find things like that? Even in peacetime, we don't have things like that in France, and in England I don't suppose they are making such things any more.' Françoise looked sour; she didn't like it when the young Mam'selles spoke together in English. She couldn't understand them and automatically assumed they were talking about her.

Ruth ran upstairs to her bedroom. Earlier

that day, the idea had come to her and she had searched in her suitcases, untouched since she had arrived in France so many years ago now. She had found tissue paper and some coloured wrapping paper and set to, to fashion four paper hats.

There was still some stiff, blue paper in the kitchen which had held sugar in the days when it had been more readily obtainable, and in larger quantities. With it, Ruth fashioned a pirate's hat for Michel and a rather pretty Regency style bonnet for Annette. For herself, she cheated a little, using an old beret as a basis to make a wig of huge, white tissue paper curls, and for Françoise she made a pointed dunce's cap with streamers from it turning it into a medieval French lady's head-dress.

She had puzzled over making crackers until she found a long, cardboard tube which had once contained Annette's drawing paper. She could cut this into four, and cover each piece in coloured paper. She thought up the silliest jokes and riddles which she could remember from childhood Christmases, which, even translated into French, would probably be totally incomprehensible to Françoise and Michel. She found some small trinkets to put inside three of them, and a cigar she had begged from Claude to put in Michel's. There was no possibility of making a snap, so when they were pulled, everyone would have to shout 'bang!' which might add to the amusement.

Françoise, encouraged by Annette, had made a big effort to produce a very special meal. To go with the farm chicken, which would be fresh and flavoursome, even if not very large, she had a variety of root vegetables from her store. She didn't have the means to make a Christmas pudding, even had she known how, but there were still apples from the farm orchard and home preserved blackberries, which would make a very acceptable pie.

At four o'clock on Christmas day they sat round the kitchen table, solemnly wearing the hats that Ruth had made. Françoise and Michel were somewhat bemused by Ruth's efforts but persuaded by Annette to join in making this a special English Christmas, to make Ruth feel less homesick.

'Here's to Christmas 1943,' Annette said, raising her glass of Françoise's home-made wine, laced with a little brandy. 'Let us hope that 1944 will see the end of the war at last. May this be our last wartime Christmas.'

Ruth raised her glass with the others, echoing Annette's words. She could sense that Françoise and Michel were thinking that this English custom of eating their meal wearing ridiculous headgear was completely mad. She often suspected that Françoise had little patience with the English, finding them incomprehensible. She had never met any English, apart from seeing tourists before the war, until Ruth and Simon had come to stay with Annette, yet Françoise had strong opinions about the English and their strange ways.

The crackers were a success, though Ruth had a few qualms while explaining what to do with them. She and Annette struggled to explain the significance of the mottoes, but the cigar and small pieces of jewellery were well received. In honour of the day being in the English style, they finished the meal by drinking the last of the tea Ruth had brought from England with her. Stale and very weak it might be, but it brought back memories of home. Ruth knew Françoise and Michel would sooner have had coffee, but there was none left and at least this strange and rather tasteless drink was something different.

Michel was wondering if this was the moment to produce the half bottle of schnapps which one of the farm hands had claimed to have stolen from a German. Fearful of discovery, he had passed it on to Michel with a warning to drink it soon and make sure the bottle was well and truly smashed afterwards. Michel half rose from his seat, meaning to fetch it and offer it round, when there sounded a knock at the front door.

'Not those damn Germans on Christmas day!' Françoise grumbled. If it had been Alain or one of the farm hands, it was more likely they would have come to the back door.

'I'll go,' Ruth said. 'It's probably nothing important. Some neighbour wanting to wish us well and good fortune for the coming year, I expect.'

She went out into the hall, unaware that she was still wearing the hat she had made, which covered her own, blonde hair and made her look rather like a clown, or a white golliwog.

The man standing on the step had his back to her and was wearing a long, winter trenchcoat. At the sound of the door opening he turned round, eyes suddenly wide with amazement at the strange sight before him.

'Pardon, Madame,' he began in halting French, 'I was looking for a young lady who used to live here. An English lady, Mademoiselle Lawson.'

Ruth stared at him and her whole world rocked and spun round her. She couldn't, didn't dare to believe what she was seeing.

'Paul — ' she choked.

He stared at her doubtfully. 'Ruth? Is it you? What has happened? Why are you dressed like that?'

'Oh, my God! My hat!' She whipped off the beret and let her hair tumble out round her shoulders. Paul let out a sigh of relief. 'Ruth! It is you! I thought you must have moved away and I wasn't going to find you again!' He was over the threshold in one stride, the door was kicked shut and he held her in his arms, kissing her, caressing her hair, holding her so close she felt almost crushed.

'Paul! Oh, Paul!' Relief made her sob.

'What is wrong, Liebchen? Why do you cry when I come to see you again?'

'Because — because I thought you were dead!'

'Dead? Because I did not write to you? You must have realised it would be difficult and perhaps embarrassing for you to receive a letter from Germany. I thought you would have understood that. And why should I be dead? I have been in Germany, not in any of the war zones. I was perfectly safe.'

'I thought you had been killed on the train out of here,' Ruth said. 'The night you left, the railway line was blown up and a train was derailed. You must have been on it, it was the

198

only train leaving for Germany that night. I thought, if you had survived, you would have managed to let me know. When I heard nothing, I assumed you were among the dead.'

'The train? You thought I was on the train that night? Oh, my poor Ruth! If I'd realised that, I would have made sure you knew I was all right. I wasn't anywhere near a train. Someone gave me a lift in a staff car to Caen and I begged a ride with a convoy going by road. I did not even know about a train being derailed until I came back this morning and saw that the trains had only just begun to come through again. There is still wreckage everywhere and only one line operational. The Resistance group must have been very satisfied with that piece of sabotage.'

Ruth looked at him sharply, but his remark seemed to be meant at face value, without any implication.

'I was so lost without you,' she said, pulling away from him to look searchingly into his face. 'I thought I'd never see you again.'

'I was attending a course. I was worried for a while that at the end of it I might be drafted somewhere else, but I managed to persuade the authorities that since I knew the area I would be of greater use back here. And there were other reasons, too, why it seemed to them that I would best serve the Fatherland in Ste Marie de la Croix. But you,' he took her hands in his, holding them as if he thought if he let go she would disappear again. 'You look well, Liebchen. But why this strange outfit? Are you disguising yourself?'

Ruth began to giggle. 'It's an English custom,' she said. 'We wear paper hats at our meal on Christmas day. They don't do it in France, but I was trying to make this Christmas a little like the English ones I remembered.'

'An English custom? Why was I not told about this English custom? It seems my English teacher was very remiss, not to explain to me all about this strange thing the English do.' His eyes twinkled while he strove to keep a stern expression.

'You weren't here for English lessons before Christmas, otherwise I would certainly have told you,' Ruth said. 'They should be paper hats out of Christmas crackers but I couldn't make them properly without the right equipment. I did my best; they are all sitting in the kitchen now, Michel and Françoise dutifully wearing ridiculous hats to make me feel less homesick. Annette experienced an English Christmas before the war, so the understood what I was trying to do, but I suspect even she thinks English customs are very peculiar.'

'All of you, sitting round the table in strange hats? This I must see!' Paul stepped towards the kitchen door, then paused. 'I had forgotten it was Christmas day today. I travelled from Germany this morning and for me it was a working day as usual. But I did not forget entirely, Ruth. Wait while I collect my case. I came here straight from the station and my suitcase is still on your doorstep.'

He opened the front door, retrieved his case and a large carrier bag. The carrier he handed to her. 'Here are a few items which may help to liven up your Christmas. We are all short of food, throughout Europe, but I am sure the civilians here are worse off than we are in Germany. Now, please show me this English Christmas you have been celebrating.'

Ruth opened the kitchen door and three heads swivelled towards them.

'It's Paul,' she said. 'He's come back. He wasn't killed. He wasn't even on the train.'

Michel was the first to react. With the bottle of schnapps still clutched in his hand, he said, 'I am pleased to see you well, Monsieur. Our little English rose has been fretting for you. Will you join us in a glass of schnapps?'

Paul made a space on the table and tipped

the carrier's contents out on to it. Françoise gasped as she saw coffee, sugar, chocolate and some tins of food spill out from it.

'Mon Dieu! I have not seen that kind of food in one heap together for years!' she whispered.

Annette looked from Paul's face to Ruth's, and her own lit up with happiness when she saw Ruth's glowing eyes. 'Paul, Ruth is so happy and relieved that you are back here again,' she said softly, in English.

'I am sorry for disturbing your festivities,' Paul said shyly, 'but when Ruth told me — I had to see this English custom for myself. No, — please!' He gestured with his glass of schnapps as Françoise and Michel both self-consciously made to pull off their hats. 'It is charming. Delightful. And I am pleased to drink a toast with you. May this New Year see the end of hostilities between our countries!'

'Françoise,' Ruth said quietly to the older woman, 'Paul has been travelling from Germany all day. I don't suppose he has managed much to eat. Is there any of the chicken left we could offer him?'

'In thanks for what he has brought us, our scrawny bird would be a poor return, but I am sure there is something I could find from it.' Françoise stood up and reached for a clean plate. 'Captain Reinhardt, because you have brought the smile back into our Ruth's face again, let me offer you a share in our Christmas dinner.'

Paul looked astonished. 'I hadn't meant — I've come straight from the station, haven't even reported in to Headquarters yet. I only wanted to see Ruth and bring you these few things.'

'You are more than welcome, Paul,' Annette told him. 'I know it might be difficult for you, but it is Christmas day, a time of truce. I'm sure no one will miss you for an hour or so, and no one will have seen you coming here. It will be quite safe and you know you are among friends here.'

Paul looked hungrily at the plate of chicken and vegetables Françoise put in front of him. Ruth pulled forward another chair beside her own place. 'Tonight there is no war,' she said. 'As Annette says, Christmas day is truce. Eat with us for once.'

Michel looked round the table at them all; French, English and German, all sitting eating and talking together. 'This is the most extraordinary Christmas I have ever known,' he announced, and poured out another round of schnapps.

9

The morning after Christmas day, Ruth woke
to reality. She lay, watching the pale, cold
light filter through the curtains and wondered
if it had all really happened yesterday. Paul
had come back. He was not dead, had not
even been involved in the train derailment
and he had come to see her before he had
even reported to the German Headquarters.
He had come back to her as he had promised
he would, and, last night, before he left after
that incredible Christmas meal, he had told
her he loved her. She clung to the memory of
those words as she clambered unwillingly out
of bed into the coldness of the unheated
room. He would be coming to see her again,
ostensibly for English conversation, as soon
as he knew when his off-duty times were. A
great surge of happiness swept through her,
to be suddenly checked when she remembered what was to happen today, or, rather,
tonight. She had promised to assist with
signal lights to enable a plane to land
someone from England; she had also told
Alain that she was willing, eager even, to do
anything the group required of her. But she

204

had promised Paul that she would have nothing further to do with the Resistance.

It was an impossible situation. Alain and Jacques had made it clear that she was under orders, quite as much as anyone in the armed forces would be, in wartime. When she had believed Paul dead, she considered herself released from her promise. It was, after all, mainly to protect him if their friendship should ever be suspected by the German authorities. It had seemed then that the sensible thing was to concentrate all her energies into helping bring an end to the war as soon as possible; an end that meant victory for Britain and her Allies. In the cold light of the December morning, it still seemed to Ruth to be the best, the only option, but now that Paul was back, she must, for his sake as well as her own, make sure that he never found out that she was still helping the Resistance. She must never risk putting his loyalties to the test.

When she came downstairs, Ruth found that Annette had already dressed herself and was settled in her chair at the table by the window of the sitting room, sketching.

'What's that you're doing?' she asked, and was surprised when Annette self-consciously slipped the drawing under another sheet of paper.

'Just sketching. An idea I had.' Annette looked embarrassed.

'Let me see!' They had always shared everything and Ruth was unused to Annette having secrets from her.

Unwillingly, Annette pulled the sheet of paper from under its fellow. There were half a dozen sketches on it, each a different depiction of a bird with a flower, either in its beak or grasped in a claw.

'What's it meant to be?' Ruth asked, puzzled.

'Just an idea I had. Something Michel said last night. He called you our English rose and I was thinking, in bed, about it. I had to get up and put my ideas on paper straight away, while I was waiting for Françoise to prepare breakfast.'

'But what are you trying to say?'

'It's a symbol; the eagle and the rose, Paul and you. The German eagle and the English rose, you see? But there's no way I seem able to draw them together without it looking as if the eagle is dominating the rose, or trying to destroy it. Ruth, do you think it's some kind of omen? Are my sketches trying to tell me something? Does it mean that the Germans are going to win this war, after all?' Tears trickled down Annette's pretty, flower-like face. Ruth wiped them away with her

206

own handkerchief.

'Nonsense! A big bird like an eagle would have to hold something like a rose in its beak or claw. What else would it do? Just remember, if the eagle picked up the rose the wrong way, or was too rough with it, the rose would use its thorns and make life very uncomfortable for the eagle. Isn't that as symbolic as the other way round?'

Annette gave a watery giggle. 'Ruth, you are such a comfort to me! You always manage to say the right things to cheer me up and give me hope. Of course the Allies will win! Even Paul said yesterday might be the last wartime Christmas. Do you suppose he knows something? Coming from Berlin, he must be very up to date with war news.'

'If he knows any war news that we don't, you may be sure that it is bad news from the German point of view,' Ruth said stoutly. 'And we shall be up to date with some real, proper British news tonight. The man being sent from England will fill us in with all the latest news before we pass him on to Jacques' people in the mountains.'

'Be careful, Ruth. I do worry about you, whenever you go out after curfew to do a job for Alain.'

'You've no need to worry. Alain plans all his Resistance activities with military precision. He could teach the Allied Generals a thing or two, and as for the German ones — ' Ruth laughed with a confidence she did not entirely feel. 'The only reason I was caught that time at the beach, was because I was careless, too self-confident and didn't look first before I walked out on to the road. That patrol would have been easy enough to avoid if I had used my common sense. Both Alain and Jacques said so. I won't let it happen again, you may be sure.'

'The Germans aren't the fools Alain and his group think they are,' Annette said seriously.

'I know that. Paul certainly isn't, and it's going to be very difficult keeping my activities from him. I hate deceiving him, but what else can I do?'

Françoise's voice, calling them to breakfast, interrupted the conversation. Annette tucked her sketches into a folder and piled some books on top. 'I don't want Françoise seeing them,' she said. 'She might get the wrong idea. And if anyone came to the house — ' She hesitated. 'Well, let's just keep these sketches between ourselves for now.'

Alain called at the back door at dusk, just before curfew.

'A private word with you, Ruth,' he murmured.

She took him into the hall, the only empty place since Annette was in the sitting room.

'We meet by the crossroads at eleven o'clock,' Alain said. 'You know the place I mean? It's not all that far to walk, even in the dark.'

'I know it,' Ruth said. 'It's the place where the war memorial is, isn't it?'

'It's more than a war memorial now,' Alain said gravely. 'Since the Germans committed that atrocity there, the place has become a shrine to all those who fight back. After the war, we shall erect something more in keeping with how we feel now. It will not be enough merely to add the names of the dead in this war to those who died in 1914 to 1918.'

And this might be one place where the names of those killed in this war would outnumber those killed in the previous one, Ruth thought. Fleetingly, she hoped that her own name would never appear among those listed.

'I'll be there,' she promised Alain. 'Do you want me to bring a torch?'

He shook his head. 'Any torch you may have will not be powerful enough for the plane to see. We will be lighting flares in a field. Bring an old rug or blanket, perhaps, to enable us to douse them quickly if necessary.'

Ruth nodded. She remembered she had an old cloak, very old now, but still kept because no one ever threw anything away these days. She would wear it there, and if it was burnt later it would be no great loss.

She left the house about half past ten. Annette was reading tranquilly by the fire but looked up as she saw Ruth in her cloak in the doorway.

'I can manage to get to bed by myself if you are late back,' she said. 'Don't worry about me. Take care, Ruth dear.'

'If you need anything, call for Françoise. She's knitting in the kitchen.'

'No, I'd sooner not let her know that you have gone out. I noticed Alain would not speak of his instructions in front of anyone but you. Clearly, he wants as few people as possible to know the details of what is to happen.'

'Dear God!' Ruth muttered. 'It seems as if Alain doesn't trust anyone, even Françoise, and she probably knows as much as I do, since Michel is likely to be there. It will take several people to put flares round a field.'

Ruth knew the road up to the crossroads well, so there was no problem in finding her way, even though it was pitch dark with no moon. Approaching the crossroads, she saw the memorial statue looming up, a darker shadow among the darkness. Then it seemed that one of the statues moved, and she realised that there were people there already, clustered round the plinth.

'Ruth?' It was Alain who spoke. 'We are all here now. There are six of us and we are to light flares in two lines of three, along the sides of the field. Each one stays by his flare ready to dowse it and scatter the evidence as soon as the RAF have made the delivery.' He led the way over a fence into a nearby field, and four other shadowy figures followed him. Ruth kept close, afraid that she would lose them if she lingered behind. Alain crossed two fields, coming to a third which was well away from the road and not near any trees.

'This is our best place,' he said. 'Take a mark from this corner, then two of you walk a hundred paces further on, and two a hundred paces to the right. I would have marked your positions with a branch or something, but there were Germans around all day and I could not get away to come here unseen.'

Ruth felt something thrust into her hands. It felt like a lantern. 'There is plenty of brushwood near the hedge. After you have collected a bundle, walk a hundred paces from the hedge and line up with the light you will see behind you. You have matches?' A box was thrust into her hand. 'Do not light anything until you hear the signal.'

'What is the signal?' Ruth asked, feeling foolish.

'You will hear the sound of an aircraft flying low. You will know it is the one because it will be a single plane. I have been told it will deliver its passenger between the flares and be off again within two minutes. Your flares should not be lit for more than three minutes. Understood?'

Ruth felt nervous. In the pitch darkness of the field she could not be sure she was lined up with anyone else. What if she was in the wrong place and, as a result, the plane crashed in the hedge and could not take off again

With an armful of brushwood she measured a hundred paces away from the hedge, remembering that on the last occasion she had done this, Alain's measurement had been in somewhat longer paces than her own. She looked round; there seemed to be a faint, red glimmer away to her left. She lit the lantern and piled the brushwood round it, except for the side facing the glimmer of light.

She did not hear him at all, but Alain must have been skilled in moving silently and have known the area well, for he suddenly appeared beside her.

'Good, Ruth. You are in the right place,' he

said. 'Light the brushwood as soon as you hear the plane's engines.'

* * *

She didn't have long to wait. Faintly, there came a humming sound away over her shoulder, from the direction of the sea. It grew louder, and then there was a dark shape in the sky, though it seemed too high up to be making a landing.

Ruth struggled to light the brushwood, but it was damp and would not catch. He won't be able to see it, she thought desperately. Perhaps he'll fly over again but if he can't see all the markers he won't know where to land.

The plane was circling, flying slowly, then, without warning, the engine sound changed and it sped off across the night sky, out of sight. Seconds later there was nothing more than a faint drone in the distance.

What happened? Could he have seen the lights from a German patrol from that distance? Ruth thought. It must be my fault, not getting the brushwood lit in time. He didn't see enough flares to guide him in. She looked up at the sky and saw what looked like a small, low cloud drifting above the field. Seconds later, she realised what it was and began running towards it.

The parachutist made a perfect landing and was standing up, detaching his 'chute, when she reached him.

'Bon soir!' he greeted her. She replied in English 'Welcome to France! That was a splendid landing, but we were expecting the plane itself.'

'Too risky. But your flares did a good job and I seem to have landed plumb in the middle of them.' He grasped her hand in a firm handshake. 'I'm Bob, codename Rickard. I say, you do speak excellent English.'

'That's because I am English!' Ruth laughed. 'My name is — '

'You must be Ruth,' Bob interrupted her. 'I've heard of you. I'm delighted to meet you at last.'

'The British agents have actually heard of me?' Ruth said, astonished. 'But I don't do anything much for the group. I'm only on the fringe.'

'Nevertheless, you are well-known back home.' She could sense his friendly grin even though it was too dark to see his face. 'I hope we may be working together. As yet, I don't know what I shall be doing. All I know is that I am to take my instructions from someone called Jacques and I would be taken to him on landing.'

'Ruth, don't stand there chatting to him as

if you'd met an old friend on a street corner,' Alain said, coming up to them. He carried a lantern and in its glow Ruth saw his face was dark with anger. She suspected he was annoyed because he hadn't understood enough to follow their conversation. 'Go and dowse the marker lights quickly. We must get Rickard away to the chateau as soon as possible.'

'The chateau?' On her way back across the field, Ruth turned sharply. 'Do you mean you are taking him to the chateau where the Comtesse Giulia lives?'

'Ruth, you should know better than to ask too many questions,' Alain snapped. He took Bob's arm and began leading him across the field. 'Deal with the parachute,' he called over his shoulder.

Ruth and another member of the group, whom she knew only as Phillipe, stooped to gather up the parachute canopy before following Alain and the others across the field.

'I suppose we'd better burn it,' Phillipe said. 'Pity, my wife could make some lovely lingerie from all this.'

'Is Alain really taking him to the chateau?' Ruth asked him.

'Didn't you know that Jacques' family have owned the chateau for generations?' Phillipe replied. 'His wife will look after our man until Jacques can come and take him to his guerrilla headquarters.'

'Comtesse Giulia?' Ruth had said nothing to anyone except Annette about seeing Giulia with the Gestapo officer. Now, she wished she had told Alain at the time, but it was too late. If the Comtesse was indeed a double agent, they could be delivering Bob straight into German hands.

'Yes, the Italian woman. A lot of us don't trust her because of that, but Alain says that since she's Jacques' wife she's as good as one of us. I hardly know her myself but she's been married to the Comte and lived in the town for many, many years so I'm sure it will be all right.'

'I must go and remove my pile of brushwood; I forgot when I ran to greet Bob,' Ruth said. 'Take the parachute, won't you? If you burnt it, the remains would be still recognisable, so why don't you ask your wife to cut it up and make herself some glamorous undies? The Germans are less likely to discover it if she's wearing it. But tell her to make them quickly, and be careful not to hang them out on a washing line!'

Ruth ran across the field as fast as she could, stumbling over tufts of grass and rabbit holes. She snatched up her lantern, kicked the brushwood pile apart and stamped on any remaining twigs that were smouldering. In seconds, she was off again, making for the gap in the hedge where she guessed Alain would be leading Bob.

She heard Alain's voice as she drew near, in the middle of the next field, asking Bob questions about the situation in England, and Bob's hesitant, brief replies.

'Bob!' She called urgently. He stopped and looked round, and she heard Alain's snort of exasperation.

'Bob - when you get to the chateau, please be very careful,' she said in English. 'The woman who lives there, the Comtesse Giulia — well, I don't think she's to be trusted. I suspect she may be helping the Germans. Be warned.'

'I will be. Thanks, Ruth.' He turned back and Ruth heard Alain saying suspiciously, 'What was all that about? What was Ruth saying to you?'

'She merely asked if I had news of someone she knew in England,' Bob replied easily. 'Unfortunately, I couldn't be of help to her.'

Ruth wondered if Alain believed him. His English was minimal, but he'd understand that Bob was thanking her for something and that didn't sound an appropriate response to an enquiry about a mutual friend.

There were bicycles hidden under the hedge by the road. Alain and Bob and two of the men mounted them and rode off silently towards the chateau. The other two men melted away into the darkness, Phillipe, looking unusually portly with the parachute stuffed inside his overcoat.

Ruth made her way back alone to the cottage. The place was in darkness but as she came from the kitchen where she had let herself in through the back door, she heard Annette call to her.

'All well? I'm glad you're back. I couldn't sleep until I knew you were safe.' Ruth came into the downstairs bedroom and sat on the edge of Annette's bed.

'They sent someone called Bob,' she said. 'I hope he doesn't have too much to do in the town, his French isn't good enough to fool anyone, though of course he's fluent enough. Guess what — he knew my name before I told him! Seems they know about me at Special Operations in England.'

'Why shouldn't they? There aren't many English girls living here, and helping the Resistance,' Annette replied. 'I've often wondered — Simon speaks such excellent French and he knows this country so well — do you think he might be one of those working with the agents? I know he was

218

intending to join the British Army when he left here just before war was declared, but I never knew what regiment he was in, or what he was doing. I don't even know where he was posted. I haven't heard any news of him for so long now, and sometimes I wonder — he has such useful skills, surely they wouldn't waste them giving him an ordinary job. If he was in some way involved — it would explain how this man came to know of you.'

'Possibly,' Ruth said. She didn't want to think of Simon being involved with sending parachutists into France. She kissed Annette goodnight and went quietly upstairs to her own room. She was wondering, uneasily, what, exactly it was that they knew about her in Britain? It could hardly be for any of the few simple and not particularly dangerous missions she had carried out for the local group. Was it, perhaps, that word had got back about herself and Paul? Had Bob been warned to be wary of her because of that?

That's ridiculous, she told herself. Then, the thought hit her. That was exactly what had happened with the Comtesse Giulia, and she had warned Bob not to trust her for that very same reason!

Paul came the following afternoon, bringing some books. 'I hope we may resume our

English conversations?' he said. 'My use of your language has been getting rusty. I have not spoken it for some time now. In fact, while I was away I deliberately tried to give the impression that I knew very little English. There was an interpreter's job in Berlin that they might have considered me for, but I persuaded them my French was better and I was of more use to the war effort by returning here.'

'I'm so glad you came back.' Ruth rested her head on his shoulder; his arm curled round her, holding her close to him.

'I would always find a way of coming back to you, Ruth,' he whispered softly. 'One day, when this war is over, we shall be together all the time. Openly. We can live wherever you wish; France, England, Germany, - Australia, even, if you like! And it will not be much longer now. I am sure of it. We've been fighting nearly four and a half years already and that is longer than the 1914 conflict. Men cannot go on fighting each other like this for so long. There cannot be the resources, the manpower, for a longer war.'

It occurred to Ruth to wonder if Paul had learnt anything about the future of the war while in Berlin, but she didn't want to ask him. Instead, she said, 'Let's not talk about war any more today. Did you manage any leave whilst you were in Germany? How did you find your family?'

'I managed a few days in Mannheim at the end of October. My parents are well, though my brother's death has hit them very hard. He was a Luftwaffe pilot, I believe I told you. Look, I have some photographs I took while I was on leave. Would you like to see pictures of my home and family?'

The snapshots showed a spacious, wood framed house in a woodland setting. There were pictures of an extensive garden which clearly had been well-tended once, but was now overgrown and looked neglected.

'Unfortunately, my father is no longer able to look after the whole garden,' Paul explained. 'The flowerbeds near the house he keeps tended and he has an extensive vegetable garden, but the rest of the grounds have been left to grow wild. One day, I hope to bring them back to how they were when Kurt and I were children. See, here are my parents!' He held out a picture of an elderly couple, sitting in chairs in the garden, the house behind them. Ruth saw a small, rather stout man with a drooping walrus moustache but a kindly expression on his face as he smiled for the camera. Beside him, his wife was plump and sweet-faced. Ruth could see a definite likeness between her and Paul.

'They look a lovely couple,' she said. 'I'd love to meet them. I wish I could.'

'One day you will, I promise.' He said. 'But if I am not able to take you there myself, will you promise me something, Ruth?'

'What do you mean, not able to take me yourself?' A cold trickle of unease ran through her.

'One never knows what could happen in war. If I do not survive, will you visit them, one day when you are able to, and talk to them about us? I have told them about you. It does not matter to them that you are English, though they worry that I would be in grave trouble if the German authorities knew about us. But I want them to meet you, come to know you, even if I am not here — '

'Paul, don't talk like that!' Ruth burst out. 'What's suddenly got into you? A moment ago you were saying the war might soon be over, now you're talking about not surviving it. What do you mean? Do you know something?'

Paul hesitated, then seemed to come to a decision. 'Yes, I do know something,' he said. 'But it is something I can tell no one, none of my colleagues. I could not even safely tell my parents, but I know I can tell you.'

'No!' Ruth clamped her hand over his

mouth. 'Don't tell me anything! Please, Paul, I beg you! I don't want to know!'

Paul laughed softly, removing her hand and kissing her palm. 'You need not fear about the possibility of divided loyalties. I do not care if you tell your Resistance friends what I am about to say. In fact, I would be happy if you were to do so.'

'What?' Ruth's cheeks flamed scarlet, though she tried to control her expression. 'Why do you think -?'

★ ★ ★

'I am not going to ask you if you are still working for them or not. I do not think you would blow up another railway line, anyway.' His eyes twinkled at her obvious discomfort. 'However, I am sure you must know some of the people who were involved. They are your friends, have been your friends for a long time, and this is a small town. Even on the most innocent of social occasions you must see them and speak to them.'

Ruth felt frightened. She couldn't admit to Paul that she was committed to being involved with the Resistance, yet neither could she lie to him. She was being forced into an impossible position.

'Paul, I don't think we ought to talk about

223

such matters,' she urged. 'When you first came for English conversation lessons I thought we had a mutual agreement that we didn't discuss subjects that — that might — well, I intended that we should keep to neutral topics, like books and films.'

'Neutral topics!' Paul gave a harsh laugh. 'Are we always to confine ourselves to neutral topics, my Ruth? Never about the things about which we feel deeply? We have, I thought, gone beyond conventional English conversation a long time ago. Now, I want to tell you something that will show you what I mean. Will you hear me out?'

'If I must. But please, Paul, don't force me to choose where my loyalties lie. Don't make things any harder for me.'

'It's not like that.' Paul took her hands in his. 'When I left for Germany it was because I was being sent on a special staff briefing assignment. That was my official reason for going to Berlin, but it wasn't the only one. I had been invited to attend certain meetings, secret meetings, of top level military and government officials. We were all agreed on one thing; that Germany cannot win this war because we are ruled by an insane megalomaniac who will end by destroying our country and most of Europe with us, if he is allowed to continue. We came to one inescapable conclusion, we must rid ourselves of the Führer forever.'

'What!' Ruth gasped. Her hands, still clasped in Paul's, felt cold and clammy.

'Our decision was unanimous. The only sure and certain way to succeed is by assassination,' Paul continued. 'I cannot tell you how or when — '

'For Heaven's sake don't!' Ruth exclaimed. 'If anyone heard you — '

'I cannot give details because I don't know any,' Paul said, 'but I wanted you to know — so that you can tell those who might find it useful to know, that there are many in Germany whose eyes have at last been opened, those who realise what has been happening.'

'Paul, be careful! If anyone among the Occupying Forces here even suspected such a thing!'

'I know. I cannot be sure of anyone amongst the other officers at German Headquarters, even though I suspect there may well be others who share the same opinions as I do. I had to tell you, Ruth, partly as a measure of my trust in you, but mainly because I want the British and their Allies to know what the feeling is in Germany and what is likely to happen there soon.'

'I think you may find the British will hear

of this soon enough,' Ruth replied guardedly. 'Now, Paul, *please* may we talk of other things? You've shown me photographs of your parents and your home, now let me show you pictures of mine.'

They spent the rest of the afternoon looking over the photo albums Ruth had brought with her from her home in Hertfordshire, talking of country walks and the holidays in Scotland she had taken as a child. When Paul left, Ruth went into the kitchen where Annette was sitting with Françoise.

'Did you hear us?' she asked casually.

'You never speak to him in French,' Françoise replied. 'He could do with some lessons there, that one. His French is no better than most foreigners.' She realised what she had said, and added quickly 'except for yourself, of course, Mam'selle Ruth. You speak it very well, but then, you have been here so long.'

Annette looked at Ruth curiously. 'I heard you saying you were going to fetch your photo album. What was special about today? He was not asking you about England, I hope. One may pick up useful information from casual remarks and there is much to be learnt from holiday snaps of the British coastline.'

'He doesn't try to fish for information like that,' Ruth said crossly. Annette still seemed not to trust Paul entirely. 'We were just chatting — about our homes, our families. The usual, safe stuff. I merely wondered - well, it doesn't matter. I seem to have developed a headache, concentrating on his grammar and trying to listen to what he's saying at the same time. I think I'll go for a walk before curfew to try to clear it. Do you need anything from the market, Françoise?'

'I always need things,' Françoise grumbled. 'Take the basket, if you are going near the square. We shall be glad of anything you can find. Perhaps there will be some fish in, or someone selling winter vegetables.'

Glad of an excuse, Ruth picked up the shopping basket and left the cottage. She went straight to Claude's bakery in the town square.

The shop was closed, but she knocked on the door several times and eventually Claude, up to his elbows in flour, opened it to her.

'I am sorry, Mam'selle Ruth, but I have no bread at all, even for you,' he said, on seeing her. 'I am preparing the dough for tomorrow's batch. Come early and there will be plenty then.'

'I'm not wanting bread today. This is a social call,' Ruth said. 'I was wondering how your family was. Perhaps I might come in and have a little chat with your wife, Claude.'

Claude, straight-faced, shook his head. 'It is not possible, Mam'selle. My wife and family have gone to visit her relatives in the country for a short while. I do not know when they will be back but it will not be for at least a few days.'

'I see.' Ruth hesitated, not knowing what to do next. She was not sure how else to contact Alain and she didn't want to wait until he turned up at the back door of the cottage. That could be at any time, and what she had to tell him was for his ears alone. At the cottage, Michel and Françoise were always around and could easily overhear.

Claude looked into the square, which, on this side, was largely deserted. 'Try the chateau,' he whispered. 'I think perhaps your friend the Comtesse might enjoy your company this afternoon.'

Giulia was the very last person Ruth would have thought of trusting with her information, but perhaps Claude knew that Jacques was there. It had been only yesterday that Bob had been taken to the chateau to meet him, after all.

'Thank you, Claude. I'll come for some bread tomorrow morning.' She had enough time to reach the chateau and be back before curfew, but it meant that she couldn't stay and talk with the Comtesse. If Jacques was there, she would tell him what Paul had told her, but if he was not, she would come straight back. It occurred to her, as she took the unmade road out of the town, that she hadn't heard or seen anything of Giulia since that day she had seen the Gestapo officer kissing her. The Comtesse must by now be thinking it strange that neither Ruth nor Annette had come to her party on Christmas night. She might even suspect that Ruth knew about her friendship with the German. For her own safety, Ruth decided to pretend to know nothing. Perhaps Bob would still be there and she could speak to him. That would be safer and ensure that Paul's message went straight to London.

It was already nearly dusk when Ruth arrived outside the chateau gates. She looked warily down the drive before stepping inside. There was a car parked near the front door but it had no German markings and looked like a French civilian one, though there were very few people who had a permit for a car these days.

The front door was ajar. Ruth pushed it wider and was about to call 'Hallo, anyone there?' when she realised there were several people in the hallway. One she recognised at once as Père Joseph, the rest were a trio of Gendarmes.

Père Joseph looked at her in surprise. 'Ruth!' he exclaimed. 'What are you doing here?'

'I came to visit Comtesse Giulia,' she said. She didn't want to suggest she knew there might be other people in the chateau; one never knew how safe it was to speak in front of the local police. 'I met her recently and she seemed rather a lonely person and to value my friendship. Is she here?' She mustn't claim too close an acquaintance with someone who could be about to be exposed as a double agent. The presence of the gendarmes looked ominous.

Père Joseph came towards her and put a kindly arm round her shoulders. 'I am so sorry, my dear, but I fear you are too late. Gendarme Lebrun here and I were summoned to the chateau by the Comtesse's cleaning lady. The woman found her employer lying here dead when she arrived for work. Comtesse Giulia's throat had been slit; I fear she has undoubtedly been murdered.'

10

Ruth and Annette discussed Giulia's murder for the rest of that evening. 'There are several people who might have done it, for different reasons,' Annette said. 'Her husband, perhaps, if he learnt that she was having an affair with a Gestapo officer, or one of the Resistance if they thought she was likely to betray them. If you saw her with a German, then other people may have seen her, too. It didn't look as though she went to much trouble to conceal the fact that she was on good terms with them.'

'She could have been killed by the Germans,' Ruth said. 'Perhaps, after all, she was loyal to her husband but playing a dangerous game trying to get information from the enemy for him.'

'What does the Gendarme say? It was Pierre Lebrun who was called in when her cleaning lady found her, wasn't it?' Annette asked. 'I know him quite well; we were at school together. Take me out tomorrow and we'll try to have a talk to him. He'll tell us whatever he knows, I'm sure.'

Pierre, however, could tell them very little,

except that Madame Moreau, who came to the chateau twice a week to do some domestic work for the Comtesse, had arrived that morning to find Giulia lying in the entrance hall in a pool of blood, her throat slashed. Madame Moreau had leapt back on to her bicycle and, sobbing hysterically, had pedalled straight to the Gendarmerie in the town. Investigations had subsequently established that the Comtesse had been killed some time the previous day. There was no weapon present, but it looked as if a dagger or bayonet had been used. Pierre and his officers had found no clues, nothing to indicate who the killer might have been, or why Giulia had been murdered.

'If it was a dagger that was used on her,' Pierre said, 'you can't get away from the fact that all these SS men carry them, and the soldiers have bayonets. If a German killed her, it could lead to a rather tricky situation. So far, the Occupying Forces are treating it as a civilian incident and do not wish to be involved, but frankly, I'd hate to have to be the one to tell them we think it might be one of their lot who did it.'

'Can you think of any reason why anyone should wish to kill her?' Annette asked.

'Plenty of reasons. The Comtesse wasn't much liked by most people in the town.

There were plenty who thought, since she was Italian, she should have been interned at the beginning of the war, or at least sent back to Italy. She never made any secret of the fact that she had very little use for the local people, so she was bound to be mistrusted. There's another theory going round — it's common knowledge that the Comte is a patriot. We know he's up in the mountains with his guerrilla army, waiting for the opportunity to kick the Boche out of France. There's a price on his head, so I've heard. No one here would betray him, but the Germans might be hoping to lure him into showing himself in town by murdering his wife. But Jacques is like the legendary Scarlet Pimpernel, he slips in and out of town without anyone seeing him. Or so I have been told,' Pierre added quickly.

When Paul came for his lesson, Ruth asked him if he knew anything about Giulia's murder.

'As I understand it, it appears to be a civilian matter, nothing for the German authorities to involve themselves with,' he said. 'I was sorry to hear about it. She was a young woman, and seemed to be doing no harm to anyone, as far as anyone knows.'

Ruth considered telling him about seeing Giulia with the SS Officer, but decided against it. Paul might feel it his duty to report the matter but if the Germans could be kept out of the whole affair, so much the better. Even if one of them had murdered her, there was little that the French police could do about it and Ruth had a strong feeling that whoever had killed Giulia had done it for reasons connected with her wartime activities.

'Perhaps we'll never know who did it or why,' she said. 'It's difficult for the local Gendarmerie to mount any proper investigation when there are so many restrictions laid on their activities.'

'You knew her, I believe?' Paul asked. 'I suppose that is understandable, since you were the only two non French citizens in the town.'

'I met her not long ago, back in the autumn. I was curious about the chateau and she invited me to tea there. She spoke near perfect English as she had been a student near where my home in Hertfordshire is, so it was pleasant to chat with her about that part of the country, but apart from that, she was not exactly my kind of person.'

Paul nodded. 'From what I've heard, it seems the local people felt it was not wise to become too friendly with her. She was, after all, Italian and no one could be sure on which side her sympathies lay. That makes me worry about you, too, Ruth. The local people might react badly towards you if they knew you and I were meeting. Not only the German authorities must be kept in ignorance, but the citizens here, too, or you could be in danger.'

There were only a very few people who knew about her friendship with Paul, Ruth thought; Annette, Françoise and Michel of course, and Alain and Jacques. Officially, no one else knew, but it would be surprising if some gossip about them both had not been circulating in the town by now. Uneasily, Ruth remembered Madame Duvalle, who glowered at her whenever she saw her, though had rarely spoken to her since the incident with the rotten vegetables, nearly a year ago. Ruth saw her sometimes at Claude's bakery, almost the only shop still open, but Madame Duvalle largely ignored her these days.

She was in Claude's shop the following day for bread, when the baker murmured to her 'my wife has returned from holiday earlier than expected. I believe you wished to visit her for a little chat, some time soon?'

'Now?' Ruth asked.

'Non.' He glanced up as the shop door tinkled and two customers came in. 'Later. Come round the back at one o'clock, when the shop is closed.'

That afternoon, he let her in to the bakehouse, warm and dusty, with the smell of newly baked bread about it. 'You know the way,' he said. 'Upstairs.'

Ruth knocked at the door at the top of the steep, wooden stairs. A muffled voice bade her enter and she found Alain and another man, a stranger, sitting within.

'I believe you wanted to see me officially, Ruth,' Alain said. 'This, by the way, is Georges, who comes from outside the region. He comes to tell us that the Resistance groups of the whole of France are to be unified, so we shall all work together for the liberation of France. The Resistance will henceforth be known as Forces Françaises de l'Intérieur, or FFI. Our group will no longer be alone; we shall have the power of all France behind us. Soon, the Allies will need our help even more and we must be ready. Exciting things will soon be happening.'

Ruth had heard this line of talking for so long now she had begun to doubt whether the British would ever invade France and drive the Germans out. As she saw it, the British and Americans were already too busy fighting in Italy. Less than a week ago the BBC World Service had reported the Anzio Beach landings, thirty miles south of Rome. Could they possibly have the manpower and resources to launch yet another front across the Channel in the near future? If what Paul had told her, actually happened, they might not need to.

'I'm encouraged to hear about the unification of all the groups,' she said. 'It should make things easier — and more efficient.' She saw Alain scowl and added quickly, 'I have some information to pass on to you. I have it on very reliable authority that there is a plot in Germany to assassinate Hitler.'

To her chagrin, neither Alain nor Georges showed the slightest interest.

'But of course! There are always plots to assassinate Hitler!' Alain waved a hand dismissively. 'That is nothing new to us, Ruth.'

'But this is a serious plot! It involves some very senior members of the military and in the government,' she persisted. 'I think we should be prepared. If he's killed, Germany will collapse — '

'Germany will not collapse,' Georges broke in coldly. 'There are enough Nazis to keep Germany still fighting, whatever happens to their Führer. In fact, my informants tell me that if certain groups deposed Hitler, they would form a far more formidable enemy.'

Ruth stared in disbelief. They were not

even interested in Paul's information.

'It stands to reason,' Georges said, speaking as if explaining something to a child. 'Hitler is a madman. That is a well-known fact. It therefore follows that his battle plans are likely to be irrational, mistaken and unrealistic. But, if others who are not mad, take his place, we shall be up against far more deadly enemies. Hope that Hitler stays alive and in power, Mademoiselle, for, believe me, it will be better that way for all of us.'

Ruth, effectively snubbed by Georges, rose and was about to excuse herself and leave, when a thought struck her.

'I wanted to ask. Do either of you know who murdered the Comtesse? It was a horrible death. She was a beautiful woman and I'm sure she didn't deserve an end as bad as that.'

Georges laughed harshly. 'Too beautiful to be true! No doubt about it, her husband killed her because she had a lover.'

'You mean Jacques killed her? I can't believe that!' Ruth exclaimed.

'Not Jacques himself. No, that I do not think. But he knew that she was betraying him with one of the SS officers, betraying in more than one sense, you understand. It is probable that one of Jacques' men did the deed. Maybe it was his new recruit, the

Englishman who was sent here recently. That would be a sensible choice; someone who has no official existence in this country, who is completely unknown to the authorities and who does not know the Comtesse. Be assured, Mademoiselle Ruth, no one will ever discover who murdered the woman.'

Ruth had a great deal to think about while she walked back to the cottage. Alain had taken Bob to the chateau ostensibly to meet Jacques, but suppose Bob's orders had been to murder Giulia before escaping to the guerrilla hideout in the mountains? Her warning to him must have sounded naïve if that was the case. She shivered. Bob had seemed a pleasant, affable, *normal*, man. Was he really a cold-blooded killer as well? She found it hard to believe, but war forced everyone to do things they would not normally be capable of doing.

There was something else, too, niggling at the back of her mind. Claude had made a point of suggesting she visited Giulia the day her body had been discovered. Now she thought of it, Ruth wondered how Claude knew she had even met the Comtesse, let alone struck up enough of a friendship to pay her a social visit. Could it have been that Claude knew Giulia was dead, and knowing that there were few visitors to the chateau, was making sure that her body was discovered soon, by Ruth if the cleaning woman didn't arrive? That would seem to implicate the Resistance, but, whatever the truth of it, Ruth preferred to believe that the Comtesse had been killed by the SS officer or one of his men. Of one thing she was certain, whoever had done it, and for whatever reason, it was unlikely that anyone would ever be brought to justice.

The following day was the day of Giulia's funeral. Ruth and Annette went, Ruth pushing Annette's chair across the uneven ground of the cemetery. There were few people at the graveside, Père Joseph conducting the ceremony, the official pall bearers and, at a little distance from the grave, the usual clutch of old women, come to stare. Among them she noticed Madame Duvalle, her sharp little black eyes watching everyone and everything. In her rusty old black coat and dress she looked more witch-like than ever.

'Ghouls!' Annette muttered. 'Why do they come? They didn't know her, they didn't even *want* to know her. I think you were probably her only friend, and that only recently. Poor soul; she had no family here. Even her husband hasn't come to her funeral.'

'He couldn't. It would be too dangerous

240

for him,' Ruth replied. 'There's a reward out for information leading to his arrest, though I doubt anyone here would try to claim it. Look, over there by the cemetery wall, there are a couple of German soldiers keeping a watch on everyone. Jacques is a wanted man.'

At the end of the service, as the pall bearers cleared away their ropes and prepared to depart, Père Joseph came over to speak to them.

'A sad business,' he said. 'She was young and had the expectation of a good life in front of her, once the war ended. And the police tell me they have no clues as to the perpetrator. I doubt he will ever be known, though there are theories in abundance, flying about.' He glanced over his shoulder at the group of women standing by the path. 'She had a poor send-off, for someone so distinguished in the town. She should have had the whole citizenry here to pay their respects, but she would be grateful to the few who cared enough to come today; yourselves, and her cleaning woman, Madame Moreau.'

'Is she here? The poor woman who found her?' Annette asked.

Père Joseph nodded across towards the little group of women. 'Yes, there she is, on the left, talking to a friend.'

'*That* is Giulia's cleaning woman?' Ruth

asked, surprised. The woman Pere Joseph had indicated, was standing beside Madame Duvalle, talking to her as though they were old friends. As Ruth spoke, they both looked across at her and Annette and it looked as if Madame Duvalle had been pointing them out to Madame Moreau. They both stared, then Madame Duvalle pulled at her companion's sleeve and bent her head to whisper something. With a final, baleful look, they both turned away and began to walk off towards the cemetery gates. Ruth had a definite impression that the women had been talking about her, and found it a very unpleasant feeling.

After Giulia's funeral, life reverted to the usual, rather humdrum existence that Ruth had learnt to accept as normal life, but now there seemed to be a difference, an undercurrent of suppressed excitement in the air which was shared by almost everyone in the town. The Allies' invasion *must* come soon; this *must* be the year when the French would be able to fight back and regain their country. It was only a matter of choosing the right moment. In February, a huge consignment of weapons and other supplies were successfully parachuted into Haute Savoie for the use of the Resistance. Though Haute Savoie was hundreds of miles from Ste Marie de la Croix and the local Resistance could hardly expect to benefit, when news of the drop reached Alain and his group, they were immensely heartened by it.

'It means the Allies mean business, and soon,' Alain told Michel and Ruth, on one of his visits. 'It also shows they will help us when the time comes, they will not let us down. We must be ready, too, to give them all the help they ask of us.'

Another indication that the Germans, too, believed that an invasion was imminent, came in May when Field Marshal Rommel, Supreme Commander of the Occupying Forces, ordered that France be cut off from all contact with neutral countries, which, in practice, meant mainly Switzerland. No reason was given, but it was generally suspected that the Germans feared that information about their own anti-invasion plans might be passed on to the Allies through this route.

'They're getting jumpy — but they can't stop us!' Michel chortled when he heard of the new restrictions. 'And they still haven't discovered your radio, Ruth, which is a miracle. The British and Polish troops capturing Monte Cassino is a great boost to our spirits. I only wish we didn't have to hide our delight from the soldiers, lest they realise how much we know.'

'They are all pretty worried themselves,' Ruth said. 'Paul, of course, won't discuss anything like that with me, and I can't say anything without revealing what I know, and shouldn't know. But I've heard the soldiers talking among themselves in the town, and they all seem very gloomy and worried about what will happen before long.'

One sunny morning, towards the middle of May, Annette called Ruth into the sitting room where she had been working with her sketchpad.

'I've done it! At last I've succeeded!' she greeted her friend, her face glowing with pleasure.

'What? What have you succeeded in doing?' For one glorious moment Ruth thought that Annette might stand up from her chair, even take a few faltering steps, but that was clearly too much to hope for. Annette reached into her pile of sketches and handed Ruth a single sheet of paper. 'I've worked out the picture of the eagle and the rose,' she said, 'without the eagle looking as if it's about to destroy the rose. I felt sure there had to be a way. The eagle and the rose simply *had* to co-exist together happily.'

Ruth took the picture. There was the eagle, in all its glory, but perched in the centre of a

244

bush of roses, the flowers surrounding him like an arbour.

'It's good,' she said. 'You've drawn a very good eagle. He really looks like an eagle, proud and majestic but he's also quite friendly looking, not fierce. And the roses — I can almost smell them.'

'It's meant to be symbolic,' Annette said. 'I felt that if I could find a way of doing it, then it would mean that it was possible — literally. That you and Paul — '

'If Paul survives the war, we'll find some way to be together in the peace,' Ruth said. 'He's depressed. I think he realises that the end must come soon, and it will not be good for Germany. All he wants — all we both want — is an end to the fighting and a return to normality.'

'It must happen soon.' Annette said. 'And then Simon will come back. I tell myself he will come back, but what if he cannot? Or that things have changed, and after so long, he no longer wants to?'

'He will.' Ruth picked up the sketch again. 'I've a picture frame upstairs that will fit this. Let's hang it over the fireplace. I wonder what Paul will think of it when he next comes?'

The following day Michel came in from his work on the farm with a message for Ruth. 'You are wanted,' he said. 'Claude's shop. Go there tomorrow, early, and ask after his wife and family.'

'I wish he wouldn't use that stupid code,' Ruth muttered. 'Someone who knows he has no family will hear him one day.'

Michel shrugged. 'Everyone knows Claude has no family, but only those who are in the secret, are invited to meet them.'

Ruth duly presented herself at the bakery the following day. Claude made great play of selling her some of his special bread, keeping her waiting until the shop was empty of other customers. 'Quick, upstairs,' he said, as soon as the last shopper had left. 'Alain was most insistent. Georges is here again and wants to see you urgently.'

Perhaps at last they were going to take Paul's information seriously, she thought, ascending the steep stairs and knocking on the door at the top. Alain was there with Georges, who looked her up and down as if he had never seen her before, then said to Alain, 'Is this the girl you were telling me about? The one who has contacts with the German military?'

Alain nodded. 'Yes, this is Ruth. You have met her before, I think.'

Alain was being very deferential, Ruth noted. Georges must be an important man, perhaps even more important than Jacques.

'Ruth has a good working knowledge of German and she has a useful friend among the German officers. She would be the ideal person for the work you have in mind. We do have one other agent in place but I am convinced that Ruth would be far more suitable.'

'Sit down, Mademoiselle Ruth. We have some work for you to do.' Georges waved her to an empty chair. 'We need to know the exact position of each of the gun emplacements along this stretch of coast. Can you find this out for us?'

'What!' Ruth gaped at him. 'Surely you realise the whole coastline is out of bounds to civilians, and heavily guarded? The guns would be camouflaged, too. There's absolutely no way I, or anyone else, could find out such information.'

Georges laughed. 'I was not suggesting you took an afternoon stroll along the beach, looking for them,' he said. 'We know there is a map marking the location of all the gun sites. It hangs on the wall of one of the offices in the German Headquarters. As I understand it, it would be quite easy for you to obtain a photograph of this map for us. You have been in the German Headquarters before, have you not? You know your way around?'

'No, I don't. I was there only once before,

or twice if you count the time I was arrested and kept in the cells,' Ruth replied. 'I don't see how I could possibly find this map and photograph it for you. I'd never be let further than the entrance lobby. Very few civilians ever are.'

'But you have a German friend, who works there?' Georges asked.

'I couldn't possibly involve Paul! Besides, he would never talk to me about anything like that. And if he thought I was trying to get information for the Resistance, he wouldn't hesitate to have me arrested and shot. He'd have to, for his own sake.' Ruth was shocked at the suggestion.

'I did not mean that you should ask him,' Georges said coldly. 'I am not that stupid or naïve. But, since you know this man, I do not think it could present much difficulty to find a reason to visit him at the German Headquarters. We have contacts in the building; one of the civilian cleaners has informed us that a copy of this map hangs on the wall in one of the offices. We will supply you with a miniature camera; the rest is up to you.'

'Why can't this contact of yours in the building photograph it? If they've seen it, it must be easy enough.'

'No, it is not possible. The civilian cleaners

are accompanied by German guards at all times and each room is locked whenever it is not occupied by a German officer. You are our best hope.'

'I don't see how I could do it,' Ruth said. It was one thing to visit Paul; she'd already done that and caused trouble. How could she possibly get into the office of someone she didn't even know?

'Please, Ruth. Say you will think of some way.' Alain leant forward to touch her arm. 'We need this information. The Allies need it. Britain has asked for it and they are expecting us to provide them with it as soon as we can. It really is vital that we have a photograph of that map.' He looked at her reproachfully. 'I have not asked you to do anything very risky, ever since you collected that package from the beach for us. That was a long time ago now. It is time that you did something for us that you alone can do. You know you can find an excuse to see your friend in his office.'

'What is the name of this friend of yours?' Georges asked.

'Captain Paul Reinhardt,' Ruth said unwillingly.

'Reinhardt!' Georges looked astonished, then grinned at Alain. 'Now I know why you say that this girl is more suitable than your other agents. Our informant states that this map hangs on the wall of Reinhardt's office. It will be simple enough for her to see him there, and find some excuse to persuade him out of it for a matter of seconds. That will be all it needs to take photographs.' He turned to Ruth. 'What could be simpler? I cannot understand why you are making so many difficulties, Mademoiselle. It is the work of a moment, no more.'

He made it sound so easy. Ruth felt trapped. 'Let me think about it,' she said.

'Don't take too long. Britain needs that information. I give you until tomorrow evening to make your plans. You will be supplied with a miniature camera and shown how to use it properly. It will be small enough to hide on your person.' His eyes flicked over her. 'Pushed inside your brassiere, perhaps?'

Ruth glared at him. 'If I can think of some way to get into the corridor where the offices are, I'll let you know,' she said. 'But I can't make any promises about photographing the map. I don't see how I could possibly manage to be alone there, even for a second. Their security is very strict.'

'You'll find a way.' Georges looked at her with cold, calculating eyes. 'I expect you to deliver the camera with the film of the map, to me, here, in three days. Go now; you have been here long enough.'

'I will bring you the camera tomorrow,' Alain said. 'Then it is up to you. Don't fail us, Ruth.'

Paul was due to visit that afternoon. For the first time in a long time, Ruth felt uncomfortable in his presence, her mind full of what she would have to do.

'Is everything all right, Ruth? You seem preoccupied,' he asked, when she had answered vaguely to a question about grammar. Although his English was excellent these days, she suspected he had deliberately made a couple of mistakes which she had missed.

'Yes, I'm all right.' She thrust the thought of Alain and his camera from her mind. 'Look, I want to show you a picture Annette has made. She wanted to know what you thought of it.' She led him to the mantelpiece and took down Annette's sketch, now finished and framed.

'Your friend is certainly a talented artist,' Paul said. 'But it seems a strange subject. What is it meant to be?'

'It's how she sees us. Or, rather, how she hopes that we will be seen in the future,' Ruth explained. 'It's a German eagle and an English rose, our countries' symbols. She wanted a way of showing them in harmony but it took her a long time to think of a way

251

that didn't involve the eagle oppressing the rose. Now, I think, she has made them both able to exist peaceably together.'

Paul nodded. 'Yes, I see it. I only hope that it is so in reality. To me it looks as if the eagle will shortly be torn to shreds by the thorns on the rose. But not in Annette's picture. That pleases me very much, and you know why? Because I think it says that Annette approves of me at last. She may be sorry that I am a German, but she does not disapprove that you and I are friends.'

Ruth had resolutely put out of her mind all thoughts about Georges and Alain, trying to concentrate on Paul and his grammar, when an idea suddenly occurred to her, of a way of giving herself a chance to get as far as Paul's office. After their break, when he carried the tray with their coffee cups back into the kitchen, she took the opportunity to look through the pockets of his greatcoat, lying across the back of a chair. She hated doing it but it looked as if this might provide her only chance. In one of the pockets, her fingers closed over a wallet and she pulled it out, thrusting it for now under the chair. If Paul noticed its absence while he was still here, she could 'find' it quite innocently, but if he left without it, it would furnish a perfect excuse to take it to him, insisting that she must hand it over in person. She wondered if the same young German soldier whom she had hoodwinked into thinking she was an informer, was still working on the reception desk. If she was lucky enough to come upon him again that might make things easier, if he remembered her.

She rearranged the coat a little so that it was likely to slide off the back of the chair with the slight encouragement of someone sitting down, or brushing past. It would seem more natural that a wallet should slip out of the pocket of a fallen coat.

For the rest of the afternoon she concentrated on listening to everything Paul said, picking out the least of his grammatical mistakes and correcting his pronunciation frequently.

'You are a hard task master, Libertine,' he said, when it was time to leave. 'I have told you I did not come merely to have English lessons, but to enjoy your company. Can we not dispense with this schoolmistress approach?'

'I have to earn my coffee,' Ruth protested. 'But you are right, I have been too fussy. If your English is too perfect it sounds just as foreign. Most English people do not speak very grammatically, anyway.'

'You make me think you are training me to

parachute into England as a spy,' Paul said.

'What?' Irrelevantly, it crossed her mind to wonder if Phillipe's wife had indeed made herself some luxurious silk underwear out of Bob's parachute panels. If she had, she had better not display them on a washing line, for a passing patrol to see and identify.

'Silly, I was teasing you. Going to England as a spy would be the last thing I would want to do. Soon, very soon now, there will be no necessity for anything of that nature. I know that you must be aware of what is really happening with the war. I don't want to know how you know, but tell those who listen to news items put out by the British that soon there will be important news — stupendous news from Germany.'

'You mean-?'

'I will not say it, but you know to what I refer. Come, let me kiss you and then I must go. I have stayed later than I should and I must hurry back.' He put his arms round Ruth.

'You are on duty tonight?' she asked, responding to his passionate kiss.

'Yes, and tomorrow!' He picked up his coat, pulled it on and walked out towards the front door. He hadn't noticed that anything was missing from his pocket.

When Paul had left, Ruth retrieved his

wallet from under the chair. She suppressed the urge to run after him and hand it back to him. This was her passport to his office, if she was lucky. Idly, she flipped it open. There was a small amount of French money in it and some Deutschmarks. There was also a pasteboard card, printed and with a photo of Paul inside it. Ruth realised that this must be his official pass. There were forgers in the town, known to Alain, who would give a fortune for a few hours' study of something like this.

No, she couldn't do that to Paul. It was bad enough that she had taken his wallet without his knowledge. Unless she returned it quickly, the loss of his pass would mean he would be in grave trouble with the German Command. She thrust it into her pocket, then, feeling over conscious of it pressed against her thigh, took it upstairs and hid it under her pillow. If Alain brought the camera to her tonight, as he had promised, she would go to the German Headquarters early tomorrow. What happened then, she still hadn't planned. She would have to wait and see what developed.

At nine o'clock the next morning, she tucked the miniature camera into the top of her blouse, put the wallet into the pocket of her jacket and set off for the Town Hall.

In the main square there were the usual groups of old women in black coats and shawls, some going about the business of finding something edible to buy at the market stalls, but others who seemed to have nothing better to do than stand around, watching. As she passed, Ruth felt the eyes of a small group of them boring into her back, their expressions hostile. She tried to ignore them but she couldn't help but feel angry that they still mistrusted her. If only they knew!

She decided to stare back, her chin lifted high. Most of the women she did not know, except by sight, but amongst this group she espied Madame Duvalle, staring at her with a curious, searching expression. Ruth gave her a defiant glare. Really, the woman seemed to be haunting her! She strode on, up the Town Hall steps, aware that eyes were still fastened on her. What she didn't see, though, was Madame Duvalle detach herself from the group and slip unobtrusively round the side of the Town Hall, towards the back of the building.

The guard on the door let her in when she explained that she had a message for one of the officers. He probably thought she was a collaborator, come to inform on a neighbour; it was a common enough practice these days. It was not his business to require details, that was for the clerk at the desk in the entrance hall, and he had orders not to let civilians any further into the building, except in exceptional circumstances and always with a guard as escort.

Ruth saw at once that the man on duty today was not one she had spoken to on a previous visit. That might, after all, not be a bad thing. The other soldier might have been warned not to let her through again.

She approached the desk with a confident step, though she was feeling far from confident inside.

'I wish to see Captain Reinhardt,' she said, in slow French for the soldier's benefit.

'What is your business with Captain Reinhardt?' The soldier eyed her up and down, his expression showing plainly that he thought she was one of the local women prepared to 'accommodate' the occupying soldiers in return for favours such as special food rations, travel passes or permits.

'My business is with Kapitän Reinhardt. It is confidential,' she said, with as much haughtiness as she could summon.

'Captain Reinhardt does not interview civilians,' the soldier stated in a bored tone, turning away and busying himself with some papers at the other end of the desk.

Ruth mentally kicked herself for not

speaking first in German. She might have fooled this man into thinking she was a compatriot and make him more likely to help her. The French, she knew, never spoke in German even if they knew some. Now, it was too late; she had established herself as one of the local townspeople.

'I need to see Captain Reinhardt. I have something important to give him.' She tried to sound as if she were someone not used to her requests being refused.

The soldier leered. Clearly, he had his own ideas of what this woman wanted to give the Captain.

'You may leave it with me. I'll see he gets it.'

Ruth shook her head. 'No, I cannot do that. I have important papers — for his eyes only. Please take me to his office.'

'I told you. Captain Reinhardt does not deal with civilians. It is Lieutenant Kruger you need to speak to, if you have information for the German Command. You must make an appointment.'

'I don't want to see Lieutenant Kruger!' Ruth stopped herself, just in time, from adding 'telephone Captain Reinhardt.' If Paul came down to her she would have to give him his wallet here and lose any chance of getting into his office.

She walked away from the desk and sat down on the bench against the far wall. She had sat here on her previous visit when she had been hoping to see Paul and ask his help for Michel.

The minutes ticked away. Several people came up to the desk, to be given forms, or to hand in forms for permits. It was never busy enough for her to risk trying to slip up the stairs while the soldier was dealing with them.

An elderly cleaning woman came from a passageway at the far end, opposite the stairs. She wore a large, print overall over her inevitable black dress, and carried a bucket and mop. She began mopping the floor, very slowly, using rather a lot of water. Ruth watched her, mainly from having nothing else to look at. The woman looked vaguely familiar, though her head was covered in a scarf and she kept her back to the rest of the hall. Most of the elderly women in the town looked like that, Ruth thought, dismissing any idea that she might know her.

An officer came from a door near where the woman was working. There seemed to be quite a lot of soapy water on the floor and as he walked quickly towards the central desk he skidded, managed to right himself and then, to her astonishment, Ruth saw the woman thrust her mop between his feet, tripping him completely and causing him to come crashing to the floor. At once, the woman stepped away, continuing to mop the floor as if nothing had happened and Ruth realised she must have been the only one to see that the man had been deliberately tripped.

The officer shouted out as he fell. He was a burly man and fell heavily, remaining on the floor, winded. At once, the clerk at the desk ran to help him. She heard the officer swearing profusely as the soldier bent to help him to his feet. The few other people in the hall were watching; mainly French who tried to look concerned while privately enjoying the spectacle of a German officer in an undignified sprawl.

It came to her then that this was her chance. Everyone was looking away from her, their backs towards the stairs at this end, the desk clerk had his attention solely on the officer. In a second she was up and running for the stairs. Silently, she sped up them. At the top she paused to glance back; no one had seen her, no one had shouted to her to come back.

She remembered her way to Paul's office. Her knees quaking, she hurried on tiptoe along the bare corridor until she reached his room. If she needed confirmation, there was his name on a card fastened to the door.

Outside, she stopped. How on earth was she going to manage to take a photograph of the map without Paul seeing? She'd need to get him out of the room for a moment, and a fainting attack with a request for some water was the best idea that she had so far been able to come up with, though it seemed a feeble ploy.

Ruth raised her hand to knock on the door when there came a tremendous noise from downstairs; men shouting, a woman screaming and several loud crashes as if a metal bucket was being smashed against something hard. The door of Paul's office burst open and Paul and another officer rushed out, into the passage. She had just time to flatten herself against the far wall as they passed her without noticing. 'Mein Gott, what on earth is happening down there?' the officer gasped. They both ran towards the staircase. Ruth thought it might only be a few seconds before one of them realised that he had seen someone, a civilian, in a restricted area. Before the door had time to crash shut again she was through it, fumbling for her camera. A large scale map was hanging on the wall behind the desk, with groups of coloured headed pins stuck on it along the edge of the coastline. She took as many photos of the map from as many angles as she could, clicking frantically until she had used up all the film, hoping that some at least would provide the essential information Georges wanted. From her pocket she took Paul's wallet, tossing it on to his desk. She had a second thought, and pulled a manila file over it. Perhaps he would think he had left it here. Better he never knew she had been anywhere near the building.

The whole operation had taken less than twenty seconds, then she was out of the door and running for the stairs at the far end of the corridor, but these turned out not to be the stairs that led down to the discreet exit in the side road. Instead, she found herself back in the hall, just beyond an alcove on the opposite side to the main staircase. She was close to the cause of all the commotion. It seemed the German officer had blamed the cleaner for the slippery floor which had tripped him up, though he hadn't realised she had stuck out her mop to ensure he fell flat on his bottom. He was now shouting for her arrest, threatening her with deportation, or worse, and the desk clerk and another soldier had hold of the woman by her arms. She was struggling and screaming at the top of her voice, swinging her now empty bucket. Those citizens who had come in for permits were gathered round, enjoying the entertainment.

Some were even bold enough to shout encouragement to her. There was bedlam in the hall.

Ruth sidled round towards the audience, hoping no one would notice where she had come from. She was now facing the woman, and as their eyes met Ruth could not hide her look of astonishment. The cleaning woman was Madame Duvalle!

As soon as she saw Ruth, Madame Duvalle relaxed imperceptibly. The soldiers were at last able to drag her towards the passage leading to the cells, but before she finally went, she looked back and gave Ruth one of her usual glares — followed by a wink, brief but quite distinct.

The whole scenario became blindingly clear. Madame Duvalle had staged this distraction purely for Ruth to have a chance to reach Paul's office, but how could she possibly have known that had been Ruth's intention? Unless she, too, was in on the plan. Alain had said there were cleaners here who were members of the group, but Ruth had never dreamed that Madame Duvalle, with her antagonism towards the English, could possibly be one of them.

Ruth stared straight back at her, then gave an infinitesimal nod. No one else would have noticed, even had they been watching, but at

263

that moment both women understood each other completely. Seconds later, Madame Duvalle was dragged away out of sight down one of the passages.

Ruth drifted out of the Town Hall beside a couple of Frenchmen who had come for travel permits. Forcing herself not to hurry, she strolled across the Town Square and took a side road which would eventually lead her home.

Reaching the cottage, she hid the camera in her bedroom and lay on her bed, shaking, for some time. She had succeeded, but only because of the help she had received from Madame Duvalle, and, because of that, the Frenchwoman was now locked in the cells and in serious trouble. Assaulting a German officer was one of the most serious offences that could be committed.

When she eventually went to join Annette she said nothing about the incident, nor did she mention Madame Duvalle. Annette knew nothing about the task Georges had demanded of her and Ruth had no intention of worrying her friend by telling her. This episode had taught her a sobering lesson, learning that the woman she had thought of as an informer, was prepared to take a serious risk to help her. Coming after the death of Giulia, the woman she thought she could trust but who was probably a double agent, Ruth realised the truth that Annette had uttered long ago. 'These days, you don't know who anyone is, any more; you don't know who you can trust.' In this war, Ruth realised, no one turned out to be who they seemed.

11

Alain came that evening to collect the camera. 'I knew you wouldn't let us down, Ruth,' he said. 'Georges will be pleased with you.'

'It wasn't me; I'd never have managed it if it hadn't been for Madame Duvalle.'

'Madame Duvalle?' Annette was wheeling her chair into the kitchen and heard the name. 'What has she been up to? Has she at last been exposed as an informer?'

'No. She's one of us. I never realised it until today. I feel so ashamed of what I thought of her,' Ruth said. 'Now she's in the cells, charged with assaulting a German officer and she did it so that I could do my job. All the time I thought she suspected me of having German sympathies, she always looked at me as if she hated me.'

'It was her role to watch out for you, see that you came to no serious harm,' Alain said. 'She pretended to the other women that she didn't trust you, so that no one would suspect you were one of us. I think she may have over-played her hand sometimes but she was a good agent. I hope we may be able to save her, even now. We are losing good people all the time. Had you heard that Claude has been arrested today?'

'Claude? No, surely not! What harm did he ever do?' Annette said innocently. 'And he's the only baker left in the town. They can't arrest him!'

'It's very serious,' Alain said gravely. 'I fear we will not see him again.'

'What happened?' Ruth asked.

'I suppose one might say he has been lucky to last so long. Claude has been helping us from the beginning,' Alain said. 'It may be that he became too casual about his activities. He talked too much about his family upstairs, above the bakery.'

'Does that mean that you and Georges and the others who meet there are at risk?' Ruth asked.

'No. We can always find somewhere else to meet. Claude's little fiction that he had a wife and family living above the bakery was a little joke. We all knew that, but what he forgot was that the Germans have no sense of humour. They decided to raid the bakery and discovered what even we did not know; Claude did indeed have a family living above his shop, up in the attics. But they were not his family, they were a group of Jewish refugees he had been hiding there for the past month. He will be lucky if he is deported to Germany but I fear very much he will face the firing squad. These days, the Germans are becoming very worried and it has made them vindictive.'

'Can't he be rescued?' Ruth asked desperately. She had grown fond of Claude over the years and the thought of what was to happen to him was unbearable.

'Don't think we haven't discussed this,' Alain said earnestly. 'There isn't one of us wouldn't be willing to offer our own lives for Claude, but it simply isn't possible. The cells at the Town Hall are impenetrable, short of blowing the whole building sky high. And we have orders from London — all of us must be ready when we are needed. We cannot risk losing any more men at this time and I fear that would happen if we tried to mount any kind of rescue for Claude. If he were to be deported, we might try derailing the train again, but there is little we can do to sabotage a firing squad.'

Paul was due to visit the following day, but there was a letter for Ruth in the post, the first she had ever had from him, explaining that he wouldn't be able to come for the next few days, due to extra work at German Headquarters. He promised, though, that he would come in a week or so. 'Somehow I will manage it,' he wrote. 'I shall miss seeing you but it will not be long before I am free to come again.' He did not mention the temporary loss of his wallet and Ruth assumed that he had not even missed it. Perhaps he was too well-known to the guards to need to produce his pass to enter the building.

Ruth felt depressed by the news about Claude. She had worried about Madame Duvalle, feeling in some way responsible, and Claude's arrest was a severe blow. She missed Paul; he was comforting to talk to, even though she would never have mentioned either of her Resistance colleagues to him. There was an atmosphere of tension about the town, too, a feeling of waiting for something to happen, which she found hard to handle. One afternoon, a few days later, she could stand it no longer, and decided to go for a long walk in the woods by herself. She wanted to be quite alone, away from everyone. Even Annette's company could be trying at times.

Most of the woods were out of bounds these days but there was a strip bordering the road which had not been cordoned off with barbed wire. It was quiet and cool and no one was about, though she knew the locals went there often to snare rabbits, or bring down birds with a home-made catapult. Food was in even shorter supply with winter stores depleted and before the summer crops were ready, and blackbird or thrush pie featured on many dinner tables in the town.

She found herself a grassy knoll and sat down, leaning against a tree trunk. She closed her eyes, day-dreaming about Simon and their lives in England before the war. But what would happen after the war was over? Ruth hadn't dared think too much about the future before, but now, when she felt it couldn't go on much longer, she began to wonder — would she and Paul really be able to spend their lives together, once the world had come back to some kind of normality? After the war — the words were beginning to have a meaning, a reality. At last, she was coming to believe that there would be a time after the war, and that she and her loved ones might even live to see it. She remembered this spot from the days when the three of them, Simon, Annette and herself, had come this way to the beach on summer holidays. Annette had led the way, running along the path, the swiftest of them all.

Sitting alone among the trees which didn't change, war or not, Ruth found a peacefulness stealing over her. The early summer afternoon was warm and the only sounds here were the call of a bird in the distance and, nearer at hand, the somnolent drone of a bee. She was away from Françoise's complaining, Annette's needs which took so much of her energy; away from Alain and the others who made demands on her loyalty. If only, she thought, time would stand still and she could stay here and let the world carry on without her.

She must have dozed but the drop in temperature finally roused her. Heavens, how long have I been here! Ruth thought anxiously, scrambling to her feet. I've been here far longer than I intended. It must be getting near to curfew time.

The overhanging trees made the wood dark but when she came out on to a piece of open ground that led to a back lane, she realised with shock that it was dark here, too. She must have slept for hours and now it was dusk.

Reaching the lane, which was no more than a track for farm carts, she began to hurry. Rounding a bend, she saw four or five young girls sitting in a row on a gate, chattering and laughing. They looked up as she approached and Ruth recognised at least two of them as girls from the school where she had once tried to teach them English, the two most difficult and troublesome pupils in the class.

'Look, there's the English woman,' said one, seeing Ruth.

Ruth, about to smile and bid them 'good evening', froze as another girl said loudly, 'It's the English traitor! The one that makes love to German officers.'

Ruth gasped. 'I do not — ' she began, angrily.

'You're a collaborator, aren't you, *Mademoiselle?*' sneered a third. 'You tell the Germans everyone's secrets, which is why we have no baker any more. He and Madame Duvalle are going to be shot, and it's all because of you.'

'Madame Duvalle is to be shot?' Ruth knew that the woman would be in serious trouble for causing one of the officers to slip on the wet floor, but shot!

'You were there, informing on her at the old Town Hall,' said the first girl, pointing an accusing finger at Ruth. 'And later, they searched Claude Rousseau's shop. They wouldn't have known to do that if you hadn't told them who was in his upstairs room.'

'Truly, I didn't even know myself who was in his attic,' Ruth protested. 'I was horrified when I heard about it. I'm not a collaborator, certainly not a traitor. I have done nothing — '

'You went to the German Headquarters in

the Town Hall and immediately afterwards there were arrests made. *Of course you informed!*' The first girl, apparently the ringleader, slipped down from the gate and came towards Ruth. 'Collaborator!' she shouted, pointing a finger. She walked right up to Ruth and poked her finger painfully into Ruth's chest. The other girls began to circle round her, blocking off her escape.

'You know what happens to collaborators!' The first girl taunted. 'You should be made an example.'

'Yes, let's teach her a lesson!' Two of the other girls exclaimed eagerly. They grabbed Ruth's arms from behind and began pushing her forward towards the gate. The first girl made a scissor-like cutting gesture with two fingers of her hand. 'That's what they do to collaborators, English Miss! They shave their heads, so all the world can see what they've been up to!'

'Come on, let's do it now!' One of the girls said excitedly. 'Take her to the barn on the other side of this field. There are bound to be shears there. Perhaps her handsome German captain won't think her so attractive after we've finished with her.'

Beginning to panic, Ruth struggled to free herself but five pairs of hands gripped her tightly, giving her no chance. Seeing the expressions on every face, she knew there was no possibility she could persuade these girls to let her go. Even if she could have told them the truth, gave away all the secrets of her work for the Resistance, she doubted if they would have believed her. They didn't want to believe her. Dislike had festered since schoolroom days and now they were going to settle old scores and nothing was going to stop them.

They dragged her across the field. In the distance she saw the roof of a barn where she knew cattle fodder and farm implements were stored. They would certainly find something in there to use to cut off her hair. She shuddered at the thought of shearing clippers or a sharp scythe slashing at her head. These girls were not going to be gentle; they were going to enjoy seeing her suffer.

Inside the barn, Ruth was pushed forward and stumbled on to the floor. The place was dark but there was just enough light to see a pile of rusty farm tools in one corner and a mound of hay filling half the far end.

'Tie her to this post,' the girl in charge ordered. Hands dragged her to one of the pillars in the centre of the barn, supporting the roof, and her hands were jerked behind it. Ruth felt her wrists being tied tightly with some twine, which bit into her flesh. She knew she would not be able to break free.

'Here's what we need!' One of the girls held up a large pair of shears. She held it closely against Ruth's face, twisting her blonde hair with her other hand. 'Say goodbye to all this, Mademoiselle,' she jeered. 'Soon you will be bald, like other women who have betrayed good Frenchmen to the Germans.'

Ruth closed her eyes. She had seen women who had suffered this treatment. Not in Ste Marie de la Croix, but in other, larger towns, their heads and much of their faces covered by shawls but there had been enough visible to show them as mostly young, and terrified. The treatment hadn't been the end of their suffering by any means, for, as Ruth had been told, anyone with a shaven head was scorned and vilified by all her neighbours. Shop-keepers never had anything but the poorest quality food on offer when they came to buy, and no one would help them in any way. It would take nine months to a year for the hair to grow back to any semblance of normality, but even then, the woman — it was only women who suffered this punishment — would be known and remembered. Only escape to another town, a long way away, would provide relief, and in wartime France it was not easy to travel.

The Germans mainly turned a blind eye to these punishments, treating them as a civil matter. Only very occasionally, if the informer had been of particular use, would they help her move away to safety. In most cases, these women had done no real harm but were the victims of vengeful neighbours looking for a scapegoat. It reminded her of the witch hunts of a previous century, Ruth thought.

The girl snipped an inch off one side of Ruth's hair, holding the shears close to her ear. It was a large implement, intended for sheep and awkward to use on a human head. Ruth waited, expecting her ear to be sliced off at the next attempt.

Someone grabbed a fistful of her hair at the back, twisting and tugging at it. They all seemed to want to take a turn with the shears and an argument broke out. Suddenly, the ringleader's voice broke through the squabbling.

'Shh! Be quiet! What's that sound?'

The girls froze. Had she not been so frightened herself, Ruth would have been amused by the strange poses they held; one with the shears open in front of her, another with her hands on it trying to wrest it from her, another with Ruth's hair held in a bunch straight above her head, ready for the shears to slice through it.

'It sounds like a patrol coming down the road,' one of them whispered.

'They've stopped.'

Clearly, Ruth heard the sound of a wheezy truck coming down the lane that ran past this side of the field, close by the barn. Not many French people used trucks these days. The sound stopped, after a spluttering of the engine, and then came the sound of boots on the gravel of the unmade lane.

'Soldiers! They're coming in here!' The ringleader's face paled. 'Quick, get out and back across the field! It must be past curfew!'

'Untie me first!' Ruth begged, as the girls scrambled for the door but they were too intent on avoiding the German patrol to think about their prisoner. One hurled the shears away into a pile of straw as the others pushed the barn door cautiously open and then began to sidle out, running back across the field the way they'd come. Ruth caught a glimpse of the sky outside as the door opened and saw it was almost completely dark. It must indeed be long past curfew now.

Her relief at escaping a scalping was short-lived. Frantic struggles with her hands confirmed that she was never going to be able to break free from the twine bonds that held her to the post. What would be worse, she wondered despairingly; to be found here by a

German patrol who would cut her loose but arrest her, or to be imprisoned here all night and possibly even all next day, if the barn was not much used?

She gave up trying to release her hands. The twine had been pulled tightly and any movement cut into her wrists painfully. She would have to wait until someone came to cut her free.

She considered calling out to the soldiers. At least, they would release her, surely, and wasn't that better than being here all night? Even as she made up her mind to shout for help, she heard the engine start up again and the truck trundled off, the sound fading in the distance.

There was no point in shouting now, it was very unlikely there would be anyone about in the field or lane after curfew. The girls would have run back up to the far track and be well on the way to their homes by now. They wouldn't risk coming back and it would be unlikely they would tell anyone how they had left her. Being tied to a post for a night they'd consider part of her punishment. Annette would worry about her non-return to the cottage and perhaps Michel would go out to look for her, but he wouldn't know where she might be. Ruth reconciled herself to the fact that she would have to spend the entire night standing tied to a post in a cold, dark barn. At least, she still had her hair, except for a small amount on one side where one of the girls had tried to frighten her.

The barn was completely dark now, except for a thin shaft of paler darkness filtering through the double doors where they did not meet together properly.

The silence was disturbed by a rustling sound, coming from within the mound of hay at the far side. Rats, Ruth thought, her heart pounding.

The rustle came again. Too loud for a rat, unless there was a whole nest of them. Could a fox have wandered in here? Foxes were timid creatures, harmless enough, but what else might live in the woods and creep for sanctuary into the barn? French woods were not like the familiar English ones; wild boar still roamed in some places, and there might be other, strange creatures who might attack out of fear.

Something slithered across the floor and there was a heavy, scrabbling sound. 'Oh, no! Don't come near me!' Ruth cried out aloud, and in English.

The scrabbling stopped. There was another sound, then, unmistakably, heavy breathing. A voice said in English, 'It's all right, don't be afraid. They've gone and I can cut you free.'

Ruth's first thought was that she must be hallucinating. An *English* voice, here in a barn in the heart of France? Then she felt a hand on her shoulder, sliding down her arm to feel for her wrists. A flashlight flickered behind her and seconds later the tension of the twine eased. She moved her hands and found she could clasp them in front of her. Thankfully, she rubbed her sore wrists, and turned to face her rescuer. He was no more than a darker shadow looming beside her, taller and broader by several inches.

'Who are you?' she asked.

'Don't worry about that now. Are you all right?' he was still speaking in English.

'Yes, I think so. Thank you for rescuing me. Were you hiding in the hay all the time?'

'Yes, I was waiting for nightfall. I didn't know what to do when they left you, but then you spoke in English and I figured it was safe to come out of hiding. I guess I couldn't have stayed there all night and I couldn't bring myself to leave you tied up. What was that all about, anyway?'

'I'm not too popular with the local girls. They don't like foreigners,' Ruth said dismissively. 'They were going to cut off my hair with farm shears until the German patrol frightened them off.'

'Shave your head! The traditional punishment for collaborators,' the man said thoughtfully.

'I'm no collaborator! Quite the reverse,' Ruth said hotly. 'But you haven't told me who you are. You're English, of course. What are you doing here?'

When he hesitated, Ruth said, 'You've recently arrived here, haven't you, either by parachute or boat? And my guess is that you are wanting to make contact with the local Resistance? If that's so, I may be able to help you.'

The man let out his breath in a sigh of relief. 'I felt instinctively I could trust you. Marvellous bit of luck, coming across you like this. My name's Harry, by the way; Harry Nicholls.'

'I'm Ruth. I think it would be best if we left here. I can take you to where I live — it's safe, they are all French patriots there who can be trusted. They'll be worried about what's happened to me. You realise we have a curfew from dusk to dawn? But it's fairly easy to move around during it, so long as you can dodge the patrols. Fortunately, the Germans tend to stick rigidly to the rules, so once a patrol has come past, it's unlikely to back track again. We'll be safe for half an hour at least. Come along, I'll take you home. It's not far away; not more than ten minutes.'

When Ruth pushed open the back door of the cottage and stepped into the kitchen, Françoise rounded on her angrily.

'Where have you been? We have all been out of our minds with worry! You went off by yourself without saying anything, even to Mam'selle Annette, and she has been frantic about you.'

'I'm all right, Françoise,' Ruth said soothingly. 'There was a little trouble, nothing serious, but it delayed me longer than I expected. I'll tell you all about it later. But, listen! I have brought someone back with me.'

She drew Harry into the room. Now in the light, she could see he was dressed in shirt and jacket with the blue trousers of the local farmworkers. He had a rucksack slung across one shoulder and a revolver thrust into his belt.

'Mon Dieu! Who is this person?' Françoise cried out, recoiling. Harry seemed to fill the kitchen with his presence. He was tall, broad-shouldered and burly, and, apart from his clothes, didn't look like a Frenchman.

Annette opened the door and wheeled herself into the kitchen. 'Hallo,' she said. 'Thank God you're safe, Ruth. Has this gentleman brought you home?'

'In a manner of speaking, but I'll explain it

all to you later. This is Harry and he needs to make contact with Alain. He's recently arrived - I'm not sure by what means, but it seems there was not the usual reception committee.'

'Sit down.' Françoise gestured to the table and then put a bowl of steaming soup in front of him. He looked up at her gratefully.

'I ought to explain. A group of us came ashore by dinghy at dusk. We were part of an advance party to prepare the local Resistance for when the Allies invade.'

'They are coming? At last, they are coming?' Françoise turned from her stove, the saucepan of soup held in her hand as if ready to offer food to any invaders coming into her kitchen there and then.

'Soon; it will be soon,' Harry said. 'As yet, we don't know where the landings will take place, but the whole coast of France must be ready. We have to put in place the means to sabotage German gun emplacements and arms depots; destroy or put out of action anything they can use against us.'

He finished the soup, then stood up. 'Can you let this Alain know about us? Tell him the goods he ordered are awaiting collection. He will know what that means.'

'Where are you going?' Annette asked.

'I have left my colleagues in hiding near the

shore. I was coming to find our contact when I had to hide from some German soldiers in a truck. I heard Ruth speaking English so I felt sure I could trust her, and made myself known to her.'

'Speaking English! But you only do that when Paul — ' Annette stopped, puzzled.

'No. I was talking to myself. In the barn at the far end of the field,' Ruth said.

'Talking to yourself! In the barn! What on earth were you doing there?' Annette demanded.

Ruth explained unwillingly. 'Some of the older girls who used to be at the school, thought they'd have some sport with me. They forced me into the barn and tied me up, but they were scared when a patrol truck stopped on the road outside, so they ran away. Harry rescued me and cut me free.'

'The girls tied you up in the barn?' Annette looked sharply at Ruth, noticing where her hair was not quite level on one side. 'Mon Dieu! They were going to shave your head! Oh, the evil creatures!'

'It's all right. They didn't do much.' Ruth brushed aside Annette's concern. Turning to Harry, she said 'Can you find your way back to your colleagues, or shall I come with you?'

He hesitated. 'Someone who knows the terrain would be of immense help. We were scheduled to rendezvous at a derelict chateau just outside the town, but one of my colleagues twisted his ankle coming ashore. It's not serious, nothing a firm bandage for a couple of days won't mend, but they thought it better to send me on ahead to locate the local contact and the chateau so that they can go there directly.'

'Giulia's chateau?' Ruth wondered.

'Must be; it's the only one anywhere near that hasn't been commandeered by the Germans,' Annette replied. 'Since her death, it's been shuttered and left empty. I don't suppose anyone ever goes there. How many of you are there, Harry?'

'Three. The Major and a couple of us sergeants from the Royal Engineers. We're the sabotage crew. The Major is all right, it's my mate Tommy, Sergeant Wilson, who did his ankle on some loose shingle.'

'Bring them back here,' Annette decided. 'Michel will contact Alain in the meantime and he will take you to the chateau. He can probably find a bicycle for your sergeant to ride.'

'Thank you, Madame.' Harry saluted her, an odd sight in his French worker's clothes. 'If you are agreeable, Ruth, I'd be glad of your help.'

Ruth took Harry through the woods, using

a path which would take them to the road near the lane leading to the beach. Although the Germans had fenced off much of it, it was still possible to work one's way round to the coastal road, without too much difficulty. Ruth knew the way very well; she had come this way from the cottage countless times before the Germans came, to swim at the beach.

'This is it. I recognise that clump of trees. We came ashore just near here,' Harry whispered, when she finally led him to the edge of the wood, near the road.

'Be careful. German patrols come down here frequently,' Ruth warned. 'I was caught once, when I was coming up from the beach after meeting a contact from a rowing boat.'

Harry gave a little gasp of surprise. He shot her a look of respect, almost awe. 'Has it been difficult here, since the Germans came?' he asked.

'You could say that. But we manage to keep going. Now, stay quiet behind this bush while I listen to hear if there's anyone on the road. I'm not going to be caught twice.'

No, and not with a stranger who doesn't even look like a Frenchman, she thought. Harry had understood Françoise and replied to her in French but he seemed far more at ease speaking English to herself and Annette and it was clear he was unlikely to pass for a Frenchman under questioning. It must be his skills with explosives that had made him suitable for this raid, Ruth thought.

They crossed the road and plunged down the lane leading to the beach. Some fifty yards along, Harry stopped suddenly and looked as if he were about to push his way into the hedge on top of the bank. He gave a low whistle and, moments later, came an answering whistle and the sounds of soft rustling in the undergrowth. Two figures loomed up in the shadows and slid down the bank, on to the lane. One of them stumbled awkwardly.

'Found us a safe place to hole up till we make contact with Alain, Sir,' Harry whispered. 'Had a lucky break and came across this young English woman — '

'What!' One of the men spoke sharply, and Ruth stared towards him unbelievingly.

'It *can't* be!' she exclaimed, almost forgetting to whisper in her astonishment. 'Simon, it's never you!'

'Ruth?' The man turned to her. 'Good Lord, that's a stroke of luck! I knew we would be near you where we landed, but I never expected — !' He turned to his companions. 'Harry, Tom, this is my sister Ruth.'

'Well, ain't that a small world!' Tom, the

man with the twisted ankle, chuckled in astonishment.

'You mustn't stay here talking!' Ruth urged. 'Come up the lane to the road, but don't step out until you're absolutely sure there isn't a German patrol anywhere near. They come along here quite frequently, since it's the coast road and out of bounds to civilians, as well as being the route that leads to the coastal defences.'

They walked up the lane, Harry and Simon helping Tom between them. 'How is Annette?' Simon asked Ruth quietly, as they paused in the shadows at the entrance to the lane.

'She's well in herself. She'll be thrilled to see you. She's been so worried about what might have been happening to you. No letters have come through and she didn't know where to write, even if we could have sent letters to England.'

'I've been working on Special Operations ever since the Fall of France,' Simon said. 'I made a few clandestine trips over here, but always they were far away from this part of France and I didn't dare risk trying to contact either of you. It might have been dangerous for you if I had, as well as tricky for myself. Oh, boy! Annette's going to have one hell of a surprise in a little while.'

'She's — she's still in the wheelchair,' Ruth warned. 'There's not much more the doctors here can do for her, except give her pain killers — when they have enough to spare for civilians. But she exercises daily — and I massage the muscles in her legs — we've not given up hope that one day, when she can get to England, there'll be people who will be able to treat her, make her walk again. She lives in hope of that.'

'Ruth, you've done a splendid job, staying here with her, keeping up her spirits and looking after her,' Simon said. 'And not only that, from what I've heard. News has filtered through about the Englishwoman in Ste Marie de la Croix who has worked with the French Resistance. You are quite famous in England, you know.'

'Not too famous, I hope. I wouldn't care for my exploits to reach German ears,' Ruth replied lightly. 'Did a certain George from Dover mention he'd spoken to me?'

'There was some rumour that he'd met an English woman, but I didn't see him myself to confirm anything. We're quite a big operation, you know. I knew he was coming to a part of the coast near where Annette lived, but I didn't imagine for a moment that he'd meet you. Most of the French agents have a code name, so the fact that he'd met someone called Ruth didn't necessarily mean you.'

They made their way through the woods towards the farm, where Annette's cottage backed on to the land. Simon, of course, knew his way almost as well as Ruth, but needed her to warn him where the Germans had cordoned off parts of the area.

They reached the cottage, which was now in darkness.

'Will everyone be in bed by now?' Simon asked.

'I doubt it. Annette will be in her room on the ground floor, but Michel will be contacting Alain. He and Françoise have a room above one of the outhouses across the yard from the kitchen and Michel has a secret signal to let Alain know if he is wanted. I don't know what it is; even Françoise says she doesn't know. They are very cagey about their contacts. Even Annette and I did not know Michel was helping the Resistance until he was arrested by the Germans.'

Ruth opened the back door cautiously. There was only a single candle, stuck in the neck of a bottle, on the table, but Françoise was there, putting out bread and cheese and setting plates.

'Françoise, I have some more visitors for

you,' Ruth said, ushering the three men inside.

'Monsieur I have met,' Françoise replied, 'and here is your poor companion who has hurt his ankle. I have prepared a cold compress and bandages. And this third Monsieur — mon Dieu! It is never — it can't be! — Monsieur Simon! I cannot believe it!' She rushed towards Simon, clasping him in her arms. 'Oh, Monsieur Simon! How we have worried about you, wondered where you were! Wondered if you were safe! My Mam'selle Annette will be so happy now! It is enough to make her quite well again.'

'I was sent on this assignment partly because I know the area so well,' Simon said. 'But where is Annette? Hadn't you better find her, Ruth, and warn her she is in for a shock?'

'Warn me of what?' Came Annette's voice from the doorway. In the gloom of the single candle she took in the scene; three French labourers beside the table, Françoise cutting bread and Ruth on her knees beside one of the men, bathing his foot in a bowl of water. She looked from one face to another — three strangers, yet one voice had sounded familiar. 'Who are you all?' she asked. 'Please introduce me. Harry I think I recognise, but the others?'

'I'm Tom,' said the man with his foot in the

bowl. 'Sergeant Wilson. And the other chap is Major Lawson — codename Simon.'

'No!' The chair shot forward. Annette did almost look as if she were going to stand up and run towards him, but she had no need, because Simon was already beside her, on his knees, his arms round her.

'Simon! Oh, Simon!' Annette said, over and over again. 'You've no idea how I've longed for this moment! To see you again — but you're here in such danger!' She caressed Simon's short, curly fair head, clinging to him, stroking his face as if she still could not believe what she was seeing.

'No more danger than you are in, than you have been throughout the Occupation,' Simon dismissed her fears. 'Listen, we've come to do a job. One of your group supplied us with a very good copy of a map of the gun emplacements round the coast here. We plan to put as many as possible of them out of action, so that, come the Allies' invasion, they'll have a clear run into shore.'

'It's coming soon, then? And it will be here?' Annette asked.

'We don't know when or where, but common sense says it can't be much longer delayed. As to where, we're destroying gun emplacements and arms depots all around the coast, from Calais to Brest — not us personally, of course, but the Germans are going to find a great many of their defences are not going to work as well as they'd expected, when the time comes that they need to use them.'

'Come, eat! And I have a bottle of good wine I was saving for a celebration,' Françoise said. 'And what better celebration could there be than having my dear Mam'selle Annette reunited with her Monsieur Simon?'

They gathered round the table, Annette still holding fast to Simon's hand, as if she feared that he would disappear if she let go.

'Why don't you stay here tonight?' Ruth suggested, as the idea came to her. 'There's plenty of room. Annette's bedroom upstairs is free, and you can go to the chateau tomorrow. Alain can come here to brief you on the situation.'

'Oh, Simon, please do!' Annette said eagerly

'That seems like a good idea,' Simon agreed. 'It'll give Tom's ankle a chance to rest up. Better he's not walking on it more than he needs. A few hours should see it right. We're as safe here as anywhere. No one saw us come and I take it there isn't likely to be anyone calling here?'

'Only the Captain,' Françoise muttered, before Ruth had a chance to speak.

'The Captain? Who is this?' Simon said sharply.

'A friend. I'll tell you about him later, but he won't come tomorrow,' Ruth said quickly. She looked across the table towards Annette, who had not taken her eyes off Simon the whole evening, but now there was fear in her expression, as well as love.

12

Tom and Harry were openly delighted to be sleeping at the cottage. 'A real bed!' Harry exclaimed, 'and I thought I might be in that barn for the night.'

Annette and Simon exchanged glances, then he wheeled her out of the kitchen and into her ground floor bedroom. The door shut behind them and no one saw anything more of either of them that night.

Ruth heard the unfamiliar murmur of voices from the room next to her own, but she was tired and soon slept.

Next morning she found Annette and Simon in the sitting room when she came downstairs. They had been bringing each other up to date on their separate lives since Simon had left for England at the outbreak of war.

'Ruth — you can't imagine how wonderful it is to have Simon here again.' Annette's face was glowing, her eyes sparkling, and for a moment Ruth almost believed she would leap up from the chair and dance round the room.

'I know, dear. I'm thrilled too.' Ruth couldn't bear to think that Simon wouldn't be staying here for long. He had work to do, dangerous work, and once he left the cottage it would be too risky to return.

'You've been doing some of your paintings, I see.' Simon moved across to the fireplace. 'I'm glad you've kept it up. What is this one, darling?' He peered at the picture Ruth had framed and hung there. 'It looks like a bird sitting on a bush. Hmm, rather a large bird to be sitting in a flowery bush like that. What's it meant to be?'

'It's the eagle and the rose,' Annette said. 'I was trying to portray them together, but it took such a long time to get it right. Each time I could only come up with the eagle with the rose in its beak, or somehow dominating the rose. I didn't want that but at last, with this, I think I have achieved what I wanted to express. The eagle is quite happy in the midst of the rose bush, even if he is, in reality, too big for it. The roses are big, too. They're very special roses.'

'It's certainly a very unusual subject,' Simon remarked. 'It's not just a picture, though, is it? There's something symbolic about it, isn't there? What does it mean?'

When Annette hesitated, Ruth said, 'She was trying to portray two symbols, the German eagle and the English rose, in harmony together. And that's because I have a German friend who visits here.'

'Is that what Françoise was hinting at last night, when she mentioned the Captain? Is he a German officer?'

Ruth nodded. She stuck out her chin defiantly. If Simon was going to give her a lecture on the inadvisability of fraternising with the enemy, she would stop him in his tracks, right there. She wasn't going to stand for him telling her how she should behave. He hadn't lived here under the Occupation, and he hadn't met Paul.

'Paul came here at first because he wanted to improve his English with conversation lessons and I was the only native English speaker in the town,' she explained defensively. 'He came regularly over several months, and we've become friends.' She waited for Simon's words of censure, but instead he smiled broadly at her.

'Sis — that's wonderful! You've acquired a tame German for us! You clever old thing! That's one of the most useful things you could have done — '

'Now, look here — ' Ruth began hotly.

The door opened and Françoise put her head in. 'Your breakfast is ready,' she said. 'The other gentlemen have started already. If you're talking about Captain Reinhardt, Monsieur Simon, I can tell you he is a good man. He had my Michel released from arrest when I thought he might be deported to Germany. And he brings us coffee and sugar and one or two other food luxuries that we haven't seen since 1940.'

'He certainly sounds a treasure!' Simon began to wheel Annette out of the room. 'You must see we meet this Captain Reinhardt as soon as possible. He could be very useful to us.'

'No! That's the last thing that must happen!' Ruth said, horrified. 'You will all have to be gone before he comes again. Don't you realise, if he saw three strangers here who clearly weren't French, he'd have you arrested before you could do anything?'

Simon turned his head and gave her a sly grin. 'Would he now?' he said thoughtfully. 'I hardly think so. There are three of us, and only one of him.'

Françoise had used nearly all the food in the house to feed the three extra mouths. Since Claude's arrest, the bakery had been closed, and though one or two of the local people had tried to fill the gap by baking at home and selling the bread on a market stall, the results were not nearly as good.

'You will have to go into town and see what you can find to buy,' Françoise said, watching the men at table. 'Perhaps there may be some fish, or Michel might manage to trap a rabbit, though there are very few of them left now.'

'Yes, I'll go soon.' Ruth wanted to stay and hear what Simon told his companions. Françoise, not understanding English, ignored them, muttering that if Ruth didn't hurry, the best of what little was there, would all be gone.

Simon told them at once about Paul. 'Guess what my sister has done!' he said as he joined them at the table. 'She's only found herself a tame German who'll do anything for her! He's already shown how keen he is, rescuing Michel from arrest and bringing them food from German supplies. He's exactly what we want, chaps!'

'He didn't rescue Michel,' Annette said crossly. 'The Germans let him go because they hoped he might lead them to other Resistance members. It had nothing to do with Paul, anyway. He couldn't have used his influence.'

'But he'll be coming to this house again very soon, you said?' Simon persisted. 'What's he like, this chap?'

'Oh, tall. Brown-haired. Doesn't look particularly German.' Ruth shrugged.

Tom looked across at her. 'How big is he?'

'How big? Well, medium build. Medium height too, I suppose. Why?'

'About the same size as your brother?'

Ruth frowned. 'I — suppose so,' she said.

'That's it, then!' Harry slapped his thigh. 'Look, Boss, with your fair colouring you could pass for a Jerry even better than this bloke. When he comes here, we pinch his uniform and you wear it. That would get you in anywhere where the guns are, and Tom and I pose as mechanics. Perhaps there's some way we can get hold of some German fatigues, but even if not, standard overalls might do, and with you dressed as a German Captain, no one's going to question who we are. It's a passport into every restricted area along this coast. It's the best bloody gift we could have hoped for!'

'You can't take Paul's uniform!' Ruth cried, horrified.

'We weren't going to ask to borrow it, polite like,' Tom said. 'Like the Boss says, there are three of us and only one of him. You bring him here, we'll do the rest. Don't worry; there won't be any blood. We don't want to make a mess of his uniform.'

The colour drained from Ruth's face. 'You can't!' she said. 'I won't have you harm him.'

'He's a *German*, for heaven's sake!' Harry growled. 'And you don't imagine we'd risk his escaping and raising the alarm if we merely tied him up. What we do needn't concern you. We'll see he is hidden well away from this place. There won't be anything to connect you with it so have no fears about that.'

Ruth looked from one face to another. They were all deadly serious about this plan. For them, it was an unexpected bonus and they would expect her to do her part to lure Paul to the cottage. To certain death!

Before she could remonstrate further, the back door opened and Alain joined them. He shook hands formally with each of them in turn, then settled himself at the table. 'These gun emplacements,' he said. 'As I understand it, your brief is to destroy as many of them as possible, in preparation for the Allies' invasion? It will not be easy, Messieurs.'

'We've been provided with a very good map showing their locations,' Simon said, producing it.

'Ah, yes! Mam'selle Ruth obtained this for us. She is one of our loyal members.' Alain smiled at Ruth, evidently expecting that she would be pleased by the praise.

'It cost the freedom, possibly even the life, of one of the other Resistance members to enable me to take those photographs,' she said.

'Then we must ensure it is put to the best possible use,' Simon said briskly. 'We owe it to the person who risked his life that we succeed. Ruth has come up with a good suggestion. It seems she has a German captain who visits here frequently. One of us can use his uniform to enable us to get inside practically anywhere in the gun emplacements. What do you think, Alain?'

'No! It was *not* my idea!' Ruth stormed. They all ignored her.

'Yes, using a stolen German uniform would be useful,' Alain mused. 'You speak German, Monsieur?' He looked at Simon.

'Yes, I'm fluent enough. If you could find something for these chaps to wear, so they can pose as mechanics, that would be perfect. Can you acquire German overalls, or do you know what their mechanics wear?'

'Overalls such as they wear should not be too hard to obtain,' Alain said consideringly. 'You certainly do not want to be taking anyone who looks like these two, anywhere near a restricted area.'

'I think we might as well stay holed up here until we are ready,' Simon said. 'There doesn't seem much point in moving to the chateau if we're going to have to be back here to meet this captain.'

'Ah, the chateau!' Alain accepted a cup of German coffee from Françoise. 'That was one of the things I was going to warn you about. It seems the Germans have become rather interested in the chateau recently. They may be thinking of billeting some of their troops there, or they may be searching for evidence of some kind. German staff cars have been seen there on more than one occasion, so I do not think it would be a safe place for you and your men.'

He drank some of the coffee and continued, 'You, Monsieur, know this area well, I think, so you know of the Comte Jacques whose family own the chateau. Jacques is the leader of all our local groups but he is at present in the mountains, training guerrilla fighters. He also co-ordinates the gathering of information from our agents. He comes to Ste Marie de la Croix occasionally, but always disguised now. He is a much sought-after man, you understand.'

'I've heard of Jacques' exploits,' Simon said. 'I think I met him once, before the war, though I could hardly say I knew him socially. I'm looking forward to the possibility that we may meet when this whole shindig starts. He had an Italian wife, I believe? What happened to her? Deported, was she? Or fled back to Italy?'

'Alas, no, Monsieur. The Comtesse Giulia was discovered to be a double agent. We trusted her, to our regret, and the Germans did also, since they thought Italy was their ally. It was necessary to — er, see she did no further harm to our cause.'

'She was murdered,' Ruth broke in. 'It was horrible. Someone slit her throat. The Gendarmerie were not able to establish who had done it.'

'The Gendarmerie were not encouraged to pursue their enquiries,' Alain said. 'They knew, or at least, they had a very good idea of what had happened. She was liquidated by Jacques' orders.'

'What! He ordered the murder of his own wife!' Annette exclaimed. 'How could he?'

'It was necessary, Mam'selle, to protect many other lives, French lives. Sometimes, some harsh decisions have to be made for the greater good.'

Ruth was aware of Simon's eyes regarding her thoughtfully. Alain's words had not been lost on either of them. For the first time, she wished it wasn't Simon who was here. She would defy any other British agent, or French one, for that matter, but when it came to a choice of risking Simon's life or Paul's, she could not bear to have to decide.

'I understand that Ruth's German, Captain Reinhardt, will be visiting here tomorrow,' Simon said to Alain. 'Can you let us have something suitable for my men to wear so they can pass for mechanics? It's a pity we have to wait until tomorrow but it will give you a chance to find us something.'

'It's no problem.' Alain stood up. 'German overalls are easy. If you had asked me for army uniforms, that would have taken more time and thought. But you are already provided for, or soon will be. I will bring all you need tonight. Meanwhile, stay out of sight here. Keep away from the windows and you should be safer here than anywhere.'

Ruth had thought the rest of the day would be a strain for all of them, but Tom and Harry kept upstairs and Simon spent most of the time with Annette in her room. She wandered, alone and disconsolate, around the cottage, without anyone except Françoise to talk to, and Françoise was too concerned with providing something for an evening meal, to be much company. She could not concentrate on a book, all her thoughts were concentrated on what she must do to warn Paul without giving away Simon's presence.

Early the next morning, Ruth was in the hall, shopping basket on her arm and about to visit the market for whatever she could buy to feed the extra guests, knowing she would have to be discreet about her purchases. If anyone noticed she was buying far more than usual, it wouldn't take long for someone to work out the reason why and there were plenty of people prepared to let the Germans know their suspicions.

Her hand was on the latch of the front door when Annette's door opened and Simon came out.

'Where are you going?' he asked.

'To try to find some extra rations. You three have hearty appetites,' she smiled at him.

'Can't Françoise do that?'

'Françoise is busy preparing breakfast. I always do the shopping. Look, I have to go. If I don't get to the market early, anything worth having will have gone.'

Simon's eyes narrowed. 'You're going to tip off that German officer of yours not to come, aren't you?' he said. 'You don't seem to realise how important that uniform of his will be for us.'

'I'm not going to see Paul. I couldn't, even if I wanted to. I told you, civilians aren't allowed beyond the vestibule of the Town Hall, now the Germans have taken it over as their headquarters.'

'All the same, I think I'd prefer it if Françoise did the shopping.' Simon attempted to take the basket from her. 'You can prepare breakfast, can't you?'

'Since when do I take orders from you?' Ruth said angrily. 'I've always done the food shopping. I'm good at it and the stallholders know me. Don't be ridiculous, Simon.'

'You take orders from me as of now, because, while we're here this house is our headquarters and I am Senior Officer,' Simon snapped. 'And I'm sorry, Sis, but, frankly, I don't trust you. You've shown that your loyalties are divided. You've clearly become emotionally involved with this German and that's likely to endanger our mission.'

'I suppose Annette has told you all about us,' Ruth muttered.

'She told me that you and this Captain seem to have become very close. Don't you realise, you stupid girl, that he's the enemy?' Simon's voice rose in anger. 'That he'd have you, Annette, all of us, shot without a qualm if he suspected anything about us being here? You've been playing with fire, letting your affections rule your head. I thought you had been cultivating his friendship for the benefit of the Allies, but now I see you are nothing more than a silly, addle-headed, romantic girl.'

'I'm not!'

'Do you deny that you'd warn this man off if you could?' Simon was holding her arm, preventing her from opening the front door. His grip increased painfully.

'I wouldn't let him come to his death here,

if that's what you mean!'

Simon laughed. 'And you're not stupid enough to think we'd merely ask to borrow his uniform, when he arrived for coffee and conversation — and whatever else you've been offering him.'

'How dare you!' With her free hand, Ruth struck at Simon's face, but he caught her arm deftly and pushed it away.

'Simon,' she said, striving to calm the situation. 'This isn't like you. You were never a bully like this. What has made you so horrible?'

'This is war, Ruth. And in war one can't afford to let one's feelings override one's duties. I'm sorry for calling you stupid. I know you aren't that, but I thought you would put the safety of your own brother and his colleagues before anything else. The whole future of the war might depend on the success of our mission, and that success largely depends on being able to infiltrate the German gun strongholds. Don't you see that?'

'You don't know what you are asking me,' she whispered.

'I'm not asking. I'm demanding.' He pushed her towards the kitchen. 'Françoise,' he called 'will you please do the marketing today? Ruth will be staying indoors all day.

She can prepare breakfast while you are gone.'

Françoise looked up in surprise, but said nothing. She took off her apron, lifted her shawl from the peg on the back door and took the shopping basket and purse from Ruth.

'I will get whatever I can, Mam'selle Ruth,' she said, going towards the front door.

'You see? Françoise does what she is told without argument,' Simon said. Tom limped into the kitchen as he spoke, remarking that his ankle seemed very much better this morning.

'Ruth is making the breakfast today,' Simon said to him. 'See she doesn't leave the house for any reason, or speak to anyone other than ourselves.'

'So now I'm under house arrest?' Ruth glared at her brother.

'Yes, regrettably, you are. I'm not letting anything jeopardise the best chance of success we can have.' He left the room and Ruth turned angrily towards the cooker, stirring some oatmeal that Françoise had begun cooking.

Tom sat down at the table. After a moment, he said 'Boss's right, you know. Doesn't do to have mixed feelings in a situation like this. The Germans are all alike, anyway. They'd stab you in the back for no reason, if Hitler told them to. You don't want to trust any of them.'

'I don't need your opinion, thank you!' Ruth slammed a bowl of porridge down in front of him, with such force some of it splattered on to his jacket. He looked at her in surprise, a hurt expression on his face.

'And don't be expecting any sugar on it!' she added spitefully. 'There hasn't been any for months here, except what a *German* was kind enough to give us, but of course you wouldn't want any of that!'

The atmosphere between her and the English men did not improve as the day wore on. Wherever she was, Ruth found either Tom or Harry close behind her. It became unnerving. Annette, embarrassed by what she had innocently told Simon about Ruth and Paul, avoided her, spending her time reading or sketching in the garden when Simon was not with her. Ruth was not allowed outside.

After an early lunch, which was good by wartime standards, Françoise having found some fish for sale, Simon said, 'You'd better go to your room, Ruth. You won't want to be around when Captain Reinhardt arrives.'

Harry looked up. 'Which way does her room face? Can she signal to him from the window?'

'She's at the back. It overlooks farmland,' Simon replied. 'But you've made a good point. Sorry, Ruth, we'll have to lock you in.'

'This is outrageous!' Ruth exploded. 'You come here, take over the house, give orders all the time and now you're making me a prisoner!'

'You brought it on yourself,' Simon said harshly. 'And you must realise — you're all under my orders while we're here. The whole Resistance group will take orders from us so you've no cause to feel you are in any way singled out. Come on, Ruth,' he added, more gently. 'It's only while he's here. And you know you wouldn't want to be around then. This way, he probably won't even realise you had anything to do with it.'

'I *haven't* had anything to do with it!' Ruth shouted at him. She wanted to run out of the house there and then, but Tom and Harry were standing beside both exits, the door into the hall and the back door. They had anticipated her reaction.

'But you did tell us about him in the first place.' Simon took her arm. He pushed her in front of him, up the stairs, thrust her inside her bedroom and locked the door. She heard him remove the key from the lock.

Ruth sat down on her bed, thinking hard. She had to stop Paul from coming here. He would almost certainly be killed if he came; even if Simon and his men didn't do it, he would be court-marshalled and shot once the full story came out.

She looked at her watch. It was past noon, and Paul was due here at two. Downstairs she could hear them moving about, no doubt planning their ambush. She felt sick.

Breathing deeply, to calm herself, Ruth went to the window and looked out. Her room was over the kitchen but there was a small, sloping roof immediately below, the roof of the outhouse beyond the kitchen. It would surely be possible to climb out of her window and drop to the ground from the outhouse roof. It concealed her from the kitchen window, but anyone in the outhouse itself would certainly hear her on the roof. Françoise was the only person who went there much, but even she would alert Simon if she knew Ruth was escaping. Françoise still had a strong hatred for the German race, even though she was prepared to tolerate Paul these days.

Very carefully, Ruth opened the window. It was casement and, in the French style, opened inwards. She pushed it as far as it would go against the wall. Fortunately, there was no small railing for a window-box here, so common in French homes, only a narrow sill and then a drop to the roof, perhaps six or eight feet below.

She clambered out, hung by her hands to lessen the drop, then let go. She landed on the roof, stumbled and nearly rolled off it. Only by crouching on her hands and knees was she able to maintain her balance. She listened. No sounds came from the kitchen or outhouse. Moments later, she had dropped from the roof and was edging her way round the side of the house, to the road.

Ruth ran to where the road joined the main road into town. Paul would come this way but she was still too near the cottage for safety. Anyone looking out of an upstairs window might see her.

She thought quickly. She knew Paul finished his spell of duty at the Town Hall at noon. Then, he would probably go for some lunch, either at the officers' mess in the building, or at his billet. She knew he lived in one of the larger houses on the other side of town, which had been commandeered for officer accommodation. She knew the area where it was, but not the exact address. Paul would almost certainly go back there after work, to freshen up or check for personal mail. He'd be most likely to come on to the cottage from there and that meant he would come past the war memorial crossroads, turning off to the left from there to reach the cottage. Her best, safest course was to wait for him by the memorial statues.

The place held a gloomy, depressing feel for Ruth. She could not help being reminded of the young men who had been shot by the Germans here, some two years after their occupation of the town. Annette used to like to come and leave flowers in memory of her uncles named on the plinth, but neither girl had cared for the place once they had seen the damage done to the statue by the German firing squad.

There was no one in sight when she reached the memorial. Ruth checked her watch again; now it was a little before one o'clock and she had nearly an hour to wait. She sat on the plinth, trying to enjoy the early summer sunshine. It was the first day of June today. A phrase from school history lessons came into her mind 'The Glorious First of June.' It had been a naval battle, she remembered vaguely, between the French and the English, off Marseilles, in 1794 and, surprisingly, both sides had claimed victory. This first of June was going to be anything but glorious as she planned what she must say to Paul to stop him coming near the cottage but without letting him suspect the real reason. She knew it must mean she would probably never see him again.

Someone was trudging along the dusty road towards her. As he came nearer, Ruth saw that it was a young boy, perhaps ten or eleven years old. Drawing level, he stopped and looked up at the memorial, crossing himself. He looked at Ruth. 'My grand-father's name is on there,' he remarked, nodding towards the plinth. 'When they add the names for this war, my father's will be on it, too.'

'I'm sorry,' Ruth said. 'There are a great many names, aren't there, when Ste Marie de la Croix is only a small town.'

'They ought to list all the heroes, not only the ones who died,' the boy continued. 'My grandmother is in the Gestapo cells at the Town Hall and I think they're torturing her. Some people say she will be shot, others that she will be deported to Germany, but they won't do either until they get the information they want, out of her.'

Ruth shuddered. If the woman was his grandmother, she must be quite old. The Germans ought not to be waging war with elderly women.

'She has her memorial already, though, whatever happens to her!' The boy grinned suddenly. 'She showed it to me, before the Germans caught her. See that angel at the

315

back of the group? It has her face now. A German bullet did that, it made the angel's face look just like hers, so she'll be recorded here even if they don't put her name on the plinth.'

'The angel looks like your grandmother?' Ruth asked, surprised. 'What's her name?'

'Madeleine Duvalle. She worked as a cleaner at the German headquarters for over a year, and they trusted her. They didn't know she was doing a marvellous job of collecting information for the Resistance. She was so good, most of her friends thought she was a collaborator. That was even better cover for her and she didn't seem to mind not having friends any more. They used to beat me up at school, call me names because of her, but I didn't mind too much because I knew it wasn't true. Now the Germans have caught her and they've realised just what she had been doing. They're mad at her for fooling them for so long, but they think she knows all about what the Resistance are doing, so they're trying to make her tell them before she's sentenced.' He shrugged, sitting down on the plinth beside Ruth. 'I hope the Allies come soon and rescue her, but I think they'll probably be too late. She's all I have, you know. My mother died years ago, soon after my father was blown up on his ship.

316

Grandmère looked after me, and I looked after her. Don't know what I'll do now.'

Ruth remembered her last sight of Madame Duvalle, screaming and shouting to provide a distraction so that she — Ruth — could slip unnoticed away with her photographs of the German map. She put her arm round the boy's shoulder. 'We'll see you're looked after.' She said. 'Your grandmother was brave, a heroine. She won't be forgotten.'

The boy shrugged off her arm and stood up. 'I don't need to be looked after,' he said gruffly. 'I can look after myself. I just want the Allies to come and rescue Grandmère before the Germans kill her.' He turned away, trudging on along the road, hands deep in his pockets. Ruth watched until he was out of sight, feeling shame for the unkind remarks she had made in the past about Madame Duvalle.

She was dozing in the warm sunshine when she heard the sound of a car coming along the road. There were few cars apart from German staff cars on the roads these days and she looked up quickly, her heart beginning to pound. She recognised the German car by its shape, long before she could see who was driving. If she flagged it down and it wasn't Paul, she'd have some awkward questions to answer. On the other hand, if it *was* Paul and she let him go past —

The car slowed as it approached the memorial. The driver wound the window down and called to her 'Ruth! I wasn't expecting to see you here!'

Relief mingled with panic. Now he was here, what was she going to say, to stop him going to the cottage, to stop him trying to see her again?

'I — I hoped you'd come this way. I was waiting for you,' she stammered.

'But I was coming to your home. It is Thursday, is it not? Why not wait for me there?' He looked at her with a puzzled expression, then pulled the car into the side of the road and switched off the engine. 'Is everything all right, Ruth? There's nothing wrong, is there?'

'No — I mean, yes! I wanted to talk to you. Privately. Not at the cottage.' She was talking quickly, her hands clasping the edge of the car window. She felt her palms sweating, but she couldn't let go.

'What is it, Liebchen?' Paul asked gently.

That was nearly her undoing. She wanted to shout at him: Don't go near the cottage! They'll kill you! But then he'd know and she'd have betrayed Simon and his companions, destroyed their plans and condemned

318

them to certain death. And not only them; if the guns weren't destroyed it would mean death for hundreds more Allied troops, when they came.

'I — I've been thinking.' Her knuckles showed white on the edge of the car door. 'Paul, what you told me — about the plans your friends had in Germany to — to assassinate Hitler. It's treason, Paul.'

'I suppose, technically, it is. But he's a madman. If he's not stopped he'll destroy Germany and half Europe as well. He — '

'I can't condone treason of any kind,' Ruth said, gulping. 'And I've realised that what I've been doing — making friends — more than friends — with one of the enemy — that's treason for me, too. I have to stop it.'

She saw the hurt in his eyes, and the bewilderment, too. She couldn't bear to look at him.

'It's over, Paul, you and me,' she whispered. 'I don't want to see you again.'

'What are you saying, Ruth?' The gentleness of his voice was too much. He was making it so very hard for her, harder than she had ever imagined that it could be. She took a deep breath, telling herself that if she couldn't make him understand, then he'd die. Making him hate her was better than sending him to his death.

'I don't love you, Paul. I've thought about it and I've come to the conclusion that I can't love one of the enemy.'

'You've taken a long time to reach your decision,' Paul said drily. 'Why don't I drive you back to the cottage and we can talk about all this in comfort?'

'No! I told you! I don't want, ever, to see you again. Please don't ever come to my home or try to see me. My mind's made up — '

'What has caused you to be like this, so unexpectedly?' he was looking at her keenly and Ruth wondered if he believed anything of what she had been saying. If he didn't, it was likely he would go away but turn up at the cottage tomorrow, while Simon was still there.

'You're a traitor to Germany!' she said fiercely. 'You're planning to assassinate your leader! You may not agree with him, but you must stay loyal.'

'I am loyal to Germany,' Paul said.

'No! You are a traitor! I cannot have any feelings for someone who is a traitor to their leader, whoever he is. I don't want to see you, ever again, and if I do, I shall report to the German Command what you told me about the assassination plans.'

Paul went very white. 'No, you must not do

that, Ruth. Too many good men are at risk.'

'Then stay away from me! Don't come to my home, ever again!' she stormed at him, fearful that he would insist on arguing his case further.

'If that is what you really want, Ruth.' He gave her a searching look. She stared straight back at him. 'Yes, I do. Please, don't ever — '

'Rest assured, I will not impose myself where it has been made clear to me that I am not welcome.' He started the car engine again. 'May I thank you for your hospitality in the past, and that of your friends? You cannot be fully aware of how much it meant to me, to have somewhere where I could go and forget the war for a time. Where I could be myself. Perhaps I was too much myself?'

'Please go.' She almost choked on the words, but they came out as if in anger, not the misery she was feeling.

'Goodbye, Ruth.' He wound up the window and the car slid forward. She forced herself not to look as he turned in a wide sweep and began to drive back the way he had come. She waited until she could no longer hear the car's engine, then sat down on the memorial plinth and wept.

Ruth stayed away from the cottage for as long as she could. She walked along the lanes outside the town and across fields, hardly

321

noticing where she was going. It was evening by the time she finally returned, walking into the kitchen through the back door, ready to face the fury that she knew must come.

The whole house seemed quiet. There was no one in the kitchen, though there was a pot of bones and vegetables simmering on the stove. She went into the sitting room where she found Annette, by herself, painting.

'Where are they? It's all very quiet. Are they upstairs?' she asked.

'Simon and the other two have gone. When Paul did not show up at two, Simon went to your room and found you gone. I think he realised then that Paul would not come but he didn't know what you would have said to him, so he felt it safest to move out. Alain came for them at four, and they all went away together. I don't know where, but I don't think Simon will be coming back.' Annette sighed. 'It was so wonderful to see him again, long before I ever dreamed I would, yet so terrifying, too. It was worse than before to have to part from him again.'

She looked at Ruth, seeing her tear-stained face. 'It was very bad for you, too, wasn't it? I knew at once what you must have done. I think I guessed what you were going to do, but I couldn't say anything to Simon.' Annette held out her arms and Ruth almost fell into them, sobbing on her friend's shoulder.

'I'm never going to see him again,' she said.

Annette nodded. 'I know. And perhaps I am never going to see Simon again, either. We must learn to comfort each other, now.'

13

Ruth woke from a heavy sleep. It was still dark, yet something had wakened her. She tried to clear her thoughts. Today was Tuesday, one of the days when Paul came, but he was never going to be coming to the cottage again. A deep sense of gloom descended on her. She had probably saved his life, but what if she had prevented Simon and his men from disabling the guns? If they failed, or not been as successful as they'd hoped, because of her, then the result would be counted in many more Allied lives lost. Did she have the right to risk that? She'd accused Paul of being a traitor, but how much more was she a traitor to her own country? Shame swept over her like a hot flush. The sanctimonious words she had spoken to Paul came back to her. And now, she would never be able to explain, to tell him why she had been so cruelly unjust.

In the distance, a loud thud made the walls of the cottage shake. Ruth realised then what it had been that had wakened her. Another followed, then a third. At first, she thought it was a raid, or Simon blowing up German guns, but these *were* guns. The sound came now, with a continuous regularity, from the direction of the coast. Slowly, it began to dawn on her, yet she still could hardly believe it. The Allied invasion had begun!

She scrambled out of bed and ran downstairs to Annette's room. Her friend was awake, sitting up in bed.

'It is it, isn't it?' she greeted Ruth. 'It's really happening at last — the Allies have come to save France.'

'Please God Simon managed to silence some of the gun emplacements, at least,' Ruth muttered.

'That's not gunfire from the coast; it's much further away. It sounds inland,' Annette said. 'I think Simon must have done what he had planned. Alain brought some German style overalls with him, three sets, when he came for them, and even Simon acknowledged that wearing a German officer's uniform might have caused more problems than solutions. Don't fret about what you did, Ruth. Just hope both Paul and Simon come through the next few days safely.'

The next hours were difficult and frightening. The girls and Françoise stayed together in the sitting room, unable to concentrate on anything to distract their minds from what was happening outside. In the afternoon, they saw two or three tanks rumbling past, thrusting between the hedges of the narrow road, clipping the white palings of the cottage's fence and tearing branches off a tree.

'They must be British,' Annette announced.

'I don't know. I didn't see,' Ruth replied, less certain.

There were rumblings of heavy trucks going past, mainly on the road leading to the town. They couldn't see very much but the traffic seemed to be going in both directions, the Allied troops going towards the town, the Germans leaving, or so they hoped, but could not be sure of anything.

In the afternoon, Michel came into the cottage. He was plastered with mud and looked utterly bedraggled. Françoise gave a scream when she saw him and rushed up to him, but he brushed her aside.

'It's nothing, woman. I've spent most of the day lying in ditches, that's all. It's been a wonderful sight, seeing British and American soldiers coming along the roads, and hearing the explosions. Did you hear a particularly loud one, early in the morning? That was one of the guns overlooking the sea. Major Lawson and his comrades fixed that one. I know, because Alain was with them. They fixed a charge to it, and the first time the Huns tried to fire it — boom! The lot went up, including the ammunitions store. A very pretty sight, I can tell you.'

'You've no business to be out there in the middle of the fighting,' Françoise grumbled. 'Leave it to the professional soldiers. You'll get yourself killed, wanting to be in on everything.'

'I've waited more than four years for this day,' Michel replied. 'I'm not going to hide away and miss it all, now. Besides, we are doing our bit to help. Did you hear an explosion from the direction of the Town Square, earlier? Some of us put explosives under the German staff cars, and when the top brass tried to drive them away, it was most satisfactory.'

Ruth paled. Would Paul have been one of them, she wondered. He would not have run away, but he might have had instructions to drive away from the Town Hall. The worry of not knowing what was happening was almost more than she could bear.

A short while later, a young man on a bicycle came down the street, hammering on their front door, shouting 'Evacuate your home! Mayor Roget's orders! It is not safe to stay in a house. The town is being shelled.'

'What are we to do? Where are we to go?'

Françoise demanded of him. The boy was already several yards down the road, on his way to alert as many people as he could.

'There's a field outside the town, off the main road leading inland,' he called back. He stopped, turned his bicycle and added 'they're setting up tents and a communal food kitchen. Take essentials and warm clothing, but don't stay in the house. Go as soon as you can.' He was off again, down the road, shouting his message to everyone as he passed.

'He's right,' Annette said briskly. 'The gunfire has been shaking the cottage. Much more of it and the walls might begin to crack. We are better outside.'

'But what are we to do? How will we manage?' Françoise wailed.

'Fetch a basket, biggest one you can find,' Annette ordered. 'Put it on my lap and fill it with all the food in the house. I can manage to hold more than either of you could carry.'

It seemed a sensible idea, and certainly served as a distraction to keep Françoise from worrying. When they had filled the basket, Ruth collected coats and blankets and they began their slow journey towards the field.

If they'd had any worries about finding their way to it, these were dispelled as soon as they had manoeuvred Annette's chair into the road. Little groups of people, carrying baskets and with blankets draped round their shoulders, were walking steadily away from the town. Some pushed handcarts, laden with everything of value they could bring. Even in the grim seriousness of the situation, Ruth found herself amused by the different objects that the townspeople considered essential. In among the bags of food and warm clothing, she saw a clock, some framed family portraits and a set of gardening tools. Given that there was a real possibility of looting from the abandoned homes, it was understandable that some people should want to bring precious family heirlooms as well as the more practical goods, but gardening tools!

The Mayor and the local officials, together with the Gendarmerie, had made very practical use of the designated field. It was about a mile out of the town, away from the road, and, hopefully, not on the route the Allies would take when they began their advance inland on their way to Paris. Some tents had been set up, but these were strictly for young children and the elderly. Everyone else was expected to spend the night in the open, using whatever they had brought with them, for shelter.

Food didn't seem to be a problem; at least for the immediate needs of the people. The

Gendarmerie had set up a field kitchen and a generous farmer, celebrating the Allies' landing, had donated an ox to be roasted on an outdoor spit. There was an air almost of carnival about the place. Everyone was excited; at last the liberators had come and no one doubted that the German Occupation would soon be at an end. If it had not been for worry about the safety of their homes they had been forced to leave, the townsfolk would have thought they were enjoying their Quatorze-juillet celebrations five weeks early.

'I'm sure we will be able to find you a place in one of the tents, Annette,' Ruth said, as the evening drew on. 'And Françoise, too. There'll certainly be a place for her.'

'No, I don't want to be in a tent,' Annette declared. 'I can sleep in my chair with a blanket, perfectly well. I'd like to be out where I can watch what is happening.'

'No tent for me, either,' Françoise said. 'Crowded in among crying babies and complaining old women? No, thank you! I am happy to be here, out in the open, with both of you, but I wish Michel was here, too. He is too old for fighting at his age.'

'He went back to the farm,' Ruth said. 'He's not fighting. Cows have to be milked, whatever else happens. He'll join us later, perhaps.'

The night was mild, with no rain. Ruth sat on a groundsheet with Françoise, both wrapped in blankets, with Annette in her chair beside them, watching the constant flashing of gunfire light up the sky over the town, and listening to the crump, crump, of explosions which never ceased. Annette declared that she couldn't possibly sleep, but soon both she and Françoise were dozing, while Ruth, wide awake, sat thinking of Paul and Simon, wondering what each was doing now and praying for the safety of both of them. She watched the townspeople settling down to sleep in little family groups, some of the older men — there were very few men except for the elderly and war wounded — gathering under a large beech tree for a final smoke and a chat before turning in.

Ruth supposed she must have slept at some time during the night, though she hadn't been aware of doing so. As the first streaks of dawn lit up the sky she scrambled to her feet, stretching cramped limbs, and walked slowly towards the edge of the field. There was still the sound of gunfire and explosions, but they seemed to be coming from a different direction now, no longer from the town. She thrust through a gap in the hedge and crossed a second field, making for the road. Before she reached it, she heard the rumbling of heavy vehicles and ran the last few yards, to stare at a convoy of trucks moving past. They were painted khaki and there were men in khaki uniforms in them.

She waved, and the soldiers waved back. A motor cyclist outrider coming along beside them, slowed and pulled up beside her. 'Mam'selle,' he began hesitantly.

'You can speak in English! Tell me what's been happening,' she begged.

His face showed relief. 'The town is in British hands now. We took it last night. Place is a bit of a mess but there aren't any more Germans there, you'll be glad to hear. A good many of them tried to scarper when we arrived, but we've taken a number of them prisoner. You been camping out in the fields last night?' He nodded towards the field behind her.

'Yes. Sort of. Can we go back to our homes now?'

'I was coming to speak to your town officials about that. Yes, it's safe to go back to the town, but the main square is a mess, glass and rubble everywhere. A good few of the houses have been shelled, too. You may be in for a shock when you return.'

'Thank you for warning me. Where are you bound now?' Ruth asked.

'This convoy's going on, inland. I'm off to

report to your town Mayor and the head of the Gendarmerie.'

'Good luck to all of you!' She waved at the passing trucks.

'And to you, too!' the motor cyclist returned. 'We can't imagine what it must have been like for you people, overrun by the Germans and bossed about by them for so long. Well, you won't have to put up with that any more. Sorry we had to make such a mess of your town to do it, though.'

Ruth made her way back to Françoise and Annette, sleeping near the edge of the field. Françoise was still snoring, completely covered by her blanket, but Annette was stirring.

'Where have you been?' she asked sleepily.

'Talking to a British motor cyclist. He says they took the town from the Germans and it's safe now to go home.'

'Good! I can do with a bath!' Annette stretched her arms wide. 'Let's go as soon as we can. Wake Françoise, she's snoring like a pig.'

'We might find the cottage has been damaged by shellfire,' Ruth warned. 'The chap told me there was quite a bit of damage and the town square is a mess.'

'We'll manage,' Annette said dismissively. 'Give Françoise a nudge and let's be on our way. I've missed my bed.'

When they returned, they found the cottage very little damaged by the battle. There were a few cracks in the plastering, two broken windows, and the front garden had been flattened by a tank driving too close, but nothing serious enough to hamper their return.

'But where is Michel?' Françoise grumbled, as soon as they entered the front door.

'Here, woman,' came a voice from the kitchen. 'I've spent the night in the cowshed, trying to calm the beasts. They were worse than a pack of nervous old women. Well, that's being female for you.'

Ruth didn't feel like making a crushing comment, she was too relieved to be back in the cottage and finding everything just as they'd left it. She tried to shut out thoughts of Paul and Simon as she went to help Annette have a bath and change of clothes.

There was still a great deal of troop movement on the roads, but now all of it was either British or Canadian. Françoise wanted to cook everything they had, in a celebratory meal, but Ruth discouraged her, pointing out that it might be days before any supplies of food could be brought into town for civilians, and there probably would be no shops still open anywhere with anything to sell.

For the first few days after their return, they heard intermittent gunfire and explosions, but these were further away to the east. Armoured cars came past frequently but there were no more convoys of troops into the town. When they had been indoors a week, Annette expressed the desire to see what had happened to the town square and urged Ruth to take her there.

'It'll be quite safe; there's no gunfire coming from that direction,' she said. 'We have to try to get back to normal living eventually. The sooner we begin, the better.'

Ruth was doubtful, but she, too, was curious to see how much damage the town had suffered. They set out, one warm afternoon, Ruth negotiating the newly made ruts in the road and avoiding fallen tree branches and collapsed garden walls.

The damage became more noticeable as they came near to the town. Several houses were in ruins and there was a large amount of debris, pieces of wall and shattered glass, littering the road.

'I don't think we can go any further,' Ruth said, stopping. 'This road is so full of rubble.'

'Please, just to the town square. If you take one of the side roads it may not be so bad,' Annette begged. 'I don't mind the bumps and I can push the wheels myself if you are tired.'

Though she found the going difficult, Ruth pressed on. One of the side streets was, indeed, hardly damaged at all, and they arrived eventually at a corner of the main square.

The place was a shambles. Most of the buildings edging the square were damaged, some destroyed completely. Ruth saw with regret that Claude's bakery had been reduced to rubble. There were tanks and armoured cars covering the centre of the square, but they all had either union jack or maple leaf insignia painted on them.

'It certainly is a mess,' Annette said, surveying the scene. 'But I think Françoise would say it looked much as it did in 1918, and we rebuilt well enough after that.'

Ruth's eyes turned to the far end of the square, where the Town Hall stood. Several windows had been shattered and were already boarded up, and the walls were pock-marked with shell holes.

'It's still there, though. And look!' Ruth pointed to the top of the building. A Union Jack and a French Tricolour, were flying, side by side, from two flagpoles on the roof.

'They've got their priorities right,' Annette smiled. 'Now I've seen it at its worst, and there's nothing that can't be put right, eventually. Take me back now, please. I've seen all I needed to.'

'I'm going to push you once round the square,' Ruth said. 'It's not too bad. The tanks have crushed most of the rubble. I always hated walking round the square because of passing the German headquarters, but now they've gone I want to see it close to, again.'

'Do you remember, before the war, how we used to walk right round, looking in all the shop windows?' Annette asked. 'There'll be shops like that again, soon. And we'll — ' She stopped. She, like Ruth, was remembering that perhaps she would never be able to walk round the square as she had done before her accident.

'Soon now, we'll be able to take you to England. We'll find doctors there who'll be able to treat you. You'll walk again,' Ruth said confidently.

'I hope so. But it's been five years since the car crash. I know you've made me exercise all I can, and massaged my leg muscles every day, but we have to be realistic. I may never walk again. Even Simon has accepted that as a possibility.'

'Then we'll have to show him he's wrong.' Ruth pushed the chair energetically along the side of the square. At the back of her mind, throughout all the long years she had been in

France, looking after Annette, had been the hope that somewhere in England they would find the treatment that would enable her friend to walk again. Desperately, she hoped it hadn't been left too late.

There was a soldier in khaki battledress coming down the steps of the Town Hall towards them. 'Stop a minute, Ruth. Isn't that a wonderful sight?' Annette said ecstatically. 'Not field grey; or sinister black, not a surly German but a British soldier in our Town Hall!'

The man stopped in front of them. 'Are you Miss Ruth Lawson and Mademoiselle Annette Brissaud?' he asked shyly.

'Yes, we are. How on earth did you know?' Ruth replied.

He gestured. 'The chair. There aren't many young ladies in a wheelchair pushed by another young lady in this town. You're famous. Did you know that?'

'Famous? What do you mean?' Ruth asked.

'Some of the members of the Resistance have been briefing us. They mentioned you, Miss Lawson. Seems you played quite a big part in their activities.'

Ruth shook her head. 'I hardly did anything very much. Delivered messages, translated some stolen German documents, that sort of thing, but nothing dramatic, like some of them. They blew up the railway lines and sabotaged some of the German trucks.'

'Well, we heard differently. Major Lawson said it was a tremendous help to him that you were here, providing a safe house for his advance party.'

'Major Lawson? Simon, my brother? You mean, he's still here in the town?' Ruth said eagerly.

'Overseeing the takeover of the Town Hall from the German Occupation,' the soldier said. 'He's up to his eyes in work right now, but I'm sure he'll be in touch with you as soon as he can. I'll tell him I've seen you both. He'll be glad to know you are safe after the battle.' He saluted and was gone, jumping into one of the trucks parked beside the road.

'Simon's safe! Oh, isn't that marvellous!' Annette exclaimed. 'I wish we could see him but we can't interrupt. You know, I feel so happy I almost feel I could leap out of my chair and run up the Town Hall steps.'

'Well, you can't; not yet.' Ruth spoke more sharply than she had intended. Annette turned a contrite face towards her and put her hand over Ruth's.

'I'm sorry, dear. That was selfish and tactless of me. You must be worried sick about Paul. Let's go back now. Françoise will start fussing if we're out too long.'

It was some days later that an official looking staff car pulled up outside the cottage. Ruth half expected it to be Simon, but it was a stranger, a sergeant, who stepped from the driver's seat and came up the path to the front door.

'Miss Lawson?'

Ruth nodded.

'Major Lawson's instructions, Ma'am. He says he would be obliged if you would allow me to drive you to the new Ste Marie de la Croix British Headquarters. It's in the Town Hall building.'

'Major Lawson? Major *Simon* Lawson? Why should he want me to come there?' Ruth frowned, puzzled. Simon would surely be too busy to invite her to the British headquarters, and why should he want to, anyway?

'I don't know why, Miss. Major Lawson asked me to come and fetch you. Said he hoped you'd come. It's all right, Miss,' The sergeant saw her hesitation and misunderstood it. 'It is the Major Lawson who is your brother. He did mention that.'

'What is it?' Annette wheeled herself into the hallway.

'Simon wants me to see him at the Town Hall. He's sent a car and chauffeur,' Ruth explained.

'That's wonderful! Can you fit my chair

inside? But how will I get up the Town Hall steps?' Annette asked eagerly..

'Sorry, Miss. Major said just to bring Miss Lawson.' The sergeant looked embarrassed.

Annette's face fell. 'It's probably something to do with debriefing the Resistance members,' she said. 'Give him my love, Ruth, and tell him to come and see us when he can.'

The sergeant's smile was mildly patronising. Annette sounded as if she were issuing a social invitation and only the military personnel involved could know that taking over from the Germans meant round-the-clock work, sorting through records the Germans hadn't managed to burn; rounding up and interrogating Gestapo officers and helping the local populace restore their town to order.

'Afraid we made a bit of a mess of the town when we took over from Jerry,' the sergeant said chattily as he drove Ruth through the streets. People were already busy sweeping up outside their homes, making makeshift repairs to windows and walls.

'Nothing that can't be mended,' Ruth shrugged. 'We were glad to see you. Khaki looks so much friendlier than field grey.'

'I imagine you've had your fill of Germans lording it around the place. Nearly four years of it you've had, haven't you? God knows how we'd have coped with it if they'd invaded us. Lucky we had the Channel between us.'

He drew up in front of the steps at the Town Hall. 'Ask for the Major at the reception desk,' he said. 'They'll know where he is. He'll be expecting you.'

It still felt uncomfortable to be walking in through the main doors of the building, though there were no longer armed soldiers standing guard outside. In fact, there was no one to ask her business. Inside, there was a buzz of activity, with soldiers in reassuring khaki uniform, both British and Canadian, hurrying to and fro. Ruth noticed at once a different atmosphere about the place; people called to each other, ran up and down stairs, nowhere was the formality of the German regime in evidence.

She approached the reception desk, remembering the other times she had come here. This time she spoke to a Scottish private, who was about to use the telephone to summon Simon, when Simon himself came from a side corridor to greet her.

'Ruth! Glad you came! It's a shambles here but we're gleaning some useful information about the previous occupants, all the same.'

'Are you in charge?' she asked.

'Not of the whole place, but I am in charge of Special Operations. I've been detailed to track down certain particularly nasty Gestapo officers and see they don't escape back to Germany, or off to South America, via Spain, which is more likely. That is what some of the more senior of them seem to be trying to do. I've my sights on one of them who seems to be a particularly nasty piece of work when it comes to interrogation. We found a few people in the cells who'd been badly beaten up by him. I swear I'll get him for some of the things he's done.' He took Ruth's arm, steering her down the passage towards the back of the building.

'Was there an old lady there in the cells?' Ruth asked.

'Yes. There was one old crone, shut in a cell by herself. Looked like a witch. Claimed she was part of the Resistance, but, I ask you! At her age!' Simon gave a scornful laugh.

'Madeleine Duvalle,' Ruth said.

'Yes, now you mention it, I do believe that was her name. Can't imagine what the Germans wanted to arrest her for. Must have thought she was casting spells on them.'

'She was the bravest of us all,' Ruth said quietly. 'Is she all right? What happened to her?'

'Badly bruised. Wouldn't let one of our doctors treat her, though. Scuttled off home as soon as we released her.'

'Her grandson will be happy she's safe again. He'll look after her.'

Simon gave her a curious look. 'Sounds as if the Germans had to contend with all sorts making life difficult for them. But someone like that in the Resistance! I can't see her taking orders from Comte Jacques.'

'Where are you taking me?' Ruth became aware that they had gone down several flights of stairs. She realised they were in the cellars which the Germans had used to interrogate their prisoners. Even now, the place sent cold shivers of dread down her spine.

Simon stopped and turned to face her. 'Look, Ruth. This is totally unofficial. You mustn't breathe a word to a soul about what's going to happen now, not even to Annette. It's certainly illegal and we'd both be in deep trouble if it ever got out. But, well, you've done your best for us and for France, and I reckon you deserve what I can do for you.' He opened a door leading into a small, bare room, with a stone floor and walls. A tiny, barred window gave a faint light. The only furniture in the room was a table and two chairs, one either side of it.

'It looks a grim place, but I assure you he's not kept here. This is just somewhere temporary that's safe from prying eyes.' Simon indicated that she should enter. It was then that Ruth realised there was a man sitting in one of the chairs.

Simon gave her a little push forward. 'I can only let you have ten minutes,' he said. 'Make the most of it. See you, Sis.' He slammed the door shut on her and Ruth saw the man stand up and take a hesitant step towards her.

'Paul!'

A moment later she was in his arms, clinging to him as if she could never bear to let him go.

'Ruth! My love! I never thought I would see you again! When Major Lawson interrogated me, and complimented me on my good English, I — '

'Oh, Paul! Paul, I'm so sorry! I never meant to say those terrible things to you! Please forgive me!' Ruth was sobbing into his shoulder. He stroked her hair.

'Don't fret, Liebchen. I know you did not mean them. I knew there had to be some reason why you made such a strange excuse to send me out of your life. It was so unlike you. Other reasons I might have accepted, but not those. You sounded as if you were speaking lines rehearsed for a play. It was not from your heart, what you said to me. And then, when I learnt that Major Lawson was your brother, everything made sense. He was at your home then, was he not?'

Ruth nodded. 'I didn't dare risk your coming to the cottage and I didn't know how long he would be there. I had to make sure you never came near the place again.'

'The war is over for me, now,' Paul said. 'And soon, I think, for you too. I am told I shall be taken to a prisoner of war camp but I do not think it will be for long. Germany will capitulate soon. Very soon.'

'I hope so,' Ruth whispered.

'I know it. I have told Major Lawson about the plans to assassinate Hitler and that then the German government will sue for peace. There are many people of high rank who know that he must go before he destroys us all. This is the only way. It is not treachery, Ruth. We are all loyal to Germany.'

'I know. I know you are no traitor. You couldn't be.'

'Any more than you were a traitor to your country because you became friends with a German soldier,' Paul said.

'Some people might say so. Many of the French did not trust me because they knew you came to the cottage, but they didn't know that we had become more than friends.'

'Your friend Annette approved. Her opinion was the only one that mattered to me.'

'Annette was happy for me. But even she

worried about what would happen to us,' Ruth said.

'But she did not disapprove! I remember the picture she sketched which I saw hanging over the fireplace in your sitting room — an eagle in a rose bush; our national symbols. I knew she was a friend to both of us when I saw that. I shall remember that picture all my life, as I shall remember our days together in this little French town. I will never forget you, Ruth, and, after the war is over, when we are free to travel again, I will come to England for you. Where will you be?'

'My parents live in a place called Broxbourne, in Hertfordshire. They'll know where I'll be, even if I'm not there with them. Here is their address.' She picked up a sheet of paper and a pen from the table and wrote on it. Paul divided the paper in two, put the half with her address in his breast pocket and picked up the pen.

'And if it is easier for the British to come to Germany before we can travel, then come to Mannheim and find me,' he said. 'This is my parents' address there. But write to me, Liebchen. Letters will be possible long before travel for civilians, I am sure.'

There was the sound of a key grating in the lock of the steel door. Ruth flung her arms round Paul again. 'Paul — I love you!' she

347

said. 'And we'll be together again soon.'

'And I love you, my lovely Ruth. It will not be long now and then we can be together for ever, openly and without fear of reprisals.'

Simon stood in the doorway. 'I'm sorry,' he said, 'but you'll have to go now, Ruth. I've risked my neck to let you have a few private minutes with your friend.'

'Thank you, Major. I am most grateful — more grateful than I can express for these moments you have given us together,' Paul said formally. He held out his hand and, after a moment's hesitation, Simon shook it. 'Come on, Ruth. I have to smuggle you out of here. There are some top brass in the building and they'd question a civilian here.'

'There's a back way - leads out to a side road. A discreet exit used by our informers,' Paul said with a grin. 'Ruth knows it. She'll show you.'

As they hurried up the stairs again, Simon said, 'He's actually a very nice chap, your Captain. Bit formal, of course. All the Germans are.'

'He'll learn not to be,' Ruth said innocently. 'After all, one day he's going to be your brother-in-law.'

She hadn't meant to tell Annette about seeing Paul, but as soon as she walked into the cottage Annette said, 'You're looking very happy. What happened? Are they going to give you a medal?'

Ruth laughed. 'That would be ridiculous. No, it's something much better than anything they could possibly give me. But it's confidential. You must promise not to say a word to anyone. Anyone at all.'

'When have I ever broken a confidence? Tell me what's happened, please. I want to share the good news.'

So Ruth told her about Paul. Annette's eyes shone with happiness for her friend, and with tears, too. 'A prisoner of war! But at least he is safe, now. And you will see him again, as soon as it's possible. I am so glad for you! And you saw Simon? How was he? He came through all the fighting without any injuries?' After a moment, she said, 'Let's go to the town square again. Perhaps I can see Simon this time.'

'I don't think so. He's very busy.'

'But why don't we go anyway? You know we managed it last time, in spite of all the rubble on the streets. And now it must be easier, they've been clearing it up for days. Please, Ruth, push my chair as far as the square.'

As Ruth hesitated, Annette said, 'I'm sure I can manage to wheel myself, if you don't want to go. The ground's level and maybe some kind soldier will help me over any rough bits.'

'I'll take you myself. It's too far for you to wheel that chair,' Ruth capitulated.

They set off early in the afternoon. 'See, the streets are almost completely clear of rubble now!' Annette said gleefully. 'I'm sure I could have managed to wheel myself. Look, they've even begun repairing the houses. The town will look just as it did before the Occupation, in a few months.'

'There's still a great deal to be done before France is truly free of the Germans,' Ruth pointed out. 'Simon will probably move on soon, with the rest of the army, towards Paris. He's unlikely to stay here once he's routed the Germans from their headquarters.'

'All the more reason to hope to see him while he's still here.' Annette leant back in her chair, turning her face to catch the warm sunshine.

There were rows of trucks drawn up in front of the Town Hall steps. A small group of townspeople were gathered nearby, watching the action. As Ruth and Annette drew near, some German soldiers were being marched across the square and loaded on to the foremost of the trucks. As they passed, a hissing sound came from the crowd. Ruth felt sorry for the soldiers; they looked bedraggled and dispirited. Some had bandages round their heads or arms in slings. She felt surprise that she had ever been frightened of these men. They looked defeated and a sorry sight.

'Prisoners of war,' said a woman in the crowd to Annette. 'They're being taken off somewhere — don't know where but I've no doubt they'll be better treated than the way they've treated us.' She spat expressively.

'We can't get past them to come anywhere near the Town Hall steps,' Ruth told Annette, with some relief. 'We can't try to see Simon now.'

'Let's stay and watch for a little while,' Annette said. 'We saw them arrive, like conquering heroes; we should see them leave, defeated by the Allies at last.'

Ruth would have preferred not to stay, but she could hardly leave Annette. She moved the chair as near to the Town Hall steps as they could conveniently go. There was a group of armed British soldiers standing beside the trucks to oversee the Germans' departure. The doors at the top of the steps opened and a group of perhaps twenty German army officers and Gestapo came out, under guard. Ruth glanced up, then stood transfixed. Paul was amongst them.

He saw her at the same moment she saw him, and hesitated. The British soldier behind him hurried him on, but Paul was close enough, as he reached the bottom step, to say something as he passed. He saluted her, then, seconds later, he was mounting into the truck with the others and out of sight.

'That was Paul!' Annette gasped in surprise. 'He tried to speak to you. Did you catch what he said?'

'He said 'till Broxbourne',' Ruth replied.

'What does that mean? Do you know?'

'Yes, I know.' A surge of happiness swept over her. Paul was safe, wherever he was being sent now, and it would not be for very long. His words were a promise that they would meet again.

'Let's go home,' she said to Annette. 'Our war's over. All we have to do now is wait for our menfolk to come and find us.' She turned the wheelchair and began pushing Annette back across the square. She was aware of the army trucks rolling past her along the road, but there was no need to watch them any more.

Historical Note

The attempted assassination of Adolf Hitler took place on 20th July, 1944. Many important and highly placed Germans were involved, including Field Marshal Rommel, though it was Colonel Fritz von Stauffenberg who placed the bomb. It was, as everyone knows, unsuccessful, and there were many executions as a result. Hitler finally committed suicide in Berlin on April 30th, 1945. The war with Germany ended on May 8th of that year.

Annette Brissaud became Annette Lawson in England in the summer of 1946. After lengthy treatment in a British hospital she was finally able to walk again.

Ruth Lawson was reunited with Paul Reinhardt in 1949. They married in 1950 and settled in Mannheim, Germany.

We do hope that you have enjoyed reading this large print book.

Did you know that all of our titles are available for purchase?

We publish a wide range of high quality large print books including:
Romances, Mysteries, Classics
General Fiction
Non Fiction and Westerns

Special interest titles available in large print are:
The Little Oxford Dictionary
Music Book
Song Book
Hymn Book
Service Book

Also available from us courtesy of Oxford University Press:
Young Readers' Dictionary
(large print edition)
Young Readers' Thesaurus
(large print edition)

For further information or a free brochure, please contact us at:
Ulverscroft Large Print Books Ltd.,
The Green, Bradgate Road, Anstey,
Leicester, LE7 7FU, England.
Tel: (00 44) 0116 236 4325
Fax: (00 44) 0116 234 0205